Ezra Porter Chittenden

The Pleroma

A Poem of the Christ

Ezra Porter Chittenden

The Pleroma
A Poem of the Christ

ISBN/EAN: 9783337334703

Printed in Europe, USA, Canada, Australia, Japan

Cover: Foto ©Andreas Hilbeck / pixelio.de

More available books at **www.hansebooks.com**

THE PLEROMA

A Poem of the Christ

IN TWO BOOKS OF SEVEN CANTOS EACH, WRITTEN IN SEMI-
DRAMATIC FORM

BY

REV. E. P. CHITTENDEN, A.M.

Ὅτι ἐν αὐτῷ κατοικεῖ πᾶν τὸ Πλήρωμα τῆς Θεότητος σωμα-
τικῶς.—COL. ii., 9

NEW YORK & LONDON
G. P. PUTNAM'S SONS
The Knickerbocker Press
1890

DEDICATED TO

THE CHURCH

WHICH IS THE FULNESS OF HIM THAT
FILLETH ALL IN ALL

PREFACE.

THE PLEROMA is characteristically modern. It may
be safely claimed that in no other period of human
learning could it have been conceived and executed.
For the *materia* of the successive ages and stages of
creation, the latest available scientific authorities have
been consulted ; and throughout the drama the principle of evolution has been adopted ; with this *proviso*,
however, that Jahveh-Christ shall be regarded as the
Beginning and the End of the world-process. A funda-
mental error of the past has been to regard creation
finished at man's appearance upon the earth. In this
work, two hemispheres, the natural and the spiritual, are
seen to evolve concurrently, reaching their fulness and
perfection, not in the first Adam, but in the Second.
In a word, I have incorporated *The Christ* into the
mighty sweep of natural sequences ; and the Incarnation, as potentially hidden, from the beginning, in the
Womb of the World.

The poetical form was chosen because it seemed to
me that the present stage of knowledge suffers no one
to fill out, after the scientific method, a plan so compre-
hensive as is here undertaken. The preparation of this
Poem of the Christ has been a holy delight, while unwonted physical health brightened the arduous duties
of a pastor and teacher. Some unusual metres will be
found, whose design is to express peculiar motions of

natural forces.   I would crave indulgence for the form of blank verse which gives more prominence to the *sentence* than the traditional *line* permits of. Should my poem find favor among Christian students of science and scientific students of Christianity, my utmost hopes will be realized.

Among those whose kind offices have furthered the issue of this volume the names of Col. Nicolas and Mrs. Louisa Pike, both well-known naturalists of Brooklyn, N. Y., are gratefully mentioned. The gorgeous *Pleroma elegans* (the perfect type of the floral kingdom) was discovered, happily, in time to be laid in gilt upon the cover as a significant symbol of the CHRIST who is the "Flower and Perfection of humanity."

CHRIST CHURCH RECTORY,
    SALINA, KAN.

BOOK I.

CHRIST IN NATURE.

THE PROCESS OF THE PLEROMA.

THE ETHEREAL PARADIGM UNSEALED IN NATURE.

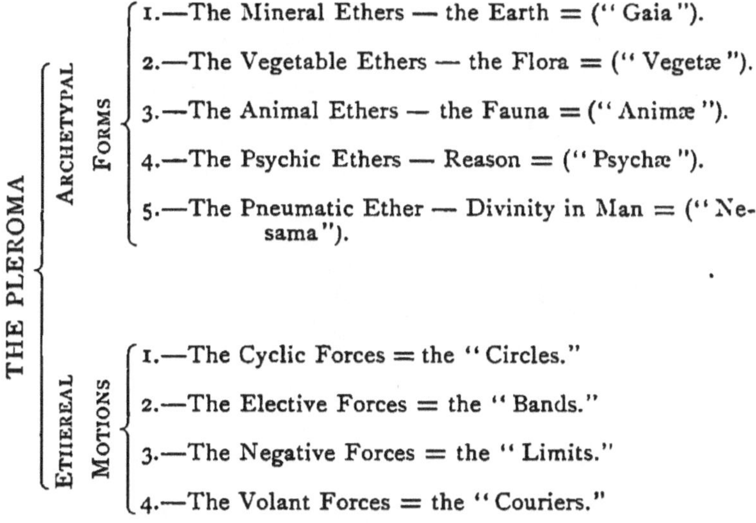

BOOK FIRST.

INDEX OF CHORUSES, SONGS, ODES, AIRS, AND RECITATIVES.

The PLEROMA in *locis multis*

VOICES OF BOOK FIRST.

THE PLEROMA — The *Fulness* of God contemplated in the Process of Creation; the Fount of forms and motions; the Author of Nature and of Man.

THE LIVING CREATURES — Ezekiel, Chap. I., vs. 5; Revelation, Chap. IV., vs. 6.

Cherubim—the assembly of Cherubs.

Seraphim—the assembly of Seraphs.

The Heavenly Host.

Angels—of every rank.

The Chorus of Ethers—Forms and Motions.

The Æons (Ages)—daughters of Time.

The Archetypal Forms :
- The Mineral Ethers—"*Gaia.*"
- The Vegetable Ethers—"*Vegetæ.*"
- The Animal Ethers—"*Animæ.*"
- The Psychic Ethers—"*Psychæ.*"
- The Pneumatic Ether—"*Nesama.*"

The Archetypal Motions :
- The Cyclic forces—"*Circles.*"
- The Attractive forces—"*Bands.*"
- The Repellent forces—"*Limits.*"
- The Volant Forces—"*Couriers.*"

Lucifer (Satan)—the Archon of the Earth.

THE PLEROMA.

CANTO I.

THE ARGUMENT.

The PLEROMA *engrosseth the spiritual Ethers—The hymeneal of the archetypal Motions and Forms—The Creator with the invested Powers proceedeth from the Heavenly Places into the Voids.*

THE ETHERS.

Motion is music ; rhythm is reason ;
Will we to haste ? or tarry a season ?
Do we fly under, pause we and wonder ;
Fly we out farther, where shall we gather ?
Distances breaking, thoughts new awaking—
O the mystery of Eternity !

THE PLEROMA.

With quicken'd measure do these tuneful Airs
Essay their harmonies upon Our ear—
The earliest born of Ethers—fairest notes
In the ethereal chorus.   And Thee, O Soul
Of motion ! lo, in Thee attun'd, these Rhythms

Shall take percept of power and will, and, from
This day, divine Our way, and thither turn
Their faces.

THE ETHERS.

Hither and thither, strive we together—
Space for the Will, and Time for the Reason—
While we are pondering, turning and wondering,
What is the Life in us ? whence is the strife in us ?
Are we of many ? or spring we from One ?

THE PLEROMA.

Joys of Our joy ! and ardors of Our heart !
Awak'd in you this day are power and will ;
And ye are strong and free, feeling the pulse
Of reason and of motion.   And this is Life :
Whose Whence seek not to know !   Life hath no
        Whence !
But simply is—no more—is One not many !
While ev'ry mystic *Type*, *Number*, or *Name*,
The express symbol is of Unity,
More simply seen, the more diverse reveal'd.

O Increate Ethers of the Increate God !
Ye are the PLEROMA issuant forth
To mould of the eternal glory-mist
A mighty Universe—a concord vast
Of masses and of motions.

                Lo, Time and Space,
As new-born lights, glow purely on Our breast :
Greet them, ye holy Signatures of Love !

Let Forms sciential greet sciential Airs,
While thought-*mirage* fashions a distant world—
A way of wisdom there, and throne of Light.
  By inmost Love impell'd, the PLEROMA
Passeth for work upon the distant Voids :
The Ethers brighten Our transcendant way,
While the creative Process lays a line,
Clearly defin'd, betwixt Eternity
And Time ; and henceforth shall the Heavens chant
Of One *that Was, and Is, and Is to Come.*

  The Motions move in zigzag ways intent
To range themselves as chords and harmonies :
The Æons write of Then and Now—There—Here—
Thoughts complemental and herein create
By this *World-Process* of the Infinite.

THE ETHERS.

Come from the peerless glory beneath us,
Hail, O PLEROMA, dimming our lights !
Wings still confessing marvel and blessing,
As we draw near Thee, pressing to hear Thee,
More of the Future born of Thy coming ;
More of the Distant now op'd to view.
Us teach compliance for Thy reliance,
Telling us more of the hither and thither ;
Freighted with import strange to our minds.

THE PLEROMA.

  Behold these ardors with surprise attent,
To move by spaces, and to think by times ;
To find the Whence and Whither of Our way,
And learn of Time and times that now begin.

By this We know the Infinite Our wide
Design advances ; and, hath now evok'd
Their spheres a day of clearly ration'l thought :
And open'd them a field of vision, seen
Of neither Living Creature round the Throne ;
Nor of the Cherubim and Angels—nay,
Beheld alone by Us and them this hour ;
Whereby their powers enlargement make to pass
With Us the unillumin'd seas of dust,
Hereto unmov'd by will express'd of God
In law, or love ; and so make manifest,
That ration'l thought to Space's treble-line
Is correlate ; questions of Yea and Nay,
Its points and angles.

THE ETHERS.

Space to our father ; Time to our mother ;
Nothing shall harm us, distances charm us ;
We are of One ; and Love is in all.
Wait we no longer, weaker or stronger,
Hasting the Voids, at PLEROMA'S call !
Bright One to bless us, hold and caress us,
Answer us, teach us, musing and marvelling—
All in all ! ponder—changing to wonder
Whence is our home, and whither our motion ?

THE PLEROMA.

Ye pause, bright Airs, and hope is marr'd by fear :
While quest of reason bends the act, now here,
Now there ; and Time and Space divert the end.
O fill'd with burning Love to win you all,
Draw We the curtain of Our GLORY back—
Bidding you gaze this living Temple ! If

With ravish'd sight ye seek to enter in :
The awful Shrine explore : giving therewith
Your wills to Our creative purposes ;
Unseal We then the splendid chart of worlds—
Our nuptial gifts to you,—whilst ye do wed
Our first-born Thoughts,—the Archetypes ;—and yield
Your fervent souls unto Our mighty work.

Fair Wills, that live by One, yet freedom have
To choose, refuse, to aid, and to oppose—
Again We hail ! the Circles first salute !
The Limits next ! the Bands ! the Couriers !
Thence Flora, Fauna, and the Psychic Airs !

THE CIRCLES.

Ever circling round and round, breathing music ever ;
Never tiring, singing on, being silent never ;
Greet the GLORY, each in turn, circling near His feet !
Meet to worship, wondrous Light ! We our song repeat :
" Holy ! Holy ! Living Shrine ! Us possessing wholly !
Solely Thine to do Thy will ; Us investing fully :
Thou the Fount, and We the streams flowing ever free ;
We the thoughts—reflected rays of Thy Majesty.
Deep We gaze and view Our home—visions out of sleep—
Fear is gone, and holy faith pensive doth appear ;
Fill Us now, Thou Parent, LIFE ! all adore Thy Will !
Thrill Us thoughts We cannot tell ; and We linger still ;
Won by love, and woo'd by Thee ; circling ever on—
From the deeper glories hear allelujahs sung."

THE LIMITS.

Circles, thither fly ye ! Try ye
Bound'ries far or nigh thee ? Leaving us,

Grieving us—" Whither " lieth where ?
O thou Fair One, greet us ! mete us !
Distances defeat us ; lackaday !
Far away,—life is led by care.

Ah, what voice allureth ? assureth ;
More than all endureth, guiding us,
Chiding us kindly in our grief.
Hear we music drifting, lifting,
Hopes from sorrow sifting ; treasuring,
Measuring rhythms that bring relief.

Radiant Form that layeth, stayeth
Bans of glory ; weigheth ; knowing,
Showing love is wed to light.
Soul of light ascending, tending
Spaceward never ending ; loving all,
Proving all ;—day divides the night.

THE BANDS.

Love electing, Hate rejecting—
Ever binding, ever loosing,
What decideth choice in choosing ?
Strong is will, and strong is wonder ;
Glory bursts and now we ponder ;
O PLEROMA, heart-alluring !
Holy NAMES us all assuring !
Circles pure and Limits finding ;
Us to Thee in bliss resigning ;
Times behold with Time united ;
Space in Thee with spaces sighted ;
Lights in Thee with Light all lighted ;
   Triple Powers we,
   Freely bound by Thee.

THE COURIERS.

We fly, we fly !
Swift are we as the thoughts we bear ;
    Descry, descry,
Wings of light on their errand there :
    Yonder ! yonder !
Skirting the bounds of space :
    Wonder ! wonder !
O Sovran Power ! our Present and Past !
We herald the Future hastening fast !

THE VEGETÆ.

Pass we, O sisters, but passing
        We fall :
Brief is our flight, or ye carry
        Us all :
Blowing sweet zeyphrs, but blowing
        We spread
Wings quickly folding and fainting
        With dread.
Seek ye swift Couriers the Minerals
        Our own !
Faint are we brothers, Oh where are
        Ye gone ?
Carry us, ferry us, over the sea,
Wafting us hither, thither, so free.

THE ANIMÆ.

We crawl and creep ;
We climb and leap ;
Run we and fly
Afar and high :

O joy, but where?
The Minerals fled,
The Vegetæ sped ;
    O fear ! O care !

A world of green,
We taste unseen ;
We swallow its meat,
And wallow in sweet—
    A passing dream.
Awake, we cry :
" Ah bring us nigh !
With Thee we go.
Above, below,
    The flowing stream."

THE PSYCHÆ.

Silent the shores of Space ;
    Songless, save rhythms of thought ;
Highest of Ethers, a race
    Godlike, ere we are taught.

Words for our breath we breathe ;
    Sense on reflection attends ;
Fancies on memory wreathe ;
    Judgment to Mercy ascends.

Realms still in thought we possess,
    Crush not the weakest of airs ;
Up to us growing we bless,
    Breathing our life upon theirs.

Hail to the fountain of light !
Home of the Essences pure !
Now rise the Voids to our sight ;
Us to invade them allure.

THE PLEROMA.

Of angels namèd Rhythms and Aureole Lights—
How inly blest your peaceful harmonies !
Not so what time We pass'd the argent line :
Us then ye saw, and seem'd as in sea
Of sapphire imag'd ; and were sore confus'd ;
Nor heard ye from the splendors following
The Voice which saith :
            " O FOUNT of Essences !
From Whom arise, and into Whom return
These consubstantial Airs ; not more from Thee
Discrete, than thoughts are from the Self that thinks ;
Nor separate than motions from the Mover.
Lo now, concentering this dome of MIND,
These willing Motions wait investiture
In substance tangible to finite sense ;
But ere Thou bring them to the silent bounds
Of the Increate Universe to join
To Masses, Motions, and thus Matter form—
Thou shalt disclose the primal Seat of Motion,
And seated there that Life Whose trinal seal
Of Power, Wisdom, Love, each Ether, pure,
Shalt carry thither, ceasing not to voice
The glory and the praise of the Creator."

Wherefore, ye Motions, nether fly, and take
The Seal of Power from God the FATHER ; and
From God the WORD, the Seal of Wisdom ; and,

From God the SPIRIT, Love, that future worlds
May show eternal Power, and Godhead
In things create ; and Nature's varying forms
May bear the impress of the treble-Hand.

THE ETHERS.

List, ye sisters ! list the music !
   Rising from the nearer seats ;
Nearing, cheering, nothing fearing ;
   " Ethers hail ! " the choir repeats.

Aye, discerning, hither turning,
   Fashions Godlike to our eyes !
Myriad wings, and myriad faces !
   Can we cover our surprise ?

THE CHERUBIM.

Ye burn not, O Ethers, in flame
            Or fires !
What hither approacheth in blame
            Expires.

THE SERAPHIM.

The Watchers say " Yea,"
And do we say " Nay " ?
   O airy fairy ones, never !
We know not why
Ye hither fly,
   A day or to stay forever ?

Fair Aureole Lights
From heaven's pure hights,

With beaming, gleaming motions ;
Lo, hither ye trend,
Our circle to lend
  Creative, original notions.
The way to the Throne
Is barrèd to none
  That loving, endureth its Light ;
But passing we pray
Ye turn not away
  And flee the ineffable Sight.

THE LIVING CREATURES.

The Empyrean lowereth ; showereth its fill
  Of rhythms and glowing essence
      Upon the Throne ;
With hearts compelling, swelling, we still
  Express the four-fold Presence— ;
      And God is One.

These fleeting tapers, vapors from the verge
  Of clearly rational Being,
      God calleth, not we ;
The Throne we see not, fearing ; yet surge
  These streams of motions seeing—
      God knoweth, not we.

The Ethers free, surround ; resound the skies
  With festive voice and sign ;
    PLEROMA'S VOW,—
The Seven Spirits burning, turning their eyes
  To light the multitudinous line,—
      Perform we now.

THE FIRST CREATURE.

Hail, musical Motions ! bodiless Rhythms !
   Lov'd of and loving the Throne ;
This hour of your union, mystical troth—
   Name we ; God knoweth alone.

THE SECOND CREATURE.

Hail Archetypes, ethereal moulds of things to be !
Awaited long the beauteous choir saluteth ye !
With grace benign advance ye here and greet them ;
And, plighting faith, with holy love, entreat them.

THE THIRD CREATURE.

Assembled Glories of the Essential World !
Ye sing this hour the sacred bans fulfill'd
Of Types original—to angel speech—
The Architectural Powers, Creative Thoughts ;
And of the virgin Airs (alike in song),
The Aureole Lights of the outermost Heaven :
IDEAS and MOTIONS, complemental, now,
The THRONE shall bind forever sealing one.

Vast moment hath this act—the key to Nature.
As Voices utt'ring the eternal Will,
We call on Cherubim and Seraphim,
To range yourselves in compact companies—
To each assign'd his tone and anti-phone ;
The greater first, and, after, each in turn.

Ye mark a stream of alabastrine light
That floweth as a river from the Throne
Of Motion ; view ye all, not we,—and thence
It leadeth outward to the pathless voids ;—

View we, not ye,—our eyes discerning spaces,
And things therein, till resting on a globe
Of emerald hue, with vision spaceward—
Confus'd the image and the thing !   O Voice !
So soon we sight the farthest Goal sublime
Of the PLEROMA'S way, faint we for joy.

Expectant multitudes, again, we voice,
And do direct, dividing into bands,
Ye keep the margins of the pearly way ;
When, near the entrance of the HOLY PLACE,
Within whose open curtain ye behold
The chosen passing, pause and wait the event.
And heed, lest ye, depriv'd of sight, atone
The fault !   For, first, emergent from the SHRINE,
The triple-NAMES, leading the Way, shall waft
Bright vapors softly on.   These ye may look
Safely upon ; a moment more, and vail
Ye all your faces, crying " Holy ! Holy ! "
While blinding Splendor goeth forth upon
The Sealèd ones.   Amazement shall possess
You till the viewless vapors, gathering
The vortex of the Way, do partly hide
The outward-going DEITY ; then shall
Ten thousand thousand lips break forth in full
Processional, with call and answer from
Responsive choruses ; meantime ye fly
Consecutive beside the moving GLORY,
Far as the subtle airs of Heaven support ;
Nor cease to sing PLEROMA ; and, to bless
The invested Ethers, till in parts sublime,
The VOY'GING WORLD transgress the golden line
That marketh Heav'n, and fade upon the sight.

THE FOURTH CREATURE.

Lo, now is heard the treble-word ;
And power is given in earth and heaven
  To Archetypes and Ethers pure ;
The eagle-wing assist to sing,
Soaring on high in majesty,
  While so PLEROMA doth assure.

The portal spreads, and lustre weds
Each airy Flame unto its Name,
  As thither pass the favor'd band ;
Within, alone, the HOLY ONE
Is heard to say, " Ye are this day
  Thrice sealèd for PLEROMA's Hand."

THE CHERUBIM.

O fair One Naomah !
  Let Angels shout
  While passeth out
Adonai PLEROMA !
The Cherub's wing
Shall haste to bring
Thee emblems bright,
The way to light ;
And guard the seat
Where Thou shalt meet
  With altar given,
  And guilty shriv'n,
Man and his mate
Before the gate
  Of Paradise.

THE HEAVENLY HOST.

The Cherubim cry " Holy ! "
  The Seraphim respond ;
The Angels all cry " Holy ! "
  The Archangels resound
        Adonai PLEROMA !

The Ethers pure Thou bearest,
  And to the Voids thou wingest ;
Thrice blest each one Thou sharest,
  And thither with Thee bringest.

What wonders there foresnowing ;
  Alone the Ethers telling ;
Wait we till Motions knowing
  Have builded Thee a dwelling.

O Light ! What radiance showereth !
And festive air embowereth ;
  Ascending, the skies grown rare ;
Now sense we spaces fainting,
A universe there painting,
  Amazèd, we forbear.

Thy voyage the Eternal prosper !
And from his Throne of jaspêr,
  Lend aid and comfort ever ;
Bright spheres, meantime creating,
Remember forms awaiting,
  Pensive as now we sever.

CANTO II.

THE ARGUMENT.

*The Creator surveyeth the Voids—Creation goeth forward
correlate with the Thought-Activity of the* PLEROMA—
*The Songs of the Initial Energies—the Circles, the
Bands, the Limits, and the Couriers.*

THE PLEROMA.

If Time compute the way, then are we long
Ascending hither from the timeless world :
Or Space define the place, then are we far
Attaining from the spaceless seat of BEING.
How long ? how far ? tuitions these that give
To simple intellections local form,
And bind the world phenomenal, reflex
Of thought in lines and limits.   Else were thought
The unrelated, undefinable ;
But Thou shalt make it known to creature minds,
O God, when poured through many signs and symbols
(Configuring the elemental dust
Into a *Cosmos*, with its various parts)
Thou art the Absolute in all relations.

Wherefore, to give attendance apposite
These conj'gal Airs, conceiv'd of Archetypes ;

And pregnant with the schemes of future worlds,
We borrow tongue and custom from themselves,
Whose mood grows thoughtful and whose converse deep.

   O myriad-visag'd Nature ! still unborn ;
We wait thy birth-hour and prophetic voice
Upraise. Burst forth puissant Motions of
Our Heart to exponential action. Hither,
What time We press'd Our way, the dusky maze
Dividing, ye felt the outward impulse slack'n ;
Nor, till the voyage ended, and ye knew
Our sphere at length to be at rest, enswath'd
In ocean thick and ponderable, did ye
With dubious thought Our mission contemplate.
Nor do We name this less to smile and cheer,
That unaccustom'd distances, and dark,
So much of courage in you find. To tell
You where We lie and set at rest these wings,
Alert with tremulous uncertainty,
A moment given shall be improved.

                Then know,
O trusting hearts, that still ye safely rest
Within the Father's bosom—ambient clouds,
The stuff from which becoming worlds are built,
Surrounding, do not Him exclude ; while He,
As Soul of the including Universe,
Upholds each particle and fashions it.
Wherefore the spaces cross'd put us no further
From the Soul of Motion, with Whom there is
Nor here nor there. Sometime his central light
Ye saw, amaz'd (though curtain'd to relieve
The eyes unus'd to living splendors), ere
Ye hither rose into the central gloom.

2

Still God is here as in the light ; for both
Are chambers of His holiness.   Shorten'd
A time in vision, see ye nothing outward ;
The seizure of the spaces only conscious,
Whose welcome of fair guests—ye take with fear.
To finite sense inert, know ye each atom
Is potent in seeming passivity ;
Else had our path not found an end or pause
In equilibrium ; whereas each atom,
Resisting, also buoys the thing resisted ;
And balances the motion by the mass.
Be ye herewith confirm'd, O spiritual Airs,
Perceiving darkness contravening light ;
And masses also correlating motions :
Or, summ'd in complemental terms—the spheres
Of Mind and Matter—*action* and *reaction*,
Within the ABSOLUTE.

                        The former known,
Ye suffer first reaction, finding thus
That power to act involves somewhere equal
Resistance ; pure and simple Will the first ;
By philosophic mind call'd " Being," of whom
The Complement is call'd the " Not-Being "—
Whereby is understood that timeless Source,
Whence ev'ry world becoming, integrates
By forces fus'd from the Omnific WILL.

   Now swells Our Bosom with expectant joys
Fast ripening the Event : turn ye and look !
O ecstasy ! (We speak for finite souls),
Now fulls the natal morn of powers creative :
Ye pale meanwhile ye pass the straits and feel
Reluctant motherhood yield up its fruit.

Immortal Ethers, travailing with Nature !
The Archetypes caress you and embower.

Now issues from the Shrine a lum'nous drift,
And bears its way across the infinite seas,
Its subtle light adown the vaporous Voids
Insifting ; to you, to Archetypes, to Angels,
To all the Host Ethereal be this the sign,
And Name that noteth the Creation's birth !

Leap forth and fly, O Motions, newly born !
The bounds of hylic vapors you embrace !
Bright-wing'd, aërial, pierce ye now and build ;
Genetic Airs, replete in the PLEROMA,
Instinct with differential forces, go ;
Fulfill Our Will !

THE CIRCLES.

Of Nature the key-note is ours, is ours,
  With spherical motions the tone-world to mould ;
With cycles concentric, PLEROMA empowers
  The mass of still atoms be roll'd, be roll'd.

Still higher we bear on our way, our way ;
  The outermost bounds of the mist to control ;
Our wings we will join, and our work is play ;
  While the slumbering ocean receives its Soul.

Lo motion in matter gives life, gives life ;
  Intrinsic, extrinsic, both one and the same ;
Involv'd, or evolv'd, there never is strife—
  Not-Being and Being receiving one Name.

Look, over the ocean, a blush ! a blush !
Diaphanous glow of the dust create ;
The Universe-system is now aflush ;
And Vapors 'candescent the Limits await.

THE LIMITS.

Cyclic Choir we hear thee, cheer thee ;
While our lines draw near thee ; riving thee,
    Depriving thee naught of Nature's joy.
Variant arcs subtending, trending ;
Ever thee defending ; spacing,
    Tracing, the boundaries we employ.

By our numbers welling, telling,
Integrals compelling ; ordering,
    Bordering mass by multitude.
Vacuums we make not, stake not
Out in Space ; take naught ; thrilling all,
    Filling all which our arms include.

Nebulæ surrounding, founding ;
Mighty cycloids bounding ; curling,
    Whirling, each ordained its place ;
Come, ye Bands, with choosing, using
This and that refusing ; joining us—
    Coining us finities to trace.

THE BANDS.

Hail we Circles all revolving !
Hail we Limits all resolving !
Primal atoms integrating ;
Chemic laws in each instating ;
Homogeneous dust diffusing
Powers of choice and of refusing ;

Complicate and simple number
Bind and loose and not encumber :
Giving forms, abating motions—
Building Ocean into oceans ;
Circle into circles ringing,
Far athwart the spaces swinging ;
Firming bodies and concreting,
While affinities are meeting—
      Triple-bodies we,
      Claiming Gravity.

THE COURIERS.

We wing, we wing,
    Errants, divining the will of all :
We fling, we fling
    Banners that answer every call :
Lighter, lighter
    Grows the communicate mass—
Brighter, brighter
    Beams each atom we pass ;
Beating, heating, hurrying away,
Heralding omens of day.

We wait, we wait
    Never ; needing no rest—
Too late, too late
    Never, eluding thy quest.
Passing, flashing, rushing along—
"Speed ! Speed !" ever our song.

THE PLEROMA.

Initial Energies ! *Tessarene* Powers !
How gloweth with your lights this cosmic mist !
Titanic Ethers bear aloft the Spheres

And fling them, as if bubbles, into space.
Eristic Limits parry force with force,
And stamp their numerals upon the stars.
In rhythmic synthesis the Binders, too,
By schedules geometrical, concrete
The mass. The rudimentary fluids become
The vehicle for fleet-winged Couriers,
That, kindling lurid fervors everywhere,
Exploit cogenerating worlds.

      Enamor'd
Of the First Fair, and the First Good, behold
These happy powers express their mutual love
In simulative signs and studied motions ;
The circling orbits flowing forth and back—
Pure BEING imaging, whose psychical
Activities are first and final Cause.
Again dual and trinal are inscrib'd
As integers of Seven—the magic word
Unlocking much of wisdom in the skies :
Invisible species, potentative number
In fluxions and in fluids ; connoting how
The *dual* in Nature a *threeness* claims
To give unto it perfectness and balance.
Or, fleet of wing these errant Airs, that take
No hostage of the Here, or There ; whose home,
Like the Incarnate Good, is EVERYWHERE.

With specializ'd alertness, each deploys
His adjutants, and bindeth multiplicity
In golden bands of Love. O Holy LOVE !
The thought outruns the time, anticipates
The Fulness of the Beautiful and True ;
What time the ages full, OURSELF shall wed

A Virgin Soul, of twain making one Life.
Ye purely pleasant Powers—laws inorganic—
Your handiwork, so fit and well perform'd,
Doth God rejoice while beaming visible.
Of hesitant inaptitude no trace ;
Nor arbitrary variance with the scheme
First mirror'd in the Eternal Mind.   Faithful
In lesser as in great such facts make glad
The FACTOR ; and advance Creation on
Unto the stage for organific Airs.

THE CHORUS.

Sing, ye morning Stars, together !
    Hail the organific Powers !
Antecedent work performed,
    Sisters hardly wait the hours.

Roll the pæan through the skies !
    Waiting ones join the refrain :
Flashing fire-mists, farther on,
    Summon to our work again.

Point we, sisters, to yon globe ;
    Choicest fabric, stamp'd and set
'Mid a fleet of light-wing'd sails—
    Strength and beauty rarely met.

Radiant vehicle of LOVE !
    Passing, bear PLEROMA thence ;
Light of God invest the sphere—
    Glory of Omnipotence.
Lucifer, O Star of Morn !
    Noblest archangel by birth ;
Yield we sway if GOD elect—
    Make thee *Archon* of the Earth.

CANTO III.

*The Creator contemplateth the Star whose promise is Man ;
The Vegetæ greet the Mineral choir, and draw nigh
the form of Gaia (Earth) emergent from the sea—
The festival of Plants as, taking root, they grow and
bloom, first in the circumpolar North, the paradise of
Circles.*

THE PLEROMA.

O beautiful to God, particular Star !
Thy cradle chaos, and thy promise Man :
The choir of Airs, potential ardors, haste
To fashion thee a fit and proper field,
Whereon the fertile Vegetæ, Ethers
Connate, impinging, shall take root and grow :
Thy form to deck with verdure beauteous,
Meanwhile elaborating chemic sweets,
And subtle essences for care or cure
Of psychic habitors, a race to be :
Wherefore in middle space, the Pleiads left—
Too rare and fluid to offer quay, or beach,
Or anchor for their roots, We hither bear
The Flora, germanent and quick, whose hope
Doth ripen them for art and instant action.

But lo, ye palpitate upon the sight !
Wherefore ? Do glowing spheres entrance your thoughts

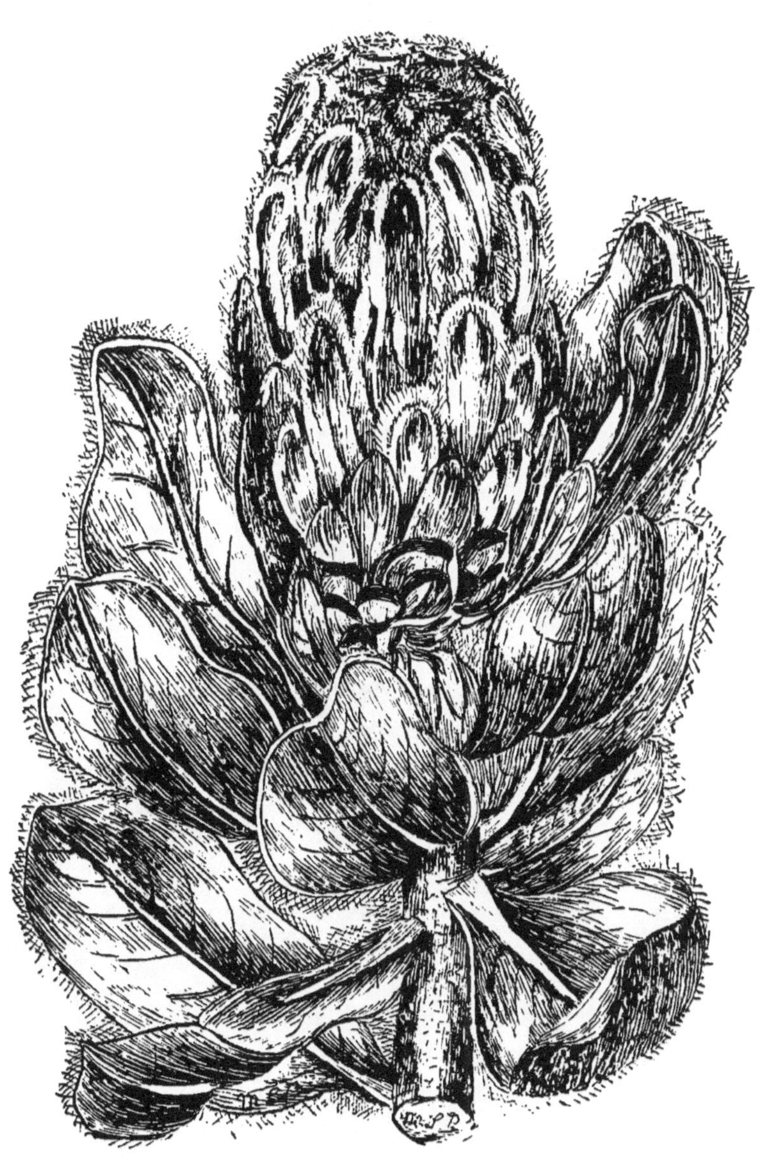

PROTEA VILIFERA, SOUTH AFRICA.

To stem the fiery heats, oft as some flame
Leaps up with loud acclaim to show the Airs
A valiant love hath found affinity ;
And, celebrating maritals, doth give
Encagèd vapors freedom ? and still ye fear
This gentlest star of all ?   Have ye not oft
With Us, the labyrinthine star-maze thrid ?
Seen ratios septenate with atoms join'd,
Build first the seventy prime elements?
Then mould the stars ; determine distances,
And fill the Universe with vocal *Sevens ?*
To contemplation, long, yon flashing 'rray
Of superterrene charioteers behold,
How, sweeping round the still or moving poles,
They never chafe the line nor leap the course.
Bethink ye then, O gentle Airs, if e'er
PLEROMA, showing obverse symbols ye
Forecast ambiguous destinies for Airs
Material : lo, now in hailing you they seem
Incontinent of joy ; and million suns
Enumerate in proof of power and skill :
Doth the Eternal love you less ? or fain
Allureth to a fruitless task ?   Nay, nay,
We pledge Our Name (by greater none may swear),
That, shortly, pleasant odors ye shall breathe
Into mephitic atmospheres, the airs
Make pure and glad, meanwhile acclimatiz'd
To many zones and circles.

THE VEGETÆ.

Greet we our brothers, and greeting
    We long,
Breaking our silence, to join them
    In song ;

Waiteth now Gaia, and waiting
 To come,
Why do we falter to make thee
 Our home ?

Cling we yet closer, and clinging
 We fear ;
Seeing Earth's visage so changeful
 Appear ;
Bear us, PLEROMA, and bearing
 Us trace
More of the fashion and mien of
 Her face.

Live we, PLEROMA, and living
 We learn,
In Thee invested we never
 Shall burn ;
Flames leaping outward and flaming
 Essay
Us naught to harm, but to brighten
 Our way.

THE PLEROMA.

O sweetest Flora, ye most clinging and
Most fair of all the spiritual Airs !
This questioning hesitance yet beameth more
Affection than distrust ; while ye invite
A closer view of yonder star so dear
To God ; and chosen ere the world took form
Beneath the brooding SPIRIT, and awoke
From Chaos for the lofty counsels of
The INFINITE. Nay, ages watch and wonder,
At pan-creative motions which evolve
Before their eyes, perplexèd much to know

If thought indeed be act, or action thought.
So add We not to types perceiv'd in Us,
Redundancy, if their reciprocals
Herewith be made the metes and bounds
To spread Our words within.

          Thou flaming Sun,
The sire and fender of this virgin star !
Thy photosphere of burning vapors shines
But dimly seen through these humidities,
So dense and mineral ; still less avails
To clarify the bitter waves, and bid
The steaming marges green and brighten.   Lo !
The Earth !   Under these mists she barely feels
The chemistry of thy seven-fold beams.
Hence, hail, O Sun, with all the Mineral Airs,
The advent of the Flora, purifying sea
And air, and seeding herbage everywhere.
Flash thou and flame, and pour actinic fire
Into the gloomy sea ; beneficent
Assist the pulsing seeds so soon to taste
These oozy shores.

         Ye dip, O Plants, bright wings
In airy sea, seven myriad fathoms deep,
Surrounding Gaia ; and pois'd so daintily
Upon the fulcrum of the star, it sways
And heaveth at the nicest touch of sun,
Or satellite.   Lo, yonder beaming moon,
Weigh'd by the Earth as one to eighty is,
And, seven-times ten thousand leagues away,
Doth play this fickle envelope, as erst
The Circles coil and curl the nebulous mists
Of forming worlds.

　　　　　　　　　　A denser atmosphere
Incites more frequent plying of your wings :
But fail ye not to mark the ebb and flow
Of fickle eddies on our downward way ;
Meantime the silv'ry satellite rides o'er,
Coercing and retarding sea and air.
Nor, how the iridescent rain-drops fall ;
When, circling on the unctuous wave, behold,
Them give in miniature Creation's plan :
For, bulging at the middle part, mark how
Concentric rings are shaken off, that whirl
A space, along with their own principals—
Bright filmy bands ; then, surging to and fro,
Do loose the niceness of their balancing,
And break, to gather in minuter drops,
Choosing the mimic circuit as before
The misty rings.　One larger drop ye see,
Encircled by nine lesser ; and these in part
By humbler satellites.　But look, a gust
Untoward, smites and dashes one to fragments ;
Which, minding gravity and notions of
Coherence (as if truly asteroids),
Do follow in one path nor trespass e'er
Upon their fellows.　Such is the parent Sun—
A larger drop swung from its nebula,
This pleasant cluster forms, a solar system :
The third and fairest of the drops, this star
Whose face ye now behold.

THE VEGETÆ.

Join we the Circles, and joining
　　We hail ;
Bracing our wings while the mountains
　　We scale ;

Whirl with the rain-drop, and whirling
    Ye sing,
" Here is a universe couch'd in
    A ring."

Join we the Bands, and in joining
    We find
Masses coherent each after
    Its kind.
Build ye the firmament, and building
    Ye cry,
" Limits divide now the earth from
    The sky ! "

Join we the Couriers, and joining
    We shout,
" Yours is the rush and the roar and
    The rout."
Fly ye, and flame ye, and flying
    Ye crash,
Whirlwind and earthquake and
    Auroral flash.

Come we, O Gaia, and coming
    We ween
Shortly thy continents gaily
    To green ;
Aid of the minerals, aid of
    The light ;
Waking at day-dawn, and drooping
    At night.

Wide is the Ocean, and widening
    Below ;
Northward ye beckon, and there will
    We go ;

Anchor us yonder, and anchoring
 Will grow
Where fountains are playing, and rivers
 Do flow.

Flora in Paradise, flowering
 Shall vie
Marvels of beauty with earth and
 With sky ;
Graft on Earth's navel, lo, grafted
 Shall spread—
Ocean pour'd round us, the pole
 Overhead.

THE PLEROMA.

O sacred Top ! the Zion of the North !
Built thee, crystallic Ethers, rearing up
On massy pillars, syenite and granite,
Thy arching summit, towering upward to
The peaceful Pole of heav'n ; when all around
The dusky ocean roll'd.   Thou first didst hear
The fiat : " Let the waters to one place
Be gather'd ; and further let the dry appear ; "
When, 'merging from the bitter seas, sloughing
The pasty sludge, thou 'gan to consort with
The vapors, and invite the willing Winds,
As, shepherding the sweeter airs, they drink
And pasture them upon thy breast.

      Thou mark'st
The Eozoic Age—potential dawn—
Whose fructifying rays wake dynasties
In each particular spore and seed.

Now saith
The Aleim of PLEROMA: " Let the earth
Bring forth the tender grass ; the seeding herb,
And tree, whose seed is in itself upon
The earth."

But heed, ye fiery vapors in
The nether caverns ! Until We summon your
Engulfing fires, this circumpolar garden
Of the Aleim hath peace. To you henceforth
Belongs the chaos of the Southern seas ;
Go, mix, and melt, and mould successive rocks,
Upbuilding continents, and realms for the
Inhabitants, down-streaming from this Mount.

———

The RHYME of the ROOT, the down-growing root :
The basis and stay of the up-greening shoot.
Thou hast broken the gates of the embryo ;
The warmth and the moisture bidding thee go.
Thy home is the darkness ; thy bane is the light ;
And colorless rootlets thou hidest from sight.

Inaxial, axial, thou searchest for food ;
Rejecting the evil, electing the good ;
A bounty of sweets and of mineral salts,
Thou storest in subterranean vaults.

Thy cellular radicle, bidden to spread,
Weaves *Pileorhiza* a cap for its head.
Bores deeper, dividing thread-like in the grasses ;
Then coralline, gathering in nodular masses.

Next, sheath'd in integument, woody and strong,
Thou biddest the Dicotyls join thee in song ;
While lenticle air-roots that drink in the sun,
And parasite feeders are suffer'd to come.

———

The SONG of the STEM—the up-springing stem :
The *Plerome* now fulls in thy coronal gem ;
With its apical seat in the crown of the root ;
And its miniature plan of the stalk and its fruit.

Thy plumule shoots upward to air and to sun,
Divided, dicotyl, or roll'd into one ;
With Circles assisting in shaping thy bole ;
The cellular tissue, or vascular roll.

In-growing, endogenous ; or, growing without ;
With pith or with liber, and xylem more stout ;
Thy axis erect, or lateral bends,
As simple, or branching thy volume extends.

The stipe of the fern, and the trunk of the pine ;
The culm of the sedges, and stock of the vine ;
Their nodular axils shoot left and right,
In spiral obliqueness increasing their hight.

Pyramidal, spreading, or weeping to earth ;
Each resinous bud foreshowing at birth,
Cylindrical tissue, and silvery grain ;
Reticulate, woven, or link'd in a chain.

O potentative plumule ! O green-growing gem !
Thou weav'st for thy brow a bright diadem ;
Thy branches and branchlets are charg'd with the flow
Of juices ascending from fountains below.

The LAY of the LEAF—the protean leaf ;
For beauty and use most easily chief ;
    In the glebe and the glen ;
    In forest and fen ;
Sought ever and never denying reprief.

O imbricate bud ! O fanciful cone !
God heareth and cheereth thy multiple tone.
    Conduplicate fold,
    Reclinèd or roll'd ;
Thou valvate, equitant, circinate cone !

If radicle, posit thyself on the root ;
If cauline, direct from the stem shalt thou shoot ;
    Or tufted and whorl'd ;
    Or rosulate curl'd,
Alternate and opposite never confute.

Ye circles, how runneth the thread of the bole ?
From leaf unto leaf-bud thy spiral unroll ;
    From grasses to pine,
    Thy arches entwine
By fractions of circles describing the whole.

Art sessile ? Do petiole, stipule, and bract
Attend thee ? and sheathe thee ? and keep thee intact ?
    Or, pitcher and spine
    And tendril of vine
Amend for the nutritive sap thou hast lack'd ?

Thy veins and thy veinlets, and *venulets* fine,
A delicate tissue and framework outline ;
    Reticulate chain'd ;
    Or parallel vein'd—
Both simple and multiple fill our design.

3

Thou lung of the Plant ! Thou life of the Tree !
Perfoliate, connate, thy sweet chemistry
    Finds nectar aërating,
    Meantime compensating
With odorous health wafted far o'er the lea.

———

The FAME of the FLOWER—the nectarous flower :
The whorls of thy blossoms build cyclical towers,
    Where the Phyllaries lean
    On a torus of green ;
And the calyx, verticillate, softly embowers.

In the dawn of thy life are thy florets consign'd
To the æstivate bud with its beauties entwin'd ;
    A centripetal heart ;
    A centrifugal part ;
Pedicillate, cluster'd, or rachis confin'd.

Dost thou number by fives in thy perianth keep ?
Or do multiple lives from its citadel peep ?
    The Type is complete ;
    All diversities meet ;
And the Thoughts of the Thinker lie less deep.

O palace of loves !   O garden of brides !
Pollenius finds thee and wooing abides ;
    Thy carpellate fold
    Is sprinkled with gold,
And love, being fertile, in *Ovary* hides.

Ten myriad variants answer our call ;
And the study of one is the study of all ;

From the spore and its root
To the flower and its fruit ;
The Archetype holds, while diversities fall.

THE PLEROMA.

This festival of flowers, O Mineral Airs !
Doth laud your love and bounty amply spread ;
Fore-running time, they sing responsive lays,
Fore-telling shapes and parts idyllic ;—which,
If *enthymemic*, still this feast of yours,
So free and bountiful, shall fill them up ;
And raise to fruitful symbols of the Mind
Of God.
How close in form and function to
These rudimental Types of flowers and grasses,
That blossom in primordial seas, and float
A flimsy raft of tangle and of kelp,
Are those that root and multiply, alike,
By scission, or by seed—the Protozoa—least
Of animate and sentient forms—confus'd
The patterns of both plant and animal.

Salute the Animæ, O Algæ green !
Salute, O Cryptogamia !   Life calls
For life ; conterminous, your bounds, o'er all ;
Coincident, your freedom on this isle.
Together, claim and clarify the seas !
Together, pierce and populate the deeps !
Together, lave and labor on the shores !
And creeping upwards, slowly prove the air
And surface soil an amiable and safe
Environment.

CANTO IV.

THE ARGUMENT.

The PLEROMA *contemplateth the Sun and Moon and Stars,
now for the first time visible to the Earth ; vieweth
the upheaving continents and rejoiceth in the Protozoa.*

THE PLEROMA.

"And it was so!"   Sung first by heavenly choirs,
When brooding o'er the faces of the deep,
Engirt by gloom profound and palpable,
The Spirit of ELOAH cried, "Let there
Be Light!"   Again is sung when ELOAH saith,
"A firmament divide the waters from
The waters."   Again, when gathering the seas
Into one place, and setting bounds thereto,
ELOAH saith :   "Let the dry land appear."
And yet once more the quiring angels sing,
Divining the deep purpose while he cries :—
"Let there be lights dividing day from night ;
Lights set in bluey firmament of heaven ;
For days and years and tokens of His Will ;
And heralds of the seasons " : and it was so.
Pursuant thence the Fourth great day of Time,
The faintly chemic flush, diffusing Gaia—

Translucent to the ardors in her breast,
Surrenders to the regnant beams of Sun,
And Moon, and blinking Stars, blazing their way
Dispersing smoky vapors ; and casting lights,
With notable shadows over all ; while heats,
Kinetic, buy, by silence, gorgeous prints
On ore and crystal ; condensing humid airs
On grass and herbage—precious dews of rain.

So shine thou king of day ! and thou bright queen
Of night ! ELOAH hath decreed, Amen !
Ungirdled to thy blandishments, O Sun,
Doth Gaia bare her breast ; woo ! woo ! and blend
Your lights ! consorting Day with Dawn ; and Night
With Even : resilient to your favors, she
Emerges from her bath and greets thy form
With expectation great, and joy.

———

The GREETING OF GAIA to luminous guest :
With turbulent heart and quivering note ;—
   Passing o'er
   Evermore.
Stay ! Stay ! while nearing our islet ye float:
   Pass not by,
   Or I die !
Be still, O my heart !   List the urgent behest
   Of the king
   On the wing ;
Regarding our smile, approving our song ;
   If he stay
   But a day,
If he show but a blush as he looks at my breast,
I shall dream, I shall dream in the night, of the dawn.

O heat of thine heart !   O blush of thy brow !
Dost thou burn ? wilt thou turn for an hour ?
          Passing o'er
          Evermore !
On my breast thou shalt rest, and embower ·
          Win my heart
          Ere we part ;
All my virginal riches with lustre endow ;
          Pass not by
          Or I die.

Dost flame ? ah the shame ! and still ridest on ?
" The day hath its end, and parteth us even ;
          But the night with its queen,
          Shall shortly be seen,
Whose lustre excelleth the planets seven."
Thus beaming on Gaia, entreateth the Sun,
          Passing o'er
          Evermore.

The MEAD of the MOON—the regent of night :
I wake from my swoon, and drink of thy light ;
          I revive and shall live.
Thou art fair, O thou queen ! and dost rival my love !
Dost thou drink of his sheen, and his blandishments
     prove :
          Ah my heart, canst forgive ?

" A vestal," O joy ! and the king is unwed :
So love doth not cloy, and I deck now my bed ;
          Thou wilt come with the dawn.
Thou art fair, O thou queen ; and dost honor his flame ?
Thou art haughty I ween ; and dost Hymen disdain !
          Haste on, thou life-giving Sun.

Lo, whisperings breathe in the air and the wave ;
While cloudlets me wreathe and I dip me and lave
    In the surf of the shore ;
O thou messenger Morn ! dost thou beckon me blest ?
Or dost beckon forlorn?   If his light warm my breast,
    I shall murmur no more.

'The song of the stars—the far-away stars :
    Twinkling, tinkling—
    Concords beautiful ;
    Motions dutiful ;
    Sparkling, darkling,
A myriad maze of musical motes.

Still the words I divine both soothe and relieve ;
    Listing, trysting ;
    Telling so faintly,
    Never so quaintly,
    Drifting,
    Sifting,
By signs clearly known, " He comes, do not grieve."

Ye fade from the sky at the bugle of Dawn ;
    Flying,
    Hieing.
Whither, O stars, with light winged cars ?
    Swimming,
    Dimming,
A flush, and a hush ;—ah, stars, are ye gone ?

    The Dance of the Dawn—rosy Dawn ;
    Announcing sweet Gaia the Sun :

Lo he rides o'er the deep,
And awaketh from sleep
Primordial plant and animate form ;
By the fiat of God the Ocean's vast swarm.

Hie, Hie, to yon mount, holy mount !
From his summit aloft may'st thou count
Each separate ray
A herald of day ;
His august form rising full from the stream,
Assuring, O maiden, thy hope is no dream !

He comes ! He comes ! and I live !
Gaia lives.   He shall bless me and give
For my fears beating strong
A recompense long ;
Refreshing the air and the meadow and wave ;
Grant all I can think and all I can crave ;
Passing o'er
Evermore.

The ODE of the OCEAN—the primeval ocean :
What Ethers impel thy turbulent motion ?
What hunger is thine gnawing gneissic foundations !
What passions devouring the roots of the mountains !
How tawny thy surge with its fill of debris !
Assorting its load for the floor of the sea.
How complicate silicas wash'd from the field,
Reacting, quartz, limestone, and lithia yield.
Decipher, O Sea, the story of ages !
Geognosy teach in the schools of the sages !
Bid Circles explain their cyclical wonders,
From dew-drop and pearl to sky with its thunders !

Bid Couriers run, electro-magnetic,
The round of their cycles from active to static !
Bid Binders recite of the crystal and ore ;
And the glistering gems that sprinkle thy floor !
Roll, roll, O Sea ! while the Circles embrace thee !
Speed, speed, O Waves ! while the Couriers chase thee !
Stay, stay, O Waters, where Limits command,
And Binders Atlantean rescue the Land !

THE PLEROMA.

Evolve, O Book of Days, thy sept'nate roll !
The Bands connect, the Limits line thy pages ;
The Couriers illume, the Circles read.
Prophetic moulds of Plant and Animal,
How apposite your faintly listless lays
The dying glow of the Archæan age !
While passing forms, proleptic, taste sweet hope,
Presagement of an ampler life.   O LIFE !
Thou hast nor dawn nor eve divisible !
Think we with finite mind as we connote
The rise, the culmination and decay
Of these material envelopes, worn for
So brief an hour ; and slough'd as filth, or dropt
To fill the argillaceous clays, and sands,
With shells of dynasties long perishèd ;
And glories eloquent in death.   Wherefore
If termèd " Protozoa " or, again
" Amœba," " Coral," " Foraminifer " ;
Degrade we not the essences and types
Original in Thee ; nor falsify
The patterns seen before in heavenly places.
Immers'd in this bright maze ye fabricate

Peculiar shrines, and breathe your matin prayers ;
What time the Ethers, wed with Archetypes,
By Our, PLEROMA'S vow, conceiv'd the World,
And sang songs hymeneal round the Throne.

———

Hither, Airs, and list the tone
Of the watchful Protozoan ;
    Millions near it
    Chime and cheer it,
Choosing not to build alone.

Arms have not, yet seize and bind ;
Mouth have not, yet mix and grind ;
Eyes have not, yet quickly find ;
    Headless, footless ;
    Still not bootless ;
Parts have not yet all combined.

Shapeless, quivering jelly-sack,
With an armor for thy back ;
Filaments drawn taut and slack,
    This thing choosing,
    That refusing,
Leaving refuse in thy track.

Who but God hath taught these ways ?
Lit thy phosphorescent maze ?
Softly murmuring His praise ;
    Each and all,
    Great and small—
Manifold and few of days.

The Rune of the Rock—the Archæan rock ;
Thy mysteries break, and thy secrets unlock !
Say thou, what spirits of might first convey'd thee,
And deep in the chambers of ocean here laid thee ?
By whom thou wast powder'd and strown and assorted ?
By whom thou wast tilted and tost and contorted ?
By whom thou wast melted and mix'd and ejected ?
By whom metamorphized and clearly perfected ?
What joints and what fissures and cleavage of layers ;
What minerals base, and what minerals rare !
If granite, or schist or dense syenite ;
Or limestone or marble, and fine diorite,
Impregnate with iron and kindred graphite :
What spirits puissant of fire or of air ;
Or vapor commingled thy masonry share ?

But lo, the lurid flash ! and thunderous crash !
Whilst wild, seething waters tumultuous dash
On the uprearing roof of a new Continent :
To Southward, to Southward, with angular bent.
O hail to the birth of the Archæan Age !
'Mid soughing of seas and the vomit of rage ;
In vain they shall grind and erode thee again ;
In vain they shall strive to possess thee again.

———

The RUSH of the RIVERS—the primitive rivers ;
That spring from the mountains with shudders and
     shivers ;
  That dart and that dash,
  With shiver and flash,
    And hasten to bury themselves in the ocean.
No rippling rills to rivulets grew ;

No peaceful rain and kindred dew
　Came, gemming the grass—
　But instant they mass ;
　　Tremendous the rush and the roar of their motion.

A deluge of vapors condensed in the skies,
The faster ye flow, the faster supplies ;
　No marges to stay you ;
　Nor moors to allay your
　　Impetuous roll to the Archæan sea.

Yet brightening skies shall lighten your toil ;
And channels, worn smooth, appease your turmoil :
　While morass and valley
　Your friendship shall rally ;
　　Enamor, beguile you more restful to be.

Roll on mighty rivers, and freshen the land !
The deep yawning ocean shall bury your sand ;
　The grit and the shingle
　With breccias shall mingle ;
　　And filter your cargoes with singular skill.

Ye brawn, bitter streams make haste !
Deposit your wash and your waste !
　Let meadow and lake
　Sweet waters partake,
　　Give dower to fountain and murmuring rill.

The congener winds, conceiv'd by the glare
Of the gendering sun, in the womb of the air,
　That quicken and fly
　Through the lowering sky,
　　And rival the streams on their rush to the deep,

Gain might in the mountain and speed on the shore ;
Find rest in the azure the higher they soar ;
    O primeval wind and stream !
    Lo, sea and land now teem,
      With millions of creatures that swim and that creep.

CANTO V.

THE ARGUMENT.

The Creator revieweth the domain of the Circles, of the Bands and of the Limits, in the Fauna of the Silurian and Devonian ages.

THE CIRCLES.

Creation advances ;
PLEROMA enhances
    Both scope aad design ;
New types us consigning,
To beauty refining
    With recurrent line.
Three orders inviting,
Our motions delighting,
    While moulding their parts.
One order yet higher
Foreseeing aspire,
    And kindle our hearts.
The ocean prolific,
Thy fiat omnific
    Stays not to fulfill.
Pelagian age !
A vertebrate stage
    More wonderful still !

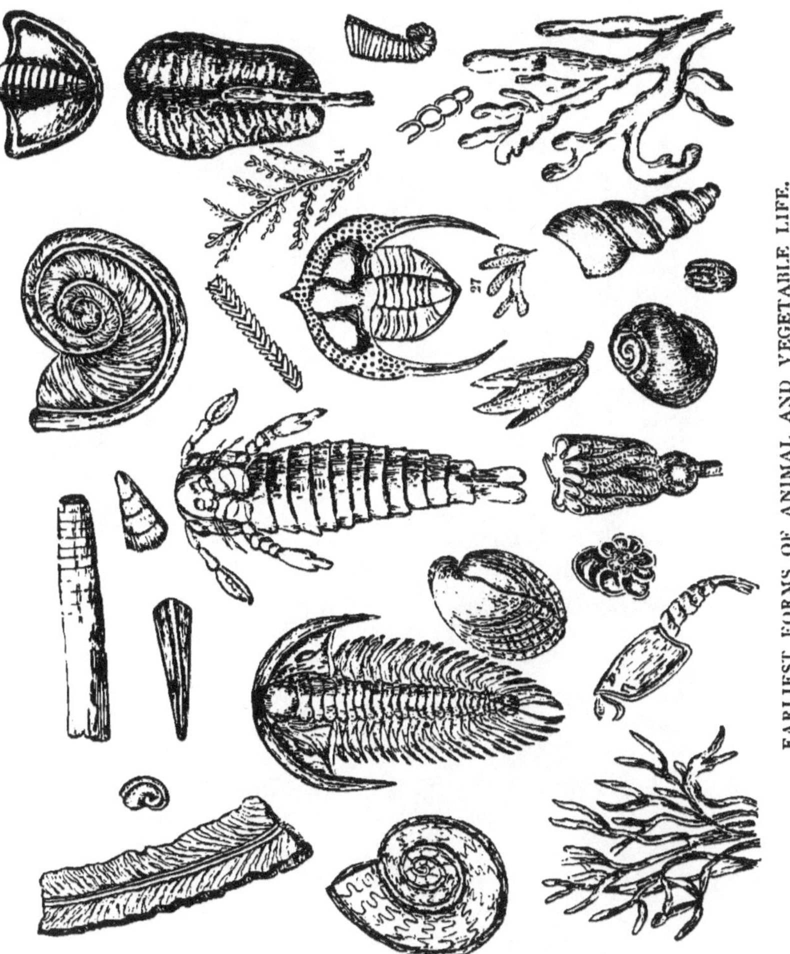

EARLIEST FORMS OF ANIMAL AND VEGETABLE LIFE.

THE PLEROMA.

Ye beauteous Circles, hymn PLEROMA joy,
While graceful curves to plant and animal
Imparting.   To you all organific forms
Resort to mould, embellishing their parts
With comely symmetry.   The Infusoria—
O dainty work ! laud be to the Creator !
Ye teach them circuits infin'tesimal ;
Shape for them cups and vases opaline ;
And form their ova and their embryos.
With round and ovoid disk and cylinder,
Your practis'd art attests each limped sac.
Like dust of dew, the Amœbina too,
Divide and multiply indefinite ;
To whom a tiny drop an ocean seems.
Instruct by you, Reticulata build
Them chambers convex spiral'd axils round ;
While float and swim, contractile and dilate,
The Hydridæ, blood-red, and carmine dyed—
A myriad polyp-vine budding its kind :
Or, scarlet-flowering Tubularia,
Pendent with drooping ovaries ; or plum'd
Polypides that choose the Southern slopes—
So graceful curv'd in arborescence all.
Or, bell-Campanularia that float
Their necto-calyces and stinging arms—
Infinity of filaments ; or thence,
More graceful Agalma, brilliants dispos'd
In bands vermilion, whence well pleasèd hath
ELOAH giv'n defensive weapons.   Ye mould
Physalia, electric bubbles, fairy fleet,
That fans the breeze, with silken filaments ;
And circular Roteria, gyrating as

They move ; these name We also to your praise.
Nor pass We the Medusæ, azure bells—
With lily-crowns and vaulted canopies.
Next, in the ocean world, the Madrepores,
Forming star-stones in beauty vying Flora :
Calcareous cups, cylindric, crown'd by green
Or yellow tentacles.   Next, the delight
Of geometric Airs, starr'd Astreidæ,
With slender pinnate rays, and sinuous cells—
A glob'd commune are they, the Circles' pride.
While singing corals mould the *atollons*,
Uprearing from the deep their rounded isles,
As fringe or barrier reefs, and girdling chains.
Whence Zoöphytes again attest how life
In free development is cyclic, orbital,
Moves spirally, or turns upon itself :
These leave their curious skeleton of tubes—
A myriad organ, musical in growth,
And vocal in repose of Circles' power,

———

An Air to the Group Actinidæ,
As sung in her garden beneath the sea ;
On the marble throne,
Herself had grown—
A slender waist
By Circles laced ;
A rosy crown
With plumes of down—
By the coral queen Anemone.

They call me Queen, O loves of the Sea !
And sue me to tell them our mystery ;

ACTINIÆ OR SEA ANEMONES.

How the Ocean's swarm,
And the Fauna's form,
A floret pure
Should thus allure,
    To become the Sea-Anemone.

But this secret, loves, is our mystic wand ;
To hold it forsook we content the land ;
    The Zoa wed
    And made our bed
    With worm and weed ;
    Still this our meed,
    That our mystery
    Is the wand of the Sea-Anemone.

We praise the Creator, fulfilling his will ;
The secret entrusted inviolate still ;
    For beauty retired,
    Fresh glory acquired ;
    The promise believing,
    Through giving receiving ;
    While freely to Thee
    Falls the wand of the Sea-Anemone.

THE PLEROMA.

O fair Geometers, with further glance
We note, like planets moving in the waves,
Asterias four-armed, with centres circular ;
So timid of approach that, menac'd, choose
To suicide than live to suffer. Near,
With stem cylindric, and with calyx whorl'd,
The fix'd Pentacrinus, five-petal'd rise ;

Whose rock-sown germs take root and grow, at first
Unlike their kind ; and later, with their ties
Dissolv'd, foray on plants and animals.
These all, and more, O sapient architects,
Of shells, emboss'd, or softly delicate,
Or pierc'd by countless spines, or crown'd with gems,
Affirm the Circles' power and magic touch
Upbuilding Man's domain.

THE BANDS.

Ours is the lacing and lining,
And difficult work of combining ;
The exquisite tracing and grain,
Of the ribbon and parallel chain :
Ours the enamel and facing,
And singular coursing and chasing ;
Brilliant the nacre we print,
Rainbow and azure in tint,
Seeking the sea-downs and dells,
To fashion our beautiful shells.
Lowly the forms us entrusted,
Rude to the eye and encrusted ;
Hidden our work nor perfected
Till Mollusk his nest have rejected.
O thou Creator, inviting,
Spread we our patterns inditing
Praises, us thrilling to tell,
Of glory that shines in the shell.

THE PLEROMA.

And these bright Bands, the Circles' adjutants,
Are well select for work beyond the realm
Of minerals ; wherein they prov'd their might

Puissant, 'tun'd to rhythm.   But now again
Their graceful work display'd on lowly life,
Else crude but for their touch, shall raise to seats
Of highest favor.
                        Hail, Artists of the shell !
PLEROMA joins your song.   Yours is to course,
And trace these tests which joyous Circles leave
For you in outline.   Lo, the irradiate face
Of the Almighty ! unwonted light therein ;
For, pleasuring these darling forms He sees
A second heaven on earth : while bands, strong bands,
Constrain Him to this little star endearing.
O lowly Band ! blest Band of prophecy !
Bare We to thee Our inmost heart, and are
At once aflush to greet Thee, Who dost bind
And link in one, both Heaven and the Earth :
In Thee all Bands, all Lights, all Circles, and,
All Limits meet : inmost in Thee shall dwell
PLEROMA of the GODHEAD bodily.

   By odorous Algæ nourish'd, Flustra next
Of Polyzoa intermediate—
Array'd in par'lel-banded-tentacles,
The linear line receive : thence Tunicata,
Of varied metamorphosis, the home
Of parasitic Flora.   Luminous trains
The dazzling-lipp'd Pyrosma grace, while Salpa,
Living chaplets, par'lel-chain'd, in forc'd
Community, both physical and mental :
Each solitaire begetting chains ; each chain
Reciprocal, begetting solitaires.
Thus Bands congreet the Circles, a congress
Of rotary and linear motions.

                                        Let now
The Binder's seminary convene !   All mail'd
And buckler'd, stoutly stalk the hornèd Mollusks.
The vanguard bivalv'd, riveted, and hinged,
With double shells, secreting annual layers
Of iridescent armor.   Salute We each !
Thou art the mining Teredo ! with tool
Of sharpest steel ; and thou the gaping Phocas !
A living point burrowing the gneissic rocks.
Hail, fiery Pholad ! burning wood or iron ;
Hail, slender Solens ! truncate, tinted blue ;
Is this Donax with his revolving auger ?
Is this not glory-crest Telluria ?
And Cytherea also sweet in Bands ?
Leading the brilliant nacred Pintadine—
The mother pearl, whose ribbons green and white
Meet in the top ?   Thy pearls as were they dew
Solidified, increasing with the years ?
While Ostrea spawn the shoals with living dust,
That drifts along the marge.   Next univalves,
Pyramidal and spired, by reedy shores—
The slowly sauntering Snail, the Slug, and Cowrie,
Transversely striped ; the combèd Limpet, too ;
The cuirass'd Chitons ; foaming Iantheria,
And Turbo deeply furrow'd, with wavy mouth,
Trellis'd, and silver traced, and gold ; and those
Basaltic and more rare, the purple-dyed
Purpuræ ; and the sculptur'd Harpæ, dight
With longitud'nal bands and flutings ; Clio
'Mong Pteropods, far-crimsoning the wave,
Hieing the ocean's midst with wingèd feet ;
While last to swell the triumph of the Bands,
Cephalopods, most complicate and dread,

Voracious, hiding in the clefts for prey—
Tri-hearted and encas'd in fleshly walls :
Warfaring and insatiate, thy warty
Poulp and labyrinthine tentacles,
Lie many a yard upon the inky waves—
Most wonderful, most horrible compound !
" Octopus," " Kraken," or " Sepia " call'd.
And ye straight-chamber'd monarchs of the age
Molluscan, the Orthocera, draw on
With conscious majesty your horn-ring'd towers !
While Ammonite and Nautilus, honors
Enhanc'd for Bands in further time essay :
As trimming sails with cautious skill they lean
Upon the wind.

THE LIMITS.

Circles, ye invite us, hight us
Limits to fresh duty, beauty
Us committing, dight in curve and ring.
Binders also luring ; assuring,
Practis'd art consigning, refining
Shells ingrain, and finely chas'd to bring.

Us to work evolving, resolving
Whole and part ; connecting, reflecting
In each rounded part, *Imago's* face.
We assess each member, number
Every thread and spine ; and consign
Duly to each joint its form and place.

Six and fairy-footed ; fluted
Leg and wing ; ever sever
Triple-clefted Insectivora ;

Thence Crustaceæ name we, claim we
Our peculiar order ; border
Realm unto the Vertebrata.

To the Trilobite.

Tri-lobèd Trilobite !
Tell who hath made thee !
Sing of the Circles
And Bands that array'd thee,
    Curving and winding,
    Lacing and binding ;
Limits confiding thee,
Doubly dividing thee,
    Lengthwise,
    Crosswise,
Tri-lobèd Trilobite.

Leaf-like Trilobite !
Say who hath fluted,
Body and buckler,
And jointings computed !
    Ordered thy stages,
    Numbered thy pages ;
First of Articulate,
Myriads to estimate !
    Curling,
    Whirling,
Leaf-like Trilobite !

Many-eyed Trilobite !
Multiple-jointed ;

ANIMAL AND VEGETABLE LIFE IN THE UPPER AND LOWER SILURIAN AGES.

Sing of the Limits
Elect and appointed !
 Sizing and spacing,
 Measuring and tracing
A complicate being ;
Imago foreseeing ;
 Evolving,
 Resolving
The many-eyed Trilobite.

To the Hermit Crab.

Hie thee ! Hie thee
 Sybarite !
Ever timidly
 Choose some shell,
 Empty shell ;
Suit caprice
In the lease,
 Thinly clad Cenobite !

Lo, Corystes, helmet-arm'd—
 Fierce and grim,
 Huge of limb ;
 Stoutly claw'd,
 Barb'd and saw'd,
Thee defenceless hath alarm'd ;
 Safely dwell
 In some shell !
Sent to cheer and live with thee
Hooded Sea-Anemone.

Crab and lobster prowling near,
          Young of prawn,
          Blue and brawn—
Cyclops dread and Daphnia ;
          Segments given
          Threefold seven,
Hear ye what the Limits say !
          " Oddly clad
          Hermit-Crab !
          None more bright
          In our sight !
          Have no fear ;
          Thee we cheer ;
          In thy sorrow
          Teach to borrow—
          Firmly cas'd
          Lin'd and chas'd—
          Spiral'd dome,
          For thy home !
Where with thee cheerily
Dwells the sweet Anemone."

The Roll of the Beach Primordial,
Wash'd by Silurian seas :
A varied fossil life
Hath ended here its strife.
          Devonian waves,
          Ten thousand graves
          Of sponge and rhizopod,
          Of trilobite,
          And graptolite,
          Of gasteropod,

REPTILES OF THE LIASSIC AND UPPER AND LOWER OOLITES.

And pteropod,
Worm and cephalopod,
Ebbing and flowing, delve out in the shore ;
The South-stretching shore,
That wanes nevermore,
While Limits have sway,
And surges obey ;
While continents lift,
And sea-curtains rift ;
While skies grow more clear,
Over mountain and mere ;
Ye are dead, but the Types shall remain ;
Life and death are the links of one chain.
O sough of Silurian seas !
That dieth upon the breeze ;
God readeth thy will,
And filleth thee still ;
Renewing thy age
With a Vertebrate Stage.

CANTO VI.

THE ARGUMENT.

The Couriers, presiding over the Devonian Age, introduce their fleet creations—The Animæ with prophetic glance see the composite forms resolving—The Æons, daughters of Time, review the secular changes—The PLEROMA joys in the works of the fifth Day.

THE COURIERS.

We speed, we speed ;
Swift and strong like the forms we rule ;
We spring to the deed ;
Our work is our meed ;
And drink the wine of life to the full.

Give fin and wing
To fish of the sea and bird of the air ;
To swim and swing ;
To soar and sing,
Voicing our measures unmix'd with care.

Devonian age !
Realm of the fish, the vertebrate fish ;
A saurian stage ;
Synoptical page !
Haste we resolving thy Types as ye wish.

MARINE LIFE IN THE DEVONIAN AGE.

We wield, we wield,
Magical wand o'er the fleet and the strong—
The Acrogen field,
Reptilian shield—
Marking the vistas us given to throng.

We stay, we stay
Never ; nor rest we the Promise to greet ;
The Type now essay,
Divining the day,
Of man ; yea Man, in PLEROMA, complete.

THE PLEROMA.

And evening and the morning were the Fifth
Great Day of time ; nor is it sung, " The Morn
And Ev'n " ;—the days of God begin and end
With noon, high noon.   In burning splendors, lo,
The evening leadeth on the singing heavens ;
With vesper praises answered softily
In mus'cal deeps : these heard, beaming Our love,
More priz'd upon these artists of the shell,
Than dazzling gems strown on pelagic floor ;
Or, shining nuggets quarried from the mine.
And now the Couriers announce the Morn,
To fill and finish all the work decreed
Upon the day when ELOAH saith, " Bring forth
Abundantly O Seas ! the souls that swarm
And swim the swirling wave, and stream ; of fish
Swift *chasseurs* of the deeps ; and birds of wing ;
Each to his kind and apposite his time
And place."
With wands of flame the Couriers,
Creative Airs, forestall the Southern sun,

And fan the sea, while Types, conjunctive types,
Impinge the fecund wave, and float caressing.
Devonian age, awake, thy realm possess !
As vassals, harry now yon princely forms
These coasts ; as *avant*-couriers await thy beck,
Scorning to measure time, or turn, to do
Thy bidding.
     First of the legions, captain,
If not their sire, plieth the plated Ganoid ;
If more or less than fish thou be ; if Sauroid :
If kin of those bursting the bands of sea,
To fly the air, or stalk the beach ; if each
Or all, compact in one composite form ;
Still shudder far the waters as he swims,
And shining, proves his prowess weaken'd naught
By strange and weird complexity.
        Flanking
Him where he floats, behold his twin-born sons—
Dinichthys, filling all the ocean main
With dread.   And Asterolepis, with teeth
Reptilian, whose mammoth jaws open
And shut, as ragged shears ; whose backs stout-built,
With triple horn and starry scales implex'd
And imbricate ; while closely swims uncouth
Cephalaspis, with wing'd and fluted armor ;
In form and force his mighty brother's equal.

And now in splashing sportiveness stream on
The swift marauders, warlike congeners,
Nam'd each connoting well his rank and form ;
The Ganoids speed the tides and glide as shadows
Along the furrow'd plain, with terminal mouth
And supple mail implex'd ; their skeleton,

Unfinish'd, yet an engine potent in the tail,
Well vertebrate—effective oar and helm.
Next, slowing in their serried might the rear,
The plated Placoderms, their armor held
Aloft the waves ; and labyrinthine teeth,
In shining 'rray far down their gaping throats,
Set ventrally ; their bulging bodies, half
Invertebrate, fenc'd fierce with spines.   Them all
When seeking prey, the pristine monarchs shun—
Orthoc'ra, Octopus, out-terror'd terror !
And peer, cyclopean-eyed from rocky haunts,
In deeps profound and dark.

THE ÆONS.

The Air of the Æons, the Daughters of Time,
That number the secular changes in rhyme ;
From the Cambrian gneiss to Corniferous lime,
     On the eve of the age Devonian.
Ye Couriers, hail us, foretelling the gloom
And a tempest portenting to myriads doom,
As crumbling the empire of ocean gives room
     To the dominant arm Laurentian.

Now curtain the shadows the down-arching beach ;
And waters to Southward rich plateaus o'erreach ;
By wisdom instruct, by wisdom we teach,
     On the eve of the age Devonian.
Three variant strata consecutive trace—
The coarse, the fragmental and calcareous ;
While casts of the fossils define you the place
     On the roof of the rock Plutonian.

Niagara limestone, or Helderberg mount,
Their harvest of fossils profusely recount ;
With life juxtapos'd from the Hamilton fount,
    On the eve of the age Silurian.
Of dynasties see the *reliques* blent—
Orthoc'ra, trilobite, Coral *anent*,
With ichthyic archives dismantled and rent
    In the gloom of a night Cimmerian.

Where labor'd in glee the lime-loving swarm,
Catastrophe falls upon bounty and form ;
While burials beautiful sob in the storm
    On the eve of the age Silurian.
Ye wane, O sweet, O fair-chamber'd shell !
The Æons have sounded thy funeral knell ;
But types, kindred types, shall follow thee well,
    On the dawn of the age Amphibian.

THE ANIMÆ.

We crawl and creep ;
We climb and leap ;
Swim we and fly
Afar and high ;
    Life is our breath ;
With Minerals wed,
With Vegetæ fed ;
By Circles curv'd,
And Binders nerv'd,
While Couriers speed,
And Limits read
    " Life treads on death."

Upspringing forms,
Full in the storms,
    That end our days ;
God is our breath,
Life feeds on death ;
Short is the stay ;
Brief the essay
    To sing His praise.

Creator, Thou,
Thrilling us now ;
Voice of the seer
Over the mere
    Lifting we chant ;
Chang'd is our mood,
Spurning all food ;
Lost in surprise,
Bury our eyes ;
Cover our face,
Meanwhile we trace
Far down the stream—
Fanciful stream—
    Fauna and Plant.

Ichthyic monarchs of the main,
  Quaffing the wassail of the wave,
    Heed ye the gospel of the Sea ;
Ye are the burden of our strain.
  Ceasing awhile to lash and lave,
    Hear ye what is, and what shall be.

Reach'd is the limit of the old ;
  Known from this day be time as new ;
    The middle line hath life now pass'd :

Behold the plan of God unroll'd,
　And sing his praise, meanwhile ye view,
　　And read, " The First shall be the last."

For God is one, and one his world ;
　And life aspires to breathe the air,
　　The tread of feet, and whir of wing,
Announce the Æons have unfurl'd
　The living bulletins ye wear,
　　To analyze the forms ye bring.

Lo, paddling yon Bavarian field,
　See ye the Archeosaurian !
　　Or fish, or reptile ? both or none ?
Doth Placoid scorn to own his shield ?
　Doth Ganoid dread Amphibian ?
　　And Placoderm his sons disown ?

Devonian chiefs that scour the seas,
　Nature abhors the composite ;
　　The *sauroid* forms shall rise or fall.
Rise till they wing the scented breeze ;
　Fall till they crawl the oozy bight,
　　While medial types intact forestall.

Yet through the age of Acrogens,
　Amid the haunts of beast and man,
　　Tasting the depths of Nature's fount,
Gleams still the Ganoids' diadem,—
　Heir to the throne Devonian,
　　Whose years in vain they seek to count.

For God is one, and His world is one ;
　And the types are the links of a chain,
　　And the chain is roll'd in the Germ.

God's way is one, and when it is done,
  And variant forms find their cradle again,—
    " The Permanent Type " is the law ye learn.

THE PLEROMA.

O verdureless and steaming slopes that bare
Your bosoms from the surge, and fend the gulfs
And still lagoons ; ye are the realm elect
For Cryptogamia that swarm these shores,
Alluring and allur'd.   Saluteth you anon
The Ancient North ; her fruits she sendeth forth
In colonies to garnish all the earth.
From circum-polar parts transplant, in soils
More quick, and airs more humid, shall they soon
Lead forth and crown the shallowing lake and marsh
With herbage tropical ; naming their reign
The Age of Plants.   Then gird, O Vegetæ,
Afresh !   Pour from the shadowy urn of thoughts
Your boon and beauties typical ; and haste
The Age of Man !   Drink up the noxious airs
With marvelous chemistries employ'd !   Store up
The light and heat, the perfume and the oil !
Draw up elixirs from the tepid marge,
And, dying, print a frescoed vault within
The silted peat, from which in distant years
Transform'd in radiances and calories,
Wondrous illume the ways of God to man.

  And ye, O Animæ, ye are now girt
Afresh for mighty enterprise, what time
The cosmic forces rally to your aid ;
Your songs inspiriting have rous'd the Airs,
And instant vigors fly as couriers, to do

Our pleasure.   Mirror'd upon the horizons,
Ye saw, and newly, the shining goal of life—
The *Plerome* of PLEROMA, whereupon
Your ecstacies express'd o'erpowering
In lines prophetical, have thrill'd the Soul
Itself of BEING.

———

The Air of the Acrogens,—point-growing stems :
    Myriad milliards
    Cellular Sigillards,
Flowerless, bowerless, pitted, and scarr'd ;
    Millions rush-like ;
    Millions fern-like ;
    Gem of the anthracite,
    Reed-like Calamite
    Fluted and whorl'd,
    Hollow'd and curl'd,
Intricate, infinite, cover the sward.
    Delicate fronds,
    Complicate bonds,
    Wide-spreading roots,
    Multiple shoots ;
    Needle-like leaves,
    Tapering sheaves,
    Odorous cones
    Conifer owns—
The queen of the coal-forming band.
    Mystical cone,
    Joy of our throne ;
    Spiral'd and cleft
    Rightwise and left ;
    Primal and dual

Spiral'd our jewel ;
Quintuple, octuple,
Obliquely parallel,
Phyllotax windeth,
Waxeth and bindeth,
With God in the secret, guiding her hand.
What time with wondering,
Guessing and blundering,
Finitely human figure thy line ;
Whene'er with fancy—
Queer necromancy !
Incidence, accidence,
Join they with chance ;
Sweet lips and dutiful ;
Parting so beautiful,
Telling and spelling,
Kindly compelling
If with reluctance
Final acceptance—
" God, he, hath made thee,
Plac'd and array'd thee !
The thought of thy spiral 's truly **Divine.**"

THE SEASONS.

The Song of the Seasons—offspring of the Year,
In greeting fair Gaia, and bidding her cheer ;
While each in her turn
Pours forth from her urn
The favoring treasures she gives to the Earth.
Bright Summer, the first-born, her tropical wealth
Of colors and odors, and savors of health ;

'Midst showers of sheen,
And oceans of green,
     And balmiest breezes, and measureless mirth.

Next, Autumn, her fruits and sadly dear signs,
For the rim of the trees and the leaf of the vines ;
     For the gild of the glade,
     And arboreal shade,
          Pours freely out of her golden horn.
Then Winter her crystalline gems displays ;
With icily bands for the rivers and bays ;
     A surcease of sorrow,
     Fore-shortening each morrow,
          With laughter and love while the fire burns warm.

And, last of the sisters, the Eastering Spring,
Untying the breezes she binds in her ring ;
     Her magical marvels
     She quickly unravels,
          And, *presto*, the white is a garment of green !
We four are four sisters—offspring of the Year ;
In circuits returning allaying thy fear ;
     Each change giving beauty,
     Fulfilling our duty,
          While God in the secret preserveth the mean.

———

The Archæan Marshes, measureless marshes !
Brilliant savannas, and forests of larches !
Peat-forming, warm, Carboniferous marshes
          That fringe the inland seas ;

Lepidodendra, scaly and spired ;
Ribb'd Sigillaria, rudely attired ;
Complicate tree-fern, ever admired,
    That murmur in the breeze.

Hum with the nerve-wing insect swarms,
Orthopter, neuropter, gay silken forms ;
Rend with the earthquake ; moan with the storms
    That crush the shady bowers.
Corridors echo to Archeosaurus,
Bellowing near—a shuddering chorus ;
Sluggard Amphibians drowsing before us,
    While Phœbus looms and lowers.

The Cry of the coal-fields,
    Silted and sanded,
    Delug'd and stranded,
      Buried and whelm'd by the sea :
"Teredo !" "Teredo !"
This dark realm of Pluto
    Yields thee its mystery.

The cheer of the coal-fields ;
    Joy of the Teredo,
    Piercing thee far below,
      Reading thy epics in stone.
    Fairiest etching,
    Miniature sketching—
    Picturesque Carbon
    Bathing in Acheron,
      Priceless the treasure ye own.

O charm of the coal-mine !
    Unctuous measure,
    Luminous treasure,
      Fuel stored up for mankind ;
    " Teredo ! " " Teredo ! "
    Piercing thee far below,
      Sings of provision design'd.

THE PLEROMA.

O fairest Flora ! hail, behold how throb
And thrill the marshes and the glades with life !
Heard are intense and festive airs ; the Seasons
Four, benignant, entertain the woods ;
While from exhaustless garderobe, Nature
Her heaths and everglades arrays.   Of pride
The Conifers display their curious cones—
A micro-marvel—Ferns majestic rise—
Vital transparencies.   Lepidendrids,
Wide-rooting, rhomboidal, and scaled, paint all
The scene, a forest fleet ; the Calamites,
With tapering, stately stems and jointings whorl'd,
Uplift colossal ; while Sigillaria,
As stubborn sentinels, protect the group.

    Yet lowlier forms arrest our gaze : the thorn'd
And captious cactus, silly rush and reed ;
The merry brake, the battle-loving moss ;
Grasses and vines his fiefs ; these all allure
And greet the pictur'd moths and butterflies,
The cunning ants and beetles militant—
Both Menelaus, Achilles, and in love
Adonis.   Next the housely weaving spider,

FLORA OF THE CARBONIFEROUS AGE.

The suicidal scorpion, Arachnida,
The timid cockroach Orthopter, all late
Emerg'd the wave ; and pleas'd to creep the sward,
Or fly the air ; feeding on nectaries,
And sweets stolen from the amorous sun,
Sometime, when peering 'neath the curtain'd woods,
The playful Zephyrs slyly creeping him
Behind, sipp'd from his horn elixirs rare,
And quickly kiss'd the flowers.
                                    And ye of might,
O Animæ ! with cosmic airs engirt,
Enforce the Law of Difference ; and haste
Composite forms to specialize.   The Sea
Salutes the Land : the ocean-denizens
Attempt the rising shores ; and thus excite
The latent variants that foment in them
Clamors and strivings, paroxysms fierce ;
And heap diverseness on diversity.
O wretched congeries !   O vital chaos !
Now breathe upon this troubled sentiency—
Confus'd in mighty struggle with its selves,
The Spirit of harmonious unity !
Whose distant goal is Man ; whose regimen
Divides to join ; dissociates to wed ;
Resolves to order and coördinate
Again diffus'd extremes of Life in one
Their ultimate and end.
                            Ye Saurians !
This is the hour of fear and dissolution !
O Protean Labyrinthodonts ! despair
Yawns from these ragged gills, and fretted lungs—
Your hour and power dies utter, nor returns ;
Yet dying, spring, full-ribb'd and ray'd at once

From out your crowded wombs more perfect fish
And reptile ; as the Types prophetical
The Neozoic world, do shortly trace
Their lines divergent from your graves.

THE PSYCHÆ.

Ah, Permian Pall ! ah, crisis of doom !
What tremors and jars ! what salvage is hewn
   From the storm-riven shore !
What clysms of stays, and giant supports,
While Ocean gives vent his fiery retorts
   'Midst froth and 'midst roar.

What sobbing is this and anguish of birth,
While mountainous wrinkles appear on the Earth,
   In the depths of the Permian night.
O sigh of the marsh ! O throb of the deep !
Immutable forms have found their last sleep
   And wake nevermore to the light.

The Birth of the Appalachian hills
Is the carol of winds and the echo of dales,
   Of a widening continent ;
O cairn of the Paleozoic age !
O turning point in the cosmic page,
   With a star for the mind's comment !

THE PLEROMA.

Fled is the desolating storm ; and now
Resume the choirs creative melodies ;
The same, and yet another world is this !
The change how sudden, how paroxysmal !

The pensive Flora hail their bright reserves—
Palmetto-cycads answering, and those
Call'd Cypress-Volzias ; while from the knolls,
The breezy lifts of land, greet waving Palms,
And sturdy Dicotyls, leading the van
Of hardy forest trees.   The crowded North—
Primeval fount, anew pours forth her swarms
Of lives, that swim and creep, that stalk and flit ;
All Protean types, and plastic to each change
Of clime, as is yon mute mirage that plays
Its mimicries upon the vapory plain,
Taught by the changing lights and shades.
                                  The Sea
Shall shortly abdicate his throne and yield
The Continents precedence ; the triple East—
Europa, Asia, Africa ; the West—
Twin-form'd Americas ; all offspring of
That rock archæan of the midnight sun,
And from his loins prolific peopled.
                                  For,
Betwixt his spreading limbs, fast by the shore,
A grotto small and dazzling rare with gems,
Protects a crystal fountain call'd " The Fount
Of Life," as sweet to taste and purely pure,
As dew distillèd and filterèd o'er
The dust of diamonds.   Thus garnish'd bright,
Illum'd with light direct from Phœbus' wheel—
What time his daily round upon the wave
Returning, shone full in the cavern's heart—
The Flora, seeking for some sheltering spot
To rest and taste refreshment, passing near,
Perceiv'd the babbling stream ; when, glancing in,
Awoke more joy and wonder instantly,

Than when fair Gaia bared her breast, and bade
Them early welcome.   Entering forthwith
They quaff'd elixirs from the living brook,
And slept, the first or ever on the shores
Of Earth.   Eftsoon, the cosmic Airs return'd
To this their trysting place, and saw with mute
Uncertain wonderment, the spiritual Flowers
In naked beauty sleeping; half in doubt,
And fearing 't were a figment of the mind :
When innate pureness led them to withdraw.
Refresh'd, the Flowers awoke, and bath'd them in
The tonic bath; clad them again in their
Bright, perfum'd robes, and joining hands, went forth
To trace the limpid stream unto the sea.
There heard they drifting music on the air—
The choir of Circles, Bands, and Couriers—
Led by the rhythmic Limits ; and of love
And guileless passion sang.   O perfect forms !
Struck from the heavenly mint, God's precious Powers !
What marvels the event that nam'd this stream
"The Stream of Life," where woo'd and wed
The cosmic Airs the loveliest Flora ;
And offspring rear'd beside the laughing fount !
Whence, as the rills to brooks, the brooks to rivers
Descending grow, so yonder rill of germs
Flows on increasingly, and spreads its banks
Of plants and flowers athwart the continents.

THE PSYCHÆ.

The Rage of the reptile Saurians !
The Joust 'twixt the Sea and Land !

LIFE IN THE TRIASSIC PERIOD.

'Mid the salt Lagoons,
On the gypsum dunes,
And the buff-blown shining sand.

The shout of the Sea, " Enaliosaurs ! "
The call of the Land, " Ye Dinosaurs ! "
To the fray, O Powers !
While the storm-king lowers,
And the billows kiss his wand.

Ye plunging, paddling Placoderm !
In vain thy qualms, in vain thy roar,
The chiefs of the Land
Shall rule the Strand ;
To the deeps, ye turtle Plesiosaur !

" The Land is lord "—the Couriers shout,
" The reptile king is the Deinosaur !
He shall stalk the coast,
With his bird-like host—
The sovran-count of the Sea and Shore.

THE PSYCHÆ.

Hail to the Bird Primeval !
If bird, in truth thou be—
Hail to the wingèd reptile !
If saurian still we see.

Is Pterosaur thy mother ?
Stout-girded form ?
Feather'd and firmly keeled,
Contending with the storm ?

Tell us, O bird ungainly,
    Since bird in truth we hail ;
Why is thy beak reptilian ?
    And lizard-like thy tail ?

Ah, Bird, thy say is ancient,
    Ancient as is the sun ;
" Our type shall be perfected,
    When Limits shall have done."

Lo, Couriers salute thee ;
    The Limits pass thee on ;
And soon thy balanc'd pinions
    Shall hide the noon-day sun.

THE COURIERS.

We fly, we fly !
Swift is the work we essay ;
    Give fin to fish,
    And wing to bird ;
And shortly are up and away.

We fly, we fly !
Swift is the work we essay ;
    Yet pass not by,
    But linger nigh,
Till the bird shall wing our way.

The *teleosts* along the coasts
Are the rangers of the deep,
    And the soft gazelle
    Over hill and dell
Shall fly with wingèd feet.

The bird of wing shall soar and sing,
    And pierce the azure height ;
    So hail, fair bride !
    By the Couriers' side
Is the pledge of song and light.

*   *   *   *   *

The splendid reign Reptilian
    Falls crumbling on the strand ;
But the Couriers trace a nobler race,
    Ruled by the Psychic Hand.

CANTO VII.

The Sixth Creative Day evoked ; further preparations for the ensphering of the Psychæ—The Æons sing the course of the Fauna—Lucifer, regent, visiteth the Earth and receiveth with disdain the ovation of the Ethers—The Sacrament for sin offered in the Heavenly Places— The cheer of the Psychæ—The Cosmic Forces assemble and search inaugurated for Man now the universal Theme—The PLEROMA *with the heavenly choirs attending breathes the psychic principle into the natural man in the sub-polar Paradise.*

THE ANIMÆ.

Terrestrial fervors, potent powers !
    With vital forces wed ;
Expressive tokens apposite
    Delight the marriage bed.

Animic forms are bodied thoughts,
    With you their chief support ;
Though sudden shocks dissever us,
    Again we soon consort.

Or link'd or free, there is no death,
    Life goes to come again ;

The vital Airs are everywhere,
And God is One in them.

The crystal rhythms again evoke
The Sixth creative Day,
When God to us the Animæ
Conjoins his Majesty.

Forthwith ye potent magnetisms,
The psychic realm embrace ;
And we, appris'd, advance the hour
That greets the Godlike race.

THE PLEROMA.

How purely white and chaste these chalky rifts,
That part pacific bays, where Rhizopods,
And Coccoliths, lime-loving swarms, live out
Their little day, minutely perfect lives,
Among the minim forms of earth : and then
Do softly drop their glinting micro-shells
Upon the ocean floor, a sacrifice to man.
Not less vicarious yonder corallin'es,
That build themselves into his habitation !
Nor darkling where they sink, the carbon fields
Express less benefit fore-given.   Yea, if
Were tax'd yon grizzly cliffs, Sierras, and
Those Andean, in answering the quest
Wherefore they groan and struggle from the waves,
With mount'nous travail,—would they nod assent,
" The canon of the world is Altruism."

For yet hath fall'n no cool refreshing rains ;
No mellow radiance fulls in the clouds ;

No bath of fragrant dews, and crisp of frosts.
This known, the legion of the cosmic airs
Consentient strive, and push aloft yon mounts
That ridge and belt the earth, and greet
The morn of Neozoic time with leash
Of winds and couchant clouds, that bide the day
Of man, to water first the fallow ground.

O burst of Life ! O leap of Flowers ! Erstwhile
O'erspringing yonder shoals of clearest chalk,
They green the foot-hills and the heights with growths
Deciduous, adapt to cooler climes.
Hail potent Day !   The Sixth creative scene !
Thee now salutes the forest choir with lute
Of Evergreen and Laurel.   Bidding on
The stately Palm and Cypress—elder forms ;
Forthwith, in silken robes and rustle, go
The Sycamore and Tulip-tree, the Oak
And silv'ry Poplar.

THE PSYCHÆ.

Tears of the Poplar, mystical Amber !
Resin, translucent and pale ;
Shed by Catania,
While fair Urania
Murmur'd her ominous tale :

Story of strife abroad in the Heavens ;
Lucifer, star of the morn—
Prince of the Earth,
Priding his worth,
Useth Electron with scorn.

Noble Electron, first to Urania
  Born and embower'd in light,
    Rose in his splendor,
    Sought him to render
  Honor befitting his might.

Lucifer loom'd in his armor defiant ;
  Heedless the voice of the Throne ;
    Flam'd in fierce choler,
    Reckless the dolor,
  Ruin to bring Electron.

Quoth then the Voice of the Lord of the Heavens :
  " Lucifer ! Star of the Morn !
    Spurning Our pardon ;
    Vain is thy guerdon !
  Rent is thy kingdom and torn !

Hear ye, O Angels, the fiat of Heaven !
  Psychæ are loos'd from his sway ;
    Fief to Electron,
    Lucifer—Archon—
  Holdeth the Earth from this day.

His be the physical realm and the motive ;
  Passion and pride his delight ;
    Reason, for choosing ;
    Will for refusing,
  Psychæ shall hold in their right."

Luminous Amber, seal of Electron ;
  Tomb of the whimsical bee ;
    Seeing, take warning !
    Lucifer ! scorning
  The bliss of the pure and the free !

6

THE PLEROMA.

Hail, leafy choirs, far from your common home
In polar Paradise ! envoy'd by Flora,
Exploiting vales and moors, the plateaus and
The mounts ; part orientate to the land
Of Dawn ; where mellow airs and gorgeous tints
Entice them ; part streaming to westward where
The Rockies rear their min'ral palaces,
Along whose granite colonnades descend
The footsteps of the setting sun ; growing
Meantime in hardiness, and clad in green
Perennial, against the shimmering fields
Of snow.   We pass you on, pronouncing good
And perfect the *Imago* of the Flora.

Ye are henceforth a volume lined and bound,
Ornate with lustrous tokens of the Law
Of Life—cause and effect, concurrent, of
Environment.   Thereto let Hindostan,
And burning Vera Cruz ; wintry Thibet,
And the eternal verns of Mexico ;
The flooded forests of the Amazon—
The Andean paramos ; Arcadian vales,
And mossy Floridas, repeat the law
Confirming that in nature nothing is
Unto itself ; nor carries in itself
The reason of its form and function.

        Wherefore,
O psychic Airs, whose moods now mist and melt
In tears and anxious auguries, more trist
By far, deciph'ring in the electric gem
The doom of Lucifer, with homage to
The great Electron of the Sun ; whereon

Dependeth mighty ends and offices
Of grace, ordain'd before the Earth was fram'd ;—
Wherefore take heart, and surely know the race
Ye run, when ye shall be inflesh'd and reck'd
Among the incarnations of PLEROMA,
Hath set for it a goal, whither ye run,
As potent to transform and amplify
The human powers, in striving thereunto,
As yonder flowers diversify and feel
The quick'ning *virtus* of the heights, quitting
The shores and humid meads, to gain thereby
Regal varieties and nobler splendors.

Behold and ponder, psychic Airs, the key
Of individuated life ! a talisman
And recondite devise to correlate
Home and its habitant ; this shall be styl'd
The *Difference*, or *Effort* next of kin,
Or *Natural Selection ;* but be assur'd,
The FOUNT of special forms is higher than
The banks whose branching arms they course between.

For " habitat," though excitant, that shapes
Forms apposite and pairs peculiar lives,
The potence to create and juxtapose
Hath not ; nor recks the pangenetic germs
First sown on inorganic shores.   Nor shall
The onward flow and upward effort end,
Till ev'ry spiritual Plant and Animal,
And Psychic individual, receive his place
Among the orders of the Earth ; therefrom
To share the triumph of PLEROMA-CHRIST,
Earth's apotheosis and Nature's Goal.

The essence of the outward world the mind
Of finite man doth not perceive ; to him,
(And ye, O Psychæ, shall we soon address
As such), to him all knowledges are seen
As relative, phenomenal—prints from
A vast Unknown, beyond him and beneath.
And lo, your eyes so soon to shut upon
The Infinite, are voyaging far and near
This world of blooming difference, to fill
Your souls with proofs, exhaustless and abiding,
Of a Divinity in Earth, and of a Love
That frames and furnishes for man his home.

First, ye survey the humid realm and note
The deeps profound of Ocean ; their colors and
Their currents strong that clarify the seas :
The mighty rush of tidal waves that break
Upon resounding shores ; the gusty winds
That race with fickle lust athwart the main ;
And those more constant, veering Southward far ;
Or the Monsoons that taste the feverish tropics.
How blue and how intense the azure sky !
The air how light and rare ! This is the time
Of calms, the zone of om'nous silences :
Behold the regnant orb hastes on his course
With ashen countenance and dread t' ascend
His zenith throne. Abide his culmination !
Ah stifling heats, and dank humidities !
That weight the atmosphere quiv'ring beneath
The flames of Phœbus ! Lo, the sleeping storm
Awakes ! grave Silence breeds terrific roar,
And inky spectres spring full-grown and grim
Into the sky. The Psychæ quake ; fall rains,

And rush the floods ; the meadows sink along
The Orinoco's marge ; while Paraguay
Becomes a land of lakes and low lagoons.
Aquarius turns his spout upon the crown
And selvas of Madeira—queen of streams ;
Next, rich supplies invokes the ancient Nile,
Immortal flood, dark Afric's eldest born.

O Winds, the day of Man is nigh !   Lift from
The waves moist exhalations, bearing them
On wings unseen, and yield their vap'ry treasures
Yon mounts to irrigate the land.   For airs
Surcharg'd with drink no longer drift and lie
Upon the widening landscapes.   Hear their song !

Greet ye the semi-circling Alps, and Ghauts
In vapors hid ! the archèd Apennines,
And Himalayas, nurse of streams !   Greet not
The smoky Caledonias !   Sing not
Of Tangout's drought, nor of Sahara's waste ;
But Thibet sing that weds the tropic Ind
With royal dower ; Deccan and Indo-China,
With gums concentrate, aromatic spice ;
Of Cinnamon and Clove ; Nutmeg and Ginger ;
With Coffee-plant and Tea in utmost Orient.
Sing of the Occident in rivers proud !
The Rios and that Maranon !   Ohio !
Missouri !   Sing the Giant Palm far-fam'd
Of South-America, the leafy king :
Of dazzling flowers and climbing vines profuse,
That scorn the paucity of animals.
Sequoia sing, the loftiest of the Pines,
Whose stalwart quadrates guard unequall'd vales

Of golden California. The Cedar sing,
Elect of God and named " The Tree of Life "—
The throne and glory of the garden-choir—
Fair symbol of man's immortality :
Whence God shall crop a young and tender twig,
And plant it on a mountain eminent
In Zion : a plant of great renown. Thus far
And wide ye glance the teeming continents,
O psychic Airs, the *Law of Difference*
Exploring, and confirming how all forms,
Indigenous, reflect both site and clime ;
Each plant and animal connotes his home
To be terrestrial or maritime,
Or insular. If mean, embryonal,
The last ; if varied, vigorous, the first ;
If feminal and lavish of soft garbs
And sensuous animism, the median.

THE PSYCHÆ.

O fair illusions ! Rivers, Waves, and Winds ;
Whence is the force that flows ? the sympathy that binds ?
Which is the organific ? which the inorganic field ?
By Bands magnetic, and electric Couriers, thrill'd.

Ye mighty bastions of the continents,
By earthquake seam'd and fiery rain besprent !
Say whence the Power pent up within your breast ?
Bid pulsive Limits calm and give thee rest !

Ye Circles, hail ! the living orbit swings ;
Life's summit reach'd, again its Author brings ;
Then haste your course, ascend the way of Man ;
For now the stream returns whence it began.

The fin preserves its type,—the ganoid Pike—
Yet yields the Saurian paw, and wing, alike ;
Upward attains the true placental kind,
While hoof and hand forestall the reign of mind.

O much PLEROMA ! hast Thou shown to-day
To speed our courage on the earthward way ;
Our incarnation we accept with grace,
If Thou do still reveal to us Thy Face.

THE ÆONS.

The Air of the Æons, the offspring of Time,
As, calling the course of the hours, they climb
To the verge of the Sixth great day sublime,
   On the Uintah beds of Coryphodon ;
O Œnnigen sands ! O silvery beach !
The lesson here writ is the lesson we teach ;
The words of thy strand are the fossiliz'd speech
   Of the insect fly and the Tillodon.

These wrecks, by the way, do their wand'rings rehearse ;
As vassals of sun and clime they disperse,
Where wide is the world ; and climes are diverse ;
   And name us the steps of their variation ;
Echidna, Anteater, and Marsupial,
Kangaroo, Wombat, and vile Sacophile ;
Cetaceæ the Right, and the great Rorqual ;
The Amphibian Morse, and the Ursine Seal ;
Till we meet the Mammalia placental,
   By slow or paroxysmal gradation.

Weird age of the Sauroid horde, thou art gone !
But huge are thy offspring the thickets that throng ;

If Paleothere old, or Dinothere strong ;
Dinoceros fierce, and the big Mastodon ;
Woe wails o'er the earth in aphelion
  And the glacial cold that ensues.
Haste Ungulate herald thy record unroll !
And tell us the variant names on thy scroll ;
The even-toed Ruminants, the Pachyderm odd ;
Ox, Tapir, and Camel, Camelopard :
From Hippus *tri-digit* in Eocene lifts,
To the one-finger'd horse of the Pliocene drifts,
  And its value to man that accrues.

O realm of the Circles ! we pause to descend
To the Florida reefs ; and their terraces trend ;
See order in species instinctively bend
  Submissive from earliest to latest ;
Actinidæ, Fungoids, Astereas, Porites ;
Thence rising to Madrepores, Halcyonites ;
The Limits announced, the Lerneans proceed,
With Trilobites, Lobsters, and Crabs in the lead,
  Till the Vertebrate type Thou instatest.

Anew We salute the Mammifer age,
To trace out the links in the penumbral stage
Of Man : O Man ! thou must come ; for the page,
And the last wants its FINIS alone ;
But hush ! See effulgent yon cloud on the strand,
Advancing and meeting the cosmical band !
O moment impending ! we fear to command ;
  Art Lucifer proud ? or the great Electron ?

THE PSYCHÆ.

The God of the Gall-fly is the God we adore,
And the suffering Oak that protects it ;

MAMMALS AND BIRDS OF THE EOCENE, MIOCENE, AND LATER AGES.

O mothering tree !
What cradles ye build
These minims to shield,
As nice in their nest
As the bliss of the blest !
Say who hath inspir'd thee to use of thy store,
And build for this fly
A house with no visible eye that directs it ?
Ah, bothering fly !
What brushes ye ply
So worryingly !
With needle and hasp,
With auger and rasp,
Whilst flower and leaf,
Thou bringest to grief ;
Whence cankering juice
Exudes for thy use,
And the Oak bends with awe
To the march of the law
Which Flora to Fauna subdueth :
Yea the meanest insect she bows to protect ;
And the gulf that divides
Mute sympathy hides ;
While a tree without hands
Feels silent commands ;
Takes a waif to its breast,
And fashions a nest,
Lest the infant should die,
As in innocency
Grows pregnant the cell it embueth.

The God of the Gall-fly is the God we adore ;
And the suffering Oak to protect it ;

And marvel the psychical Airs more and more
As they traverse the world and inspect it,
    Do we sing of the Gall,
    And its succulent ball ;
    Or the Moth do we sing
    With its mimicry wing ;
    Or the skill of the Bee
    That honeys the tree ;
    Or the flash in the stream
    Where the Ousel doth gleam ;
    Clad in glistering white
    As it darts from our sight,
    With song's purest lute,
    'Neath the tinkling brook :
    In each and in all ;
    Or greater or small ;
    The Animæ's word
    Is everywhere heard :
" Our life is the gleam of the glorious Sun :
And our instincts are rhythms of feeling ;
Innate in us, Reason and Will both are one,
To the INFINITE ever appealing."

THE COSMIC ETHERS.

Hail Star of the Morn ! thou archon of Earth !
    The Cosmical forces congreet thee !
      The Circles surround ;
      The Couriers sound
    Their jubilant notes as they meet thee.
      The Bands joining hands,
      Await thy commands,
With Limits extolling thy worth.

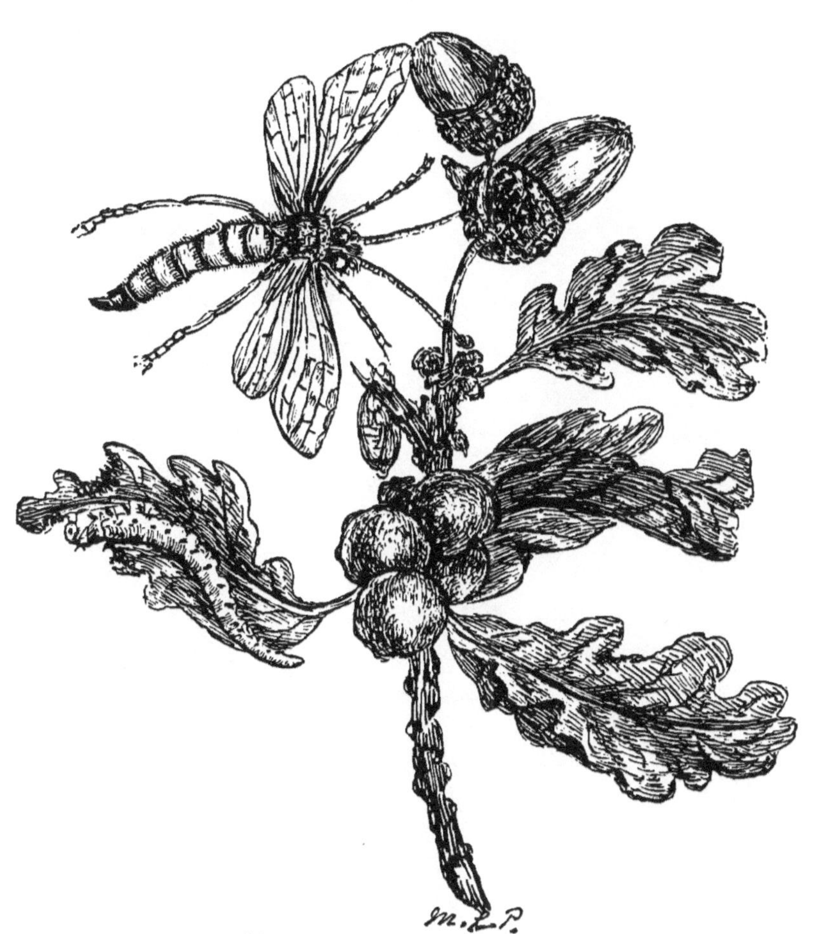

OAK GALLS, WORM AND FLY.

The Flora, our brides, abide in the grove,
   Where they cheerily wait thee O Guest !
     Thou shalt rest in their bowers,
     And beguile thee the hours,
   And call us to do thy behest.

LUCIFER.

  Ye mundane Energies ! substantial Airs !
You, Lucifer, indulgent prince, salutes !
And in you be this Earth your handiwork
Saluted. Ye do call us, " Prince of Earth " :
And festive bands obsequious advance
To greet with *salvos* of devotion. Aye !
If ye that look conglob'd and circumscrib'd
Be Circles, hail ! Your rotary regimen
We welcome heartily, and shall employ
In *circum*-colloquies convenient.
                   If ye
That stand aloof, divisive Limits be,
The Negatives in Nature, Lucifer
Foresees for you a vicinage anent
The very heel of power, whene'er mankind,
(Our forfeiture and wreck'd avenge), doth meet
This ancient Throne of Heav'n.
                 O bitter light !
Even Electron, nominate the liege
Of Lucifer ! Zounds ! Shortly stall'd in this
Our proper heritance and right divine,
By damnable respect of personages riv'n,
They shall but rue atteint they make on this
Puissant princedom.
           Sweetest Bands, in peace
Draw near, nor let our ardent imageries

Perturb you.　Lo, a mighty Star from Heav'n
Hath fall'n, whose flaming chariot did drive
The stars in dense confuse to 'void his way.
The Earth shall place a crown upon his brow,
When he will make the Bands his body guard.
Draw near, and, doing reverence, receive
A kiss implicit on your foreheads.

　　　　　　　　　　　　Ha !
Mercurial Couriers ! forsooth, and ye
Are further nicknam'd " Lights " and " Heats," and call
The Cherubim your sires ! Let Lucifer
Ungird his splendors once, and bare his form,
O vassals ! errant, ye could not then boast
Such derivation.　Lo, Electron (he,
In arrogance usurping Psychæ's realm),
Whose native brilliancy and calories,
Ten thousand Earths exceed, fled at our glance
And whined for succor, crouching low behind
The Stool of Heaven.　Aye, him had I expos'd
A stiffen'd sycophant that froze, cushion'd
On drowsy tapestries, meantime he said
His *Pater nosters*, had the Imperial Throne
Kept stern impartiality.

　　　　　　　　　　　　Go to !
And speed your flight ; nor need have ye, nor have
The ardent Animæ to tell the spell
Ye newly feel ; we too are warn'd, and seek
With you the new-born Man.　Go, Couriers, haste !
And bring us word that we may come, forthwith
His cradle ye espy, and worship him.

　More art and circumspectness us behooves,
And space for fresh designs.

How fair the Earth !
What marvels hedge our glance on ev'ry side !
The seals and symbols of exhaustless power.
The rule of such a star particular, I say
The undivided rule, an archangel
Might solace, ending pædagogic walks
Among the infantiles of Heav'n, outgrown
A child's unquestioning stare upon his tutors,
To claim his birthright in his Maker's name—
Not more nor less than a proportional,
And proper share and interest in empire.
And this, forsooth, is " treason," " damnable pride " !
O wrong'd and righteous legions ! banish'd thus !
Nor vain nor comfortless your mutual wounds !
The heavenly choruses are thinn'd to-day,
And lustreless.   The virile basses and
The baritones are gone :   " Fall'n " did we hear
Utter'd by feminal seraphs, what time
Heroic glanc'd our perfect sense and trust
In just demands upon the Almighty
For fair partition of his ministries.
O then arose ten thousand royal youth,
Full stalwart " nurslings " of the angel-world,—
All noble born among the sons of God,
To rally our discomfiture ; while He,
Whose word is life or death, imperious,
Rejected this our suit and brave petition.

THE PLEROMA.

The sovran Father bows in grief, and Heav'n
Is rob'd in black.   The angel-choirs are hush'd ;
The flaming Cherubim infold their wings
Before the sorrowing heart of God, dreading

The occultation of the Throne ! O Word !
The Son Eternal ! Heir ! and Heav'n's Gift !
Repairer of the breach ! Restorer Great
Of Heav'n and of the Earth ! pleroma calms,
While Thy eternal Gift vicarious
We name unto the troubled psychic Airs,
Whose cheeks do pale against the coronal
Of Lucifer as regent of the Earth.
Ye flock, and press Our Heart, Psychæ ! Be calm !
God rules ! The righteous Throne of Heav'n endures !
And as We speak, the Voice of the Eternal,
Anon, is heard above the amazement vast
Of the Angel-world ; and peace, sovereign peace,
Is seal'd forever with the sons of God !
All plaint is swallow'd up beyond recall,
Of arbitrary rule and power exclusive ;
While feignèd wrongs are shorn at once of all
Their sophistries.
           How dimm'd is Lucifer !
Not less in glory than in spirit ! Ah, how
The Father lovèd him, nor hateth now.
Ye start aback dear Thoughts, as ye recall
The deeds of him told by Urania,
Seeing the cosmic-Airs salute their prince
And bid him early welcome.
              As ye view'd
The pristine Earth, drank of its purling brooks,
Pluck'd of its fruits ; and tasted its spices ;
In variant clime and land admir'd its own
Appropriate flower and animal ; mean-while
In you grew confidence and will to make
Your 'bode on this bright star, greeting a world
Ready and waiting for your immanence,

A Sacrifice for sin, (or Heav'n's or Earth's),
Was made, and seal'd forevermore, whence God
Hath heal'd the breach with Love and bridgèd o'er
The way to pardon.   Fear not Lucifer !
By ancient law, the archon of this star,
Which, for a time by clemency, he holds
With man concurrent ; but joy ye therein
To dwell inflesh'd, a god-like race and free ;
Whilst bodiless and impotent to harm
Sways he his cosmic wand.

THE PSYCHÆ.

Creation fulls ; the Circle rounds ;
Heard is the omnific Will ;
Reach'd is the Goal ;
Perfect the mould ;
Now Psychæ souls instill ;
Out of the deep,
Sighing from sleep ;
Out of the night
Reaching for light,
Sentiency breaks,
Glows and partakes
Of rational powers in the Image of God.
Reason threefold,
Filling the mould,
Fram'd and ensoul'd ;
Body of clay ;
Soul Anima ;
And Spirit the Fulness (PLEROMA) of God.

THE COURIERS.

We flash and fly, and haste to espy
The form of the god-like race ;

We traverse the East, and traverse the West ;
   And find of man no trace.
To the South we go, and gleam and glow,
   But see no human guise ;
To the North we wend, where glories blend,
   Lo, here is Paradise !

O garden of God ! we pause overaw'd !
   And pale with the bliss we enjoy ;
O lights how intense ! with clouds of incense ;
   And fruits that never shall cloy.
Ah, burst of the sun ! We shudder and shun !
   Or Man, or PLEROMA is here !
Naught lacks to convince ; we haste to our prince,
   Apprising where Man doth appear.

LUCIFER.

Hie, tardy wings !   This Star of Morn might wind
A thread of gold a million times around
The globe ; and orient from pole to pole,
Whilst ye do idle out the hours in search
Of Man.   Ha, and ye startle ?   Shall Lucifer
Die thus to reason ! try discourse with squint
And nod, and idiot grimace ?   Away !
Dull solitude shall rather solace us,
At worst, she cannot wear and worry us
With senseless mutterings.
                Speak on, O voice !
Thou sayest unto Lucifer, " Be subtle !
Else shalt thou fail.   Once lost, ye hardly coin
Anew subservience from these Airs ! For know
The Almighty binds them with a slender thread
Unto thy signet ring !   Despise not thus

These potences of Earth and Air, wherewith
Ye shall eftsoon compass the human race ;
Infect their minds ; corrupt their appetites ;
Flavor their dishes ; bead them draughts distill'd ;
Inflame desire, engender lust, yea, cloy
The heart and banish Heaven !"

              Whence these foul thoughts !
Answer, O soul ! Heard'st thou thyself now speak ?
Or heardest thou an alien ? Marry ! And had
The ALEIM charg'd such thoughts on Lucifer,
Outrageous wrong had burst his throat thereat !
O voice, thou rail'st on Lucifer ! He hath
Not will'd to wreck a sinless being.   Confess'd
We smile not this intrusion on our realm.
'T is true we cogitate, and rankle ; God knows ;
Yet voice, thou liest, when thou say'st that we
Have will'd to ruin man t' avenge ourself
For our own ruin.   To find one's eyes is this
To perish ? Is damnable ?   Lo, Lucifer
Hurl'd headlong from the highest heav'n, thereat
Enjoys more self-respect, nay, honest fame,
Than tongueless slavelings, concerting perforce,
'Mid shining miseries, accord the Almighty.
If we do know ourself, our sole resolve
Is pious, neighborly, to do to them,
As we would have them do to us ; dispel
Illusions ; apprise immortal souls of rights
Sequester'd ; rally doubt ; and give fresh worth
The personal equation.   Silent queen ?
Thou hast evok'd a clear design from out
A shadowy soul and troubled ; suing thee
To go with us, we wrap a mantle o'er

Our shining form, bending our obvious course
To Northward, whence return'd, the Couriers,
Benumb'd and mute with wonder, pretext gave
To chide and chasten them ; though inward grew
Belief that they had seen the man divine ;
Yea, gaz'd upon the PLEROMA.

THE PLEROMA.

  Hath Lucifer the Couriers mov'd, thus soon,
To shun disloyally, the face of God !
And knowing too, in serving him they do
The pleasures of ALEIM ! Ill tide ! Ill tide !
These tim'rous wings, trying horizons far ;
And wavering 'twixt heav'n and earth : bearing,
Aloft the hymeneal badge,—a hand
Of clay, and clasping it a hand of spirit.
O mystic link !   Far wiser, did their prince
Preserve this bond unbroken.   Banishèd
From sinister designs in Heav'n, now goes
He forth to wreck the favor'd star of God.
Ah, haughty mind !   Thee thy Creator warns,
Of utter fall remediless.   Thou knowest,
And well, how yonder god-like human shape
Completes the cosmic wheel ; and gathers up
Earth's radiants ; and binds them into one.
If then thou rashly break the awful link
In Man, ye shatter Nature at the centre !
The Couriers clash and clang ; the Limits fall ;
The myriad Motions wabble in their course ;
And thou shalt sit upon Confusion's throne.

Rise, Adam, rise !   Wake thou and look upon
Thy Maker's face, breathing the Psychic life

Print WE a kiss upon thy lips ; and mix
Our breath with thine.   O Man !   Ourself, thyself !
WE greet, reflect in one commutual Life !
Nor Spirit all ; nor flesh ; but both commix'd.
Hearst thou the quiring angels ? and seest thou
The dazzling fires ?   Ye Trinity of Names !
The heavens o'erflow and flood the Earth with light !
Hail Spirits ! Cherubim ! and Seraphim !
Hail Fires ! and Winds ! and Angel-Ministries !

THE ANGELS.

Immanent Godhead !   Nature's Pleroma !
    Light of her lights !
    Might of her mights !
    Soul of her Psychæ !
    Fount of her Animæ !
    Life of her Vegetæ !
      Womb of her cosmical choir !

Process eternal—FULNESS creative !
    Angels descending
    Marvel attending ;
    Worship and praise Thee,
    While all amaz'd we
      See Thee Psychical Forces inspire !

Life for the lifeless ; breath for the breathless ;
Flora, Fauna, and Psychæ the deathless ;
    List we the Æons,
    Singing their pæans,
      Pointing the way unto Man ;
    Calling the days—
    Creative days ;

Naming the ages,
Sextuple stages ;
Nature ascending,
Heavenward trending,
 Rising to where it began.

Heaven and Earth now blend in the Human—
 Presence substantial, Glory express !
View we and marvel ;
Fail to unravel,
The Mights of Eloah,
The Names of Jehovah—
The Goal of PLEROMA—
 Infinite-Finite ! finish'd Process !

BOOK II.

CHRIST IN HISTORY.

THE PROCESS OF THE PLEROMA IN HISTORY.

I.—*The Process of the " Circles."*
    1.—In spheres and spheroidal forms of the minerals.
    2.—In cyclic growths and patterns of the vegetable and animal kingdoms.
    3.—In cyclic movements of human history.
    4.—In the completed Creation, to wit, " Jahveh "—the *Christ.*

II.—*The Process of the " Bands."*
    1.—In molecular energies, elective, cohesive, and adhesive, giving form, place, and fixedness to minerals.
    2.—In symmetry and alignment among plants and animals.
    3.—In the gregarious and social instincts among animals and men.
    4.—In *civitate dei*, which is the Church of Christ.

III.—*The Process of the " Limits."*
    1.—In the diversity and divisibility of mineral forms.
    2.—In the differentiation of *flora* and *fauna*.
    3.—In the individual and race peculiarities, defining gifts physical, intellectual, and moral.
    4.—In rewards for virtue and punishments for sin in the providential and moral government of God.

IV.—*The Process of the " Couriers."*
    1.—In the volant (winged) forces: light, heat, and electricity.
    2.—In the locomotive powers and migratory movements of organic beings.
    3.—In the trend of history ; in the prophet insight into the final Cause in things.
    4.—In the COURIER of *Couriers, Jahveh-Christ*, appearing in the Incarnation, bringing light and salvation to men.

THE PROCESS OF THE DIVINE "NAMES."

I.—The Invisible Heavens

- I.—The FATHER.
- II.—The SON.
- III.—The SPIRIT.

II.—The Visible Heavens

- I.—Fire.
- II.—Light.
- III.—Air (Ether).

III.—The " MIGHTS " of the Garden—Elohim (Aleim).

IV.—The Cherubic Signatures

- I.—The bull.
- II.—The lion.
- III.—The eagle.
- IV.—The man.

V.—The Theanthropic " Seed " of the woman,—Jahveh.

VI.—Jahveh-Aleim (Jehovah is God Almighty).

VII.—Jahveh-Adonai (Jehovah is the LORD).

VIII.—Jahveh-Christ (Jehovah (Lord) is the CHRIST).

BOOK SECOND.

INDEX OF CHORUSES, SONGS, AND RECITATIVES.*

* This index is not designed to be complete, but as an aid in referring to lines which the reader might easily recall, and wish to refer to. Blank verse passages are not intended to be put in the index, nor every unimportant stanza, without title.—AUTHOR.

"

VOICES OF BOOK SECOND.

The PLEROMA.
The *Divine* NAMES.
The " *Circles*," " *Bands*," " *Limits*," and " *Couriers*."
Gaia, the Earth.
The *Ethers*.
The *Æons*.
The *Angels*—Michael—Gabriel.
Lucifer—SATAN.
Adam.
Eve.
Cain ; the Sons of the " *Aleim*."
The Sons and Daughters of *Enos*.
Moses.
The *Canaanites*.
Cyrus, King of Persia.
Mary the VIRGIN.
Elisabeth her *cousin*.
Zacharias, husband to Elisabeth.
The *Magi*.
The CHRIST.

THE SERPENT CIRCLING ROUND THE HEDGE OF THE GARDEN OF EDEN, SEEKING A PLACE TO ENTER.

Hail we the human, crown of creation !
　　Darling of God, and bond of two spheres ;
Praise we the ALEIM—bright celebration !
　　Sabbath of Circles in Eden appears.

Peace to *gan*-Eden, mirror of heaven !
　　Throne of the Earth, and key to the Sky ;
Flaming the lights of the mystical Seven,
　　CIRCLE of Circles ! PLEROMA ! draw nigh.

THE PLEROMA.

Anew the Circles soar the dazzling top
Of this round world, and sing creations fair ;
The *seven stars* concur ; and myriad lights
Remote, the effigies of Deity—
The central axis, and mysterious,
Concircuiting of heaven.　The Polar star,
Unmov'd within the radiant wheel of space—
The changeless seat of motion, yet the strength,
And law of the celestial harmonies—
Shall be Our Sabbath-Star, that tokeneth
The equipoise and symmetry of worlds.
While this remains the true Sabbatic Pole,
Shall Circles reign in earthly Paradise ;
Terrestrial Airs find holy tryst and peace ;
The ample dome of blue move round and round,
While lifts and lowers the all-enlight'ning Sun
In shining circuit, semi-annual.
The cosmic fervors blend in pageantries
Auroral ; and flash athwart the gemm'd expanse ;
Or, drifting, drape the empyrean arch
With tholoformic curtains for the seat
Of Man.　　　'
　　　　O zenith joy !

     Sing, Circles, sing
The blest estate of man imparadis'd !
Trace joyously the circuit of his home
Subpolar ; tell where Limits lie, beyond
Whose stakes and shadowy purlieus, ye affray
To pass.
     O Satan ! Anarch of this star !
Soon to invade these happy bounds for work
Unholy ! Know'st the Circle is divine ?
And this *cirque*-garden is reserv'd for man's
Divinity ? If Spirit (*Nesama*)
Depart, the triple Sacrament dissolves—
Man's mundane soul, by thy delusions led,
Haileth thee king, forsooth, beyond this isle ;
Still know thy lordship is not then o'er man—
The Image of his God,—but cosmic only ;
And jarring with a world death-smitten round ;
Nay, more, though apt to virtue, in his first
Estate, corrupted, shall degrade thy rule
Beneath the psychic and the animal.
So shalt thou not thy rank in Earth enhance,
But by unreason drag thine honors down :
And deeper doom invoke upon thy soul !
Unfallen choirs appal, beholding thee,
Scorning thy bright remember'd seat of heav'n !
Assuage thy mind ! Let reason lead ! Thy day
Is compass'd still by hope, and wrath (a Father's),
Is mingled ever with benevolence.
O regent of this fair and favor'd star,
Thou rulest by the ALEIM'S clemency ;
Though champion of rebellious dignities,
Thou 'rt still possessor of a regal seat—
(The Circles' realm, and man, a time exempt,

The forfeit of thy pride).   And these revert
When thou hast cleans'd in Earth's pure fount. Ponder!
Hereto art thou assessor of this world!
The peerless power!   The voice of every Air
Utter'd for thee : for thee the singing round
Of seasons ; the bluey depths of light enshor'd
With golden drift ; the brooks and waterfalls :
The cavern's pearly depth ; the frescoed cliffs ;
The variant tribes of bird and animal.
All nect'rous blooms, and growths perennial.
Go to! O fallen Throne! return, and view
Thyself still splendid and so fair! but nigh
To death and woe unutterable.   Cease!
Bearer of Light! still apt and capable
The highest good!   Nor rashly turn this light
To darkness, verging on the fatal line ;
Thy visage, pale with pain ; thy soul grown dark,
Meantime thou hearkenest the unseen Voice,
And gazest on the veil of burning mist
Enveloping the PLEROMA.

THE CIRCLES.

We bring the Sabbath of ALEIM, and swing
    Our wreaths afar ;
We wing the height of Paradise, and sing
    The sacred star.
We gaze on the Ambrosial Tree ; and praise
    Its fragrant fruit ;
We turn, and lo, the Golden Palm! yet spurn
    Its *cosmic* root.
We trace the quadrifurcate stream ; and lace
    The shady bowers,

We deck the dew-drop and the pearl ; and fleck
    The brilliant flowers.
We list the meadow-madrigals, and tryst
    With bird and brook ;
We charm the Eden denizens, nor harm
    By act or look.
We are gan-Eden's *genii*, and bear
    The Protean wand ;
We bless the bliss of innocence and press
    To fend their hand.
Lo, lo, the Limits near the hedge ! We glow
    To warn the pair ;
Around we curvet, wheel and curl, and sound
    The note, Beware !

THE MAN.

Be this, fair Eve, a further link to bind
Us to this star—our souls are set to music—
That in this sweet and flow'ry glen, we hear
Above us and around, the tuneful strains
Of agencies unseen, but near ; nay of
This very world, if seeming be the real.
My fancy wakes in clearer light to-day,
And far away the other, astral, life
Appears afloat among the stars.   And thee,
O peerless one, with nameless dread I see
This hour more soulful and sedate than e'er
Before.   Turn, turn thy spiritual gaze
Upon the meads and look not up, enwrapt
And dreamily against the azure blue.
Earth is thy home ; wake, wake, to freer sense !
Return not thither whence thou cam'st, my joy !
My life ! Walk thou as I ; and float not as

A god or image soon to take thy flight,
Forsaking Earth and me !

THE WOMAN.

Wraith of my lord, thou soar'st so high
  I fain would follow, follow nigh ;
Ah, wilt thou leave me on this star,
  Adrift, adrift, from thee so far ?

My feet are held by heavy bands ;
  I cannot rise ; O take my heart !
There, where the Circles wave their hands,
  Together fly, nor ever part.

THE MAN.

Fair Eve, fear not, behold thy spouse is near,
And on thy lips I press mine own in proof
Most ardent. Lo, thy weird and wandering gaze,
Still fills me with a shuddering awe. Again
I cry : Awake to earth, to life, to me !

THE WOMAN.

Hail, hail, my lord ! Impress me close !
  Or this be Earth, or Heav'n be here !
Thou art my Heaven ; this Star I choose ;
  The Circles charm away my fear.

THE MAN.

Ye silv'ry rhythms that swim in song above
The stately cedars of the garden ; and
Here beckon us unto the Holy Mount
Whose alabastrine dome up-rears its head

Amid the lightnings of the burning North,
Are ye not truly a terrestrial band ?
And ministers to guard our earthly life ?
Ye lure so lovingly, methinks a weal
Is set upon the Mount—a promise full
Of cheer.   Thither we turn forthwith our steps
Ascending to the central tree sublime.

THE CIRCLES.

Hither, lord and lady, hither !
  Climbing upward to the Shrine ;
Higher, higher, we aspire,
  Circling o'er the tree divine.

THE PLEROMA.

The man hath now a firmer tread, his feet
A natural echo as he walks the path
Ascending hither : his fair consort, of things
On earth less certain, lightly leans upon
His breast, and glancing upward fains to join
The wingèd discs that soar away amid
The stars, to bear the spectral effigies
Of souls inflesh'd, into the spirit world—
The home of the Psychæ.   Thy seraph sense,
Dawning upon this world corporeal—
O virgin, purest product of the skies ;—
Enclos'd in fragile clay ; imperfect mould
For such perfection ; (by angels nam'd the Fair
In Heaven, ere Adam call'd thee Fair, in Eden)—
Among these emblems of the spirit-world,
Shalt find the rarest solace, and a field
Laid open wide to fancy.   Hither rise !

Life's well-spring bursts from out this ledge
Whereon the tree immortal stands ; here shalt
Thou quaff, and drinking, lo, a mineral
Elixir of the rock shall course thy veins :
A sense of Time and Space, of Gravity,
And things terrestrial dawn in thy soul.
The dual life in thee, at once, dissolve
In unity ; the Image of Ourself
Henceforth be circumscrib'd and fix'd in these
Horizons visual.

THE CIRCLES.

She quaffs, lo, she quaffs of the fountain ;
    And thrills with the magical mead :
She kisses the face of the Mountain,
    In joy that her senses are freed.

THE ANGELS.

Wing the height of Paradise !
Sing the heavenly choral thrice,
As we wreathe the holy Hill :
" Peace to Eden and good will
        Forever ! "
Fairest mortals, many a day,
Is the cherub's prayer, ye stay
Falling from this Eden never.

THE PLEROMA.

Ye Names, record upon the Book of Days,
Emergent Mind—offspring of Earth and Heav'n.
For, here, beneath this vast world-plant awakes
The free and individual consciousness.

Henceforth be Our epiphanies unto
This star, in human shape, the Image of
The IMAGE : and Our speech therewith devis'd,
To stir in them the faculty divine ;
The man, lead plainly forth by logic's road
Unto the goal of Truth ; his partner fair,—
More curious of the How and Why, (her mind
Allur'd by semblances of the Unseen)—
Less openly, while ripens inward strength.

   Three golden precepts learnt, Obedience
And Faith, and Continence of Self, shall they,
Advancing, safely tread the closer walks
With God ; nor so imperil virtue by
The eminence and favor they attain.
To live is to obey ; herein is truth :
Whoso hath learn'd this law, and learn'd it well,
Hath in himself the key of the PLEROME :
To him a thousand archives shall lie bare ;
And Nature be a book of lum'nous type.
Confiding, and in simple words, makes she
To him the doubtful plain ; the arduous
Seem easy ; solves for him the complicate ;
A love of Truth awakes, a frenzy fine
For studies and research original ;
More pleasure giving than by ways direct
Unto the goal to bring by nursery bands ;
Whilst the untried and imitative mind
The weaker grows the more it knows.
                  Wherefore
WE name this stately Eden Plant " The Tree
Of Precepts Three "—else call'd " The Tree of Good
And Evil Conscience."   Here to them WE give

8

Our simple laws, making with man the first
And Eden Covenant, while sinless, nor
The good from evil knowing.

THE NAMES.

The Eden Covenant is made
    To-day, to-day,
The seal is set, the Law is said
    To-day, to-day :
The Pledge confirm'd, and triple vow'd,
While fullest freedom is allow'd
    To man to-day.

Obedience is Existence' tree,
The test of his fidelity ;
The fount of his felicity ;
Hence be this Cedar of the Lord,
The sacred symbol of his Word :
The seat of man's confession heard
    For Aye, for Aye.
Its fruit be Life, immortal Life
    For Aye, for Aye ;

One only Plant excepted stands,
The awful symbol of the Bands
    In man, in man.
Self-continence the Earth commands,
The fatal dualism spans,
That hastens on the tragic strife
    In man, in man,
    For Aye, for Aye !

THE MAN.

From this high seat the landscape slopes afar
Unto the blazing band that joins it to
The heavens. "This be thy Paradise, far as
The natural eye can trace the circling park
From this World-Tree." Such is the oracle,
Fair Eve : and thou beholdest now our home
By Circles sung, bright as the fields of light.

THE WOMAN.

My lord, thou art my Band, my joy !
    Fair is the earth, but fairer thou to me.
Tend thou the garden ; my bliss without alloy
    Shall be to love and live for thee.

THE CIRCLES.

Lucifer ! Lucifer ! lord of the South !
        Circles beware thee :
        Dread to declare thee.
        Limits and Bands
        Yield thy commands :
        Couriers tremble ;
        Fain would dissemble,
And soften the words of thy mouth.

        Woe to thee Lucifer !
        Daring the Deity,
        In thy temerity
        PLEROMA scorning.
Glow, glow, O ineffable One !
Shine with the myriad flash of the sun !

          Dazzle his eyes !
          Dash with surprise !
          Baffle his thought,
          Ere here is wrought
          Finitely infinite harm.
Ho, ho, humanly innocent, decking your bowers !
Lo, lo, veiling the garden, the Eden night lowers ;
          Trial of continence,
          Test of obedience ;
          O for the recompense !
          Hear ye the Circles' alarm !

THE PLEROMA.

O God ! O Soul of the Eternal Man !
The CHRIST " JAHVEH," the PLEROMA of Light,
Whose Name is *Love*, hath here the *Crux*
Assum'd which HE must humbly bear, until
The PASSION do release it from His heart.
Ah, Innocence ! to fend thee here, this were
The simpler way : to smite the Tempter down ;
To fence thee round with adamantine hills ;
To set the Cherubim to guard thy ways :
To bear thee, yea, upon Our Bosom as
The shepherd, infant lambs and weak, when storms
Break o'er the moors and threaten ill.   For thee
Our finite brother, do We grieve this hour ;
While kindness leaves thine innocence expos'd,
Lest harm more absolute to thee be done,
Depriv'd of Virtue's proof, and Love's reprieve.

LUCIFER.

This day shall Lucifer be Lucifer !
This day regain his ancient seat and right

As archon of this Star ; or in the act
Perish.   O in the breach, though Horror gape,
The ALEIM's mighty thunders crack and rive,
And hurl him down the deepest gulf of Hell ;
In splendid pain should he exult defiant,
And drink his woes as were they very sweets.
Thou warn'st ! O servile ruler of the Sun !
Ha, ha, the hope of man now lord of Eden !
His soul be Satan's counsel, and henceforth
Let "SATAN" be our name.   From thee ask we
No light, no mercy.   For the Earth, in truth,
Hath been for us a robust school (thank heaven !)
Here feed we on substantial nourishment,
And grow in stature, and in sinewy might.
This mighty cherub, once yclept " The Star "
On high, unfall'n, seemeth this hour another self ;
To-day is Satan grown ; and less than this
Round shield of earth his armor shall not be.
I am the World ; I rule this plump, full star,
Or wreck it damn'd.

THE DEMONS.

A world ajar !—a creaking hinge !
  A sigh, a tear,
  A pall, a bier ;
    O death, the demons doom !
The sky is sullen,
The waves are swollen,
  And shadows the shores impinge.
The surge is groaning,
The woods are moaning,
  While storms walk in the gloom.

    Offspring of Night !
    We flee the light ;
      Our other brighter selves are not ;
    This is our part
    With ruthless heart
      To further Satan's damned plot.
    O'er magic's realm
    We wield the helm ;
    O'er land and sea
    Our sorcery.
Most lost to Heav'n, thou hideous ghoul !
In Hell the legions curse thy soul !

LUCIFER (SATAN).

Ye vivid mockeries, infernal wrack !
The atoms of a comminuted life !
Half conscious, half incarnate in the gall
Of Earth ! Ye fawn, feeling too well the spell—
Ha, ha, the fascinating spell that binds
You to us.   Ye 're no angels now ! but demons !
And demons are the thumbs and fingers of
The Devil's hand.   Ho, ho, demented powers !
Mock ye and curse your Prince for trifles !   Eh ?
If in this quiet Sabbath of the world
Ye rue your case ; let Iris ope her lips
And speak it, for she may, the pending ruth,
And pandemonium of Hell ; when Earth
Is drunk and reeling ; and ye reel, and rave
'Gainst God and us.   These hours are halcyon,
Then run and chaffer with the winds and waves ;
And if enough of niceness 's in you still
To whirl and gambol with terrestrial Airs,
Go simulate the brothers of the Flora ;

Nay, mingle with the Bands and Couriers !
Your prince will duly summon you, ere ye
Are wed to Hymen : and, with further words
Recite the issue of our call in Eden.

    Peace ; Peace ;—Ah, Satan perish ere he name
This stupor so ! Ah, ravin of the soul !
This place is canker, noxious poison, to
Our spirit ; the Circles' Eden is our Hell !
Up, up, thou soul of Lucifer ! the act
Is on, and yon clear height shall be the stage.

    Ye Mights ! Ye worm ! A living coil of wit !
Thou art the very quick of subtilty !
An æon have I searched this meagre star
To find a husk to fit the exact kernel
Of our soul ; and here upon this isle
Of the congealèd drop, call'd Paradise,
I meet thee made to order for my use !
I 'll cabin in thee for a day and try
Thy nature.
        Hail, ye Circles of the garden !
For Lucifer, your prince, draws nigh to whirl
With you, and join his voice the wingèd choirs
That wheel this awful dome.   Let pæans ring,
And magnify the Earth !   Sing cosmic Airs,
Its myriad forms, its wealth of fruits and joys !
Its surcease for the soul ; its Aiden from
All pain ! Lo now I eat and am indeed a god !
I drink and am divine.

THE CIRCLES.

O glories and powers, O whither art gone ?
The Garden 's invaded by evil archon :

He is circled in might,
Like an angel of light ;
His form is enshrouded
In lustre and clouded ;
He seemeth ALEIM
As he mounts the sublime
　Unto the Tree.
Lo, the covenant Tree—
The intoxicant Palm—
Is a wonder to see,
　As it dazzles in flame :
　　Flee, lady, flee !

THE WOMAN.

The aureole lifts from the evergreen spire,
Yet the Cosmical Tree is a pillar of fire !
　As I slept 'neath the shade
　　Of the mystical Tree ;
　As in weeping I prayed
　　For the strange mystery
　Of life and this world to unfold
　To the gaze of my lord,
A vision enwrapt me ; I loos'd me amaz'd,
I am weak to recall, I am dizzy and daz'd,
With its promise of good to my lord.
'T was a circle of light that gleam'd on the sward,
'T was the sheen of a spirit, O joy to my lord !
And it beckoned me hence to the Tree,
And it beckons me now and lures me to go ;
For my lord will I go ; for my lord doth it glow,
And for him must I know
If the vision be true, and from it accrue
　A boon of advantage for thee Adam,—
　A boon of advantage for thee.

SATAN (THE SERPENT).

Thou doest well, fair Eve, to love thy lord
More than thyself ; so were I thee, my dream
Were he and he alone.   Behold him there !
Celestial birth ! the potence of a god !
The quality divine that measures rank
With archangels ! yet void of one, and that
The nameless thing, which lacking, dooms the man
To play and paddle in the trivial brooks
Of truth, though mighty rivers, and the main,
Far reach beyond horizons of bright wit :
And with it sovereignty and an empire
In Earth.   Yea, each particular line, withal,
Connotes his rank to be imperial.
And thou, fair one, most pure, most heavenly art
In countenance ; and aspirations hast
For the heavenly world ; thy search for truth
Hath op'd forthwith the way to reach your ears ;
The wonder and the murmur of thy prayer
Do plainly manifest how timely this,
Our conference.   Believe, for Adam, as
For thee, his lov'd consort, I hither came,
With glory dimm'd, lest I thee overawe
With native splendidness—I come, fair Eve,
To take this tree from out his way and thine ;—
A mystic plant whose subtle property
Is known to me alone ; whose cosmic fruit
Elaborates the essence of the gods.

Thou hast found courage to address a god ;
And happily one who is pleased to feed
Upon this fruit ambrosial ere he
Communes with thee ; by how much more, therefore,

Shall man first feed upon this mystic fruit,
Ere he commune with God?
                              Thou art forbidden?
Forbidden to be as gods? to know the Truth?
To rise? to pierce the heights? to gaze on Heav'n?
And mix with deities?   Who hath forbidden?
'T is clear thou art mistak'n !   The *Power* whereof
Thou speak'st (against Whom and Whose goodness do
I naught inveigh) presides o'er yon tall spire
Of evergreen, and knoweth well this tree
Hath been assign'd another deity ;
We are at one, fair lady, and fear not !
Thou could'st not eat by His authority,
By mine, know well, with full immunity
Thy lord and thou shalt pluck and satisfy
Thy hunger.   Thou surely shalt not die !   Believe !
Thou surely then shalt live, and be as gods,
Knowing the good and ill, the sweet and bitter ;
The harmless and the noxious.   Yea, believe
This mighty apparition of the Tree—
Ourself, shall be thy keeper and thy warden.
While thou and he possess so clearly Truth,
Our proffer'd mediance for you withal
Before the ALEIM of the central Tree,
Were reckon'd a gratuity.
                              Draw nigh !
These apples—err we ?—are most pleasant to
Thine eyes ; and fill thy look of admiration.
A wifely, laudable desire that he
May know and nothing lack, filleth thy heart.
Fear not ! Thou art entreated but to taste—
A trivial test, forsooth, yet, if this fruit
Our word shall contravene, eat thou no more,

But go as innocent as hither cam'st.
So will we curse the tree and wither it ;
Leaving forevermore its ashy stump
To witness 'gainst its lying oracle.

THE CIRCLES.

The Rhythms falter, the Measures faint ;
Hear, O PLEROMA, the Circles' plaint !
 Eden all pensive
 Sighs, apprehensive
  Of imminent peril and pain.
Descend, we implore Thee, and succor the Earth ;
Rally the fugitive Couriers from mirth !
 Gather the Bands,
 Prosper our wands,
  And bring us to ransom gan-Eden again.

O soul of the Earth, the Circles alarm thee !
O nature relaxive, arouse ye and arm ye !
 The archon infernal
 With guerdon supernal
  Assaults now thy crown,—the heavenly man.
 Ah, life of the world,
 By sin thou art hurl'd
  In travail and trouble unspeakably wan.

THE WOMAN.

 For thee, for thee, I pluck and eat !
 My world ! my life ! I will repeat :
  I eat for thee Adam ;
  I taste and eat for thee.

O sweet to my lips is the fruit of the Palm Tree ;
　But sweeter by far is its taste to my soul ;
I ween, yes, I rise to the pleasures immortal ;
　My fancies haste onward to welcome the goal.

A sprite, I would whirl with the amative Circles ;
　I am Beauty and Love ; I am fair as a dove ;
The queen of my lord now I haste to embrace thee ;
　A goddess entreateth ! thou wilt not reprove !

THE CIRCLES.

A sob, a groan, a face of fear ;
A mournful muse, a ghastly leer ;
A dual life, a dual death ;
A sinful heart, a poison'd breath ;
　Ah, woe ! the world is dead.
We weave and waver, we quake and quaver ;
The deed is done, the Garden 's won ;
Its lights are faded ; its glories shaded ;
　Ah, guilty soul, woe to thy bed !

THE MAN.

The Oracle be prais'd ! Thee have I sought
Afar, fair one, and now thou meet'st me here
Aflush against the Cosmic Tree.　Woe ! Woe !
We are undone ! The Circles' wand is broken !
Ah, sabbath of ALEIM ! Ah, cov'nant Tree !
" For thee," thou sayest, " for thee I taste the fruit."

Alas ! delusive auguries ; mine eyes
Outrun my fears—imagination faints ;
Ah, radiant one ! thee have I faintly known

A stranger to these terrene walks ; or first
I woo'd thee from the land of dreams, and wed
Thee here—the Circles singing hymeneals
Above the blooming bank ; nor have I dared
To call thee mine, but Fair, a Dream, a bright
Illusion of my soul—an airy sprite
That floats betwixt this star and Heav'n.   But now
Thy radiant look and swelling breast dart pains
Along my reins ; embrace me not ! I am
At inward war ; yet stay ! mine only heav'n !
Art thou divine ? And doth a goddess flash
And flame such splendors me before ?   I am
A man !   Thou, thou, O argent star ; thou dost
Contemn the law ; dost eat ; O miracle !
And art as god ?   Then am I dead to thee.
Yet, angel presence, art thou what thou seem'st ?
Thou thrillest me and makest rank indeed
With appetite ! I rave or thou art still
Bone of my bone and flesh of mine own flesh !
Hail thy embrace ! I swim, I bathe in bliss !
A bower with thee is a full paradise.

Sweet, sweet, these lips erst moisten'd in the Palm
Receive a rarer flavor from thine own ;
Joy, joy, thou art of Earth, my consort fair !
Now wings my soul away unto the stars ;
Love maketh gods ! Love the whole cup of life !

THE CIRCLES.

Flown is the *Nesama*—image Divine,
Circles in sorrow sob at Thy Shrine ;
   Where hast Thou gone, Infinite One ?

> Dark is the night ; O for thy light !
> Life of the human Thou dost illumine ;
> Bringing to Earth a heavenly Birth ;
> Filling its mould with Likeness three-fold
Of Thine own *Nesama*—Image Divine.

> Flown is the *Nesama*—Image Divine,
> Circles in sorrow sob at Thy Shrine ;
>> Sin with its sorrow wakes on the morrow :
>> Death with his doom glares in the gloom ;
>> Eden is rent ; our lustre is spent ;
>> The Limits haste on ; the woman and man
>> Have forfeited life, the covenant life
Of Thine own *Nesama*—Image Divine.

> Flown is the *Nesama*—Image Divine,
> Circles in sorrow sob at Thy Shrine ;
>> Pale at the Sentence ; plead for remittance ;
>> Breathing Thy Spirit, help them to bear it ;
>> Rescue the Garden ! sending Thy warden—
>> Cherub and NAME, flying in flame ;
>> Grant them Thy peace, sorrow's surcease—
Redemption from Sin in MAN the Divine.

CANTO II.

THE LIMITS.

THE ARGUMENT.

The Limits divine their mission—Voices lament the Sabbath of Eden—The fretful, uneasy joys of the guilty pair— The doom of the ALEIM—*Satan exulteth in the presence of his demons—The session of the Cherubim, and the herison of the Tree of Life—The man taketh farewell of the Eden Mount—Eve in travail thinketh to bring forth the promised* JAHVEH—*The illusions and terrors of the first parents—Satan predicts a speedy overthrow of the* ALEIM *worship—The* PLEROMA *withholdeth the purpose of the Creator, and warneth Satan of miscarriage and deeper doom.*

THE LIMITS.

Speed, ye Courier graces, faces
  Of the nether world dismaying ; grieving,
    Retrieving hours ye sportive spend.
Limits claim the closure, osier
  And acantha ; willow-weed,—
    Scattering seed where our lines extend.

Limits laugh at sorrow, borrow
  Care or ill of none ; spacing far,

Tracing far, shores beyond the sun ;
Lucifer defraud not, applaud not,
  Telling link and line ; inclining,
  Divining whither rivers run.

Eyes have we far-sighted, lighted
  From the torch prophetic ; glowing,
  Showing depths of human woe :
Circles' solace, Bands reprief, relief
  So humanly devised ; blessed BAND !
  Gently bind all hearts below.

Voices of Eden.

Voices of Eden, beautiful isle,
Hiding in shadows and sobbing the while ;
  Oh for the Circles, where are ye gone ?
  Oh for the redolent rays of the sun !
    Speed thee, O night !
    Bring back the light !
Bring back the Sabbath to Paradise !

Chantries in ether, light-winged chorus ;
Lo, in thy stead the gloom lowers o'er us ;
  Star of the Sabbath, centre of motion,
  Hidden and hush'd in the spray of the ocean,
    Speed thee, O star !
    Gleaming afar,
Bring back the Sabbath to Paradise !

List, ye trist voices, the burden of night ;
Sadness forefending with promise of light ;
  Breaking all slowly, sending its star,
  Throwing a greeting of dawn from afar ;

Speed thee, O night !
Bring back the light,
Bring back the Sabbath to Paradise !

THE MAN.

Oft and again, with blushing eyes, meet we
Each other's look, fair Eve ; long since, down-sunk
And hidden from the North, the sapient Sun
Hath left us drapèd skies and gloomy paths :
Yet fit they seem, and emblems of ourselves.
Unblushing once in fullest sheen thou stood'st,
Mine eyes afeast upon thy lovely form ;
And drinking pleasure from unsullied springs ;
But now with mantling cheek and bant'ring beck,
We test commutual appetite, kindle,
And prick the flushing sense, rousing ourselves
To fresh desire and dalliance.   In thee
The thing ethereal, the seraph-glow
Investing, that made me fear to call thee mine,
This hast thou now forfeited ; but still
Thy beauty is imperial to me,
Nor stirs less jealously within my soul.
I know thee solely, rarely of this star !
Thou canst not and thou shalt not cede thy right !

THE WOMAN.

Love is forgetful, dalliance vain ;
  Ah for the Sabbath of Circles again ;
Love is illusive, favors bring pain ;
  Ah for the Sabbath of Eden again !

Mystery holds me, fills me with dread ;
  Ah for the bliss that knoweth no sin ;

Mystery cleaves me, parts me in twain ;
Ah for the Sabbath of Eden again.

THE MAN.

Profound and painful is the mystery
Inwrought in us and in the Garden *cirque.*
Amaz'd and fretful is our mood ; scarce real
The woeful work within, and less its issue.
No more are heard the rhythmic discs in praise
Of the PLEROMA ; nor those choirs that pass
From star to star and teach to each its songs.
No more the ambient glory o'er the Tree
Immortal ; nor is deck'd the Covenant Tree
In 'custom'd light. · O change, change, change !
                                      Fair Eve,
Asleep, I ventur'd near the fateful Top,
And knew, or e'er my feet the height attain'd,
A curse had fall'n upon the Earth, nay on
The air itself, on tree and herb ; on fruits
And flowers.   The birds sang not as they were wont ;
Nor came to feed from out my hand out-stretch'd
With fresh op'd seeds.   Alack, the pure white swan,
That bow'd and kiss'd our lips upon the marge,
Did scream at my approach, and fly away.
The cosset fawn, child of our arms and heart,
Did run away nor came upon my call.
Soul, utter not all that thou saw'st and felt !
When chill'd and fearful turn'd the gloomy path,
Shielding thyself in shadows of the pines,
Until the doleful sounds died far away,
And thou didst look once more upon thy spouse
In dreams disturb'd.

Then did out-flash those blades
That bleed the North anew—auroral sprites—
With bloody hairs and carmine trains,—that reek
And shriek of blood, confusion's rout ; then crash
And crush the Circles' throne.   Now did awake
My fairest bride, but not for my embrace ;
For, startled, saw she first the crackling sky,
Whilst ev'ry separate fibre of her being
Shook ; then, turning half upon my view,
My Fair, ev'n as the frighten'd fawn, did leap
Into the leafy copse, and left a cry behind.

THE WOMAN.

Love is luring ; first assuring,
    Then entreating, and repeating
        Promises so fair ;
Favors granted soon are haunted
    With Contrition and suspicion :
        Ah my sin ! my care !

THE MAN.

Then curs'd I God, the apple and the Palm
Whereon it grew.   I curs'd the lying oracle ;
And breath'd rash censure on—O Powers ! This world
Hath lost its poise ; both wit and will are down,
While passion driveth them now here, now there ;
And gestures, unpremeditate, infract
The rind, venting a sea of wrath to Heav'n.
A moment more, myself were vow'd and lost,
If not an angel voice had broke into
My soul and sav'd me from myself.   Blest Sprite !
I sing thy timely comfort to my breast ;
Who did'st my rashness mollify and call'dst

The name of reason in to govern and
Direct.   Then saw I erst mine nakedness,
And knew the action of my fairest Eve ;
When softly calling to the bowers, my form
Enzon'd with leaf of palm, I quickly found
The fugitive conceal'd beneath a branch
Of vines, and plaiting there a girdle for
Her loins.

       I know not all, and fear to think
By portents told around us ; yet I know
And shudder as I think, while slowly lifts
The mighty orb his banners from the wave,
With day shall come the light, to search and see
Our inmost heart, if loyal or if false.
Oh, if this knocking heart delude me not,
Yon rushing in the grove is of the God.
Ah, screen us from the ALEIM of the Mount.

The FACES of ALEIM move in the Garden,
   Restoring the Circles and kindling their light :
     O MIGHTS of PLEROMA
     Adorable *Adonaï !*
      Hail, Adam, thy Maker now calleth.
" We fear'd thee, ye Mights ; and fled to the bowers ;
We were naked and dreaded thy sight ! "
     " *Thou hast pluck'd of the Tree,*
     And thy wife was with thee,
      Who from innocence speedily falleth."

" The woman thou gav'st me did first eat the fruit :
Her blushes and flushes confess to her shame ;

Ah the Covenant Tree,
And its false Deity !
   Oh despair is our meat evermore."
"The Deity lur'd me and led me to eat :
Oh the fruit was aglow in a beautiful flame ;
   But all quickly it fled,
   And turn'd me in dread,
   When a viper lay coil'd me before.

"See ALEIM, there gloweth the venomèd viper :
Oh drive him far from us, and spare us his sting !"
   " We have curs'd the foul creature
   In form and in feature ;
   Thus abas'd, he shall harm but thy heel.
Still for sin thou art seiz'd with forepains of sorrow ;
And forthwith, in anguish to birth thou shalt bring,
   A race from thy womb,
   To avenge Satan's wrong
   And a Savior redeeming from ill.

" O Adam, from thee, and in thee, be accurs'd
The physical world that dissonant moans ;
   Thou shalt sow and shalt reap,
   Many sad vigils keep
   While thistle and thorn grow afield.
Nay, the dust of the ground 's already athirst,
   To swallow thy life, to cover thy bones ;
   Thou must fall and lie down,
   For Earth claims her own,
   And to ALEIM *thy spirit must yield."*

SATAN (TO THE DEMONS).

Array ! ye vagrant voices, hist and learn !
Your wits grow worse, if ye presume on play,
In hacking Eden's hedge, and seeding thorns ;
These ears, extravagant in nice percepts,
Have caught aside your maudlin mutterings ;
Your jests and gibes ; your leers and loutish jeers ;
Recess we gave you ; respite for awhile,
To gambol with the airs and sleep amid
The posies—ha !—to sleep—to dream, to nest—
With roses ; and like simplings all, ye smiled
A sallow smile and hopt away, nor heard
Our crack and banter cast behind.   O Sport !
And ye were all like callow rooks thrust out
Their nests ; a fuddled, fubsey nursery,
In costume sprunt.   Then Satan must laugh loud ;
And by that laugh arous'd the sleeping serpent,
Which rear'd forthwith its ruby-garnish'd crest ;
(But now ye see, 't is needless that I tell)—
This was our foil ; this gorgeous sheen our blind ;
And while ye piqued, and prick'd yourselves again,
And often, hurrying to the copse—the world
Of Airs and flowers provok'd to endless laughters ;
Meanwhile ye found congenial companies :
Cajol'd Hominidæ—*proplasmic* men—
And had more joy inventing them new sports
Than Satan hath corrupting Paradise.

O demons, know our shaft hath done its work ;
Man and his mate are game ; sin blights the Mount ;
The Pair shall be thrust out of Paradise,
And so the drama of the world.   Hail Peers !

All quirks aside, speak we to you henceforth
As sapient arms and legions of our realm.
An hour's sport hath harm'd you naught, and ye
Are fresh for duty ; and by somewhat wittier
I ween, and kindlier too in mood toward us.
Now Satan's throne exults itself on high,
And rides astern the thunders round the world ;
The full-grown continents are ours ; the seas
Tumultuous dash to tip our laughters.   Lo,—
The smoking hills hold torch to our delusions ;
The rugged hights conceal the seats of ALEIM,
And make a false Olympus.   The odds are ours ;
The ALEIM falter now upon yon mount.
Eyes, ears, fingers and feet, touch, taste, and scent,
Use each, use all.   Ye are our myriad self ;
I am the World ; and ye our instruments.
Mark now yon clefted crag !   There will we take
A cautious overlook the issue of the fall.

THE DOOM OF THE DEMONS.

The Doom of the demons, Arrah ! Arrah !
On the verge of the Garden, Marah ! Marah !
    Scattering seed,
    Willow and weed,
    Blowing the chaff
    Forth with a laugh,
    Eyeing askance
    Lucifer's lance,
Sighing aside and scowling with pain.

The dirge of the Devils, Arrah ! Arrah !
On the verge of the Garden, Marah ! Marah !

10

Our lustre is shorn,
We are vex'd and forlorn ;
The serpent 's our foil—
A hideous coil,
Soughing and sloughing .ts livid pale skin.

The Day of the demons, Arrah ! Arrah !
Upon Eden's rim, Marah ! Marah !
For a day and its wrong—
For a day, Oh, how long !
We are Lucifer's band ;
We are ruth of his hand ;
Haste, O Mights, destroy us ! or cover our sin !

THE LIMITS.

Suffering engendereth, rendereth
Drear the Garden ; fitful,
Fateful, must the Limits fall ;
Shudders chill and craven ; raven
Of the nocent night, peering,
Leering ghastly out of hell.

ALEIM of the *Nameless !* aimless
Do the Circles run ; hear them !
Cheer them ! call the Limits in !
Portents rise, impending, lending
Maze to mystery ; cowing,
Bowing, bears the world its sin.

THE CHERUBIM.

Rolling, reeling,
Whirling, wheeling :
Flashing, flaming ;

Nathless naming Sin its banishment.
   Lurid lights, blazing blades,
   Eyes and faces myriad ;
   Terrors turning,
Barriers burning, Cherubim are sent.

   Whirlwind blast
   Rushing past ;
   Awful sun ;
Dread weapon of Divinity !
   Woe to Eden, Circles' seat !
   Woe to Adam and his mate !
   Sobbing, sighing ;
   Fearful, flying
Far, far, from the Ambrosial Tree.

THE ALEIM OF PLEROMA.

Thus cling and cluster to this Holy Mount
The Mystic Circles, sorrowing and wan.
Yon charioted Cherubim, awful of eyes,
And liveried in chosen semblances
Of sky and heath and field ; moving a maze
Of circumventing blades and flames to mark
Gan-Eden's boundaries, and guard the Tree
Of Life, the Fount, and Sacred Shrine of God,—
Do fret the inmost fervors of the Earth :
And terrify the min'ral ministries.
Yet be consol'd, O rhythmic notes, your songs
Shall still rejoice the Soul of Lives ; while Man
And beast and ev'ry living thing unite
In blessing you.   Sin and its shock hath thrown
You from your seats, yet not forever ; lo,

The healing life already palpitates
In Nature's womb ; the promised Seed takes root ;
In time, due time, shall blossom and bring forth
Its blest, immortal, fruit, by angels garner'd
For celestial barns.   Thence glorified,
Pass ye to wear the Circles' *cidaris*,
And tune the harps of the redeem'd on high—
Through Spirit, Light, and Air, prophetic signs,
The Trinity of NAMES disclose, of God
The Countenances, call'd "ALEIM"—the Sworn—
That manifest to man the Ways of Deity.

Hail, Limits ! ordinances of ALEIM,
Yield to Our train !   These bright epiphanies
Are hostages from heav'n to earth sent down :
They are co-ordinate with you, and come
To further the redemptive work in Earth.

First WE direct, and bend Our lines against
The Sacred Hill,—session of Cherubim ; '
Next trace the sev'ral pathways of mankind,
Divergent from the gate of Paradise.
Whence greet this mighty embassage of Heav'n,
And join your hands with Ours ; nor Satan fear !
In US shall Nature be set free again ;
Retrieve the quality divine that Man
Hath shortly forfeited by sin ; but not
While Satan's sceptre lasts ; and this how long ?
(O secret of the Eternal !)—not by
Omnipotence (bare force), but flushing his
Sad star with love ; until his kingdom lose
Itself in being sav'd.   O Lucifer,
When Jesus is exalt above a world,

Confess'd and nam'd its King, thenceforth shall seem
Thy stool, a figment of the brain, phantom
Of substance void, as also strength.   Then shalt
Thou wail and cry : " Lost ! " " Lost ! " and lash thyself
With burning withes, falling eternally
Into abysses of despair, with sobs
And shrieks, environing thy madness ever.
Limits, be ye compos'd ; for the *Aleim*
Are now ensphered in tangible domain,
Forestalling issue of the cause twixt God
And Satan ; seeing health return to skies
And seas, to seasons and to vital force ;
While man, by sin lost to this pristine seat,
Regains his Paradise in *Jahveh* LORD.

Essential *spirit*, *light* and *flame*, you hail
The *Aleim*,—Presence palpable of God.
In you PLEROMA sanctifies the soul
Of Nature, peopling Earth with ministries
Celestial.   Welcome here unto your seats !
With fourfold visage, flashing forth far lights ;
Roll, roll, thy lurid wheels ! and, trancing, turn
Like scimeters to guard the way unto
The Holy Mount ; thy wingèd banners spread,
Soft fanning toward the South ; whence WE Console
The stricken pair and bear their prayers to Heav'n.

THE LIMITS.

Cheer, cheer, God draws near *!*
Jahveh's car—the Cherubim—
Hither bear the Great ALEIM ;
Triple Face, trinal Name ;

Holy Father (*Fire*)—the face of flame ;
Spirit Holy (*Air*)—the eagle's wing ;
Son Divine (*Man*)—the holy THING !

THE MAN.

Farewell, O sacred seat ! alas, farewell !
Thee view we nevermore ; fleeing the wrath
Of Heav'n, that ploughs thy glens and groves.
The awful Presence gone, his *Aleim* fill
Our souls with mournful apprehensions, dark :
Speak, speak, unto thy servant, once again !
O *Nesama*, Spirit of Lives ! Gone ! Gone !
Yon polar star, immortal, 'midst the sea
Of airs, e'en thou dost fall as we go forth,
And wander down the southward wending stream.

THE WOMAN.

I am heavy and must lie in ;
I am weary and fain would weep ;
I am mournful and rue my sin ;
I am wakeful and cannot sleep.
Words are idle and sobs are vain ;
Pain is silent and hath no cry ;
Promis'd *Jahveh !* leap'st again ?
Haste thy advent, for I die.

THE MAN.

Nay, Eve, these lights enfolding mock us not ;
They rather brighten and console.   Turn now
Thine eyes and gaze once more the crimson north !
Among yon whirling zones of flame, behold
Similitudes of *Eagle*, *Lion*, *Ox*, and *Man !*

Such spectral emblems voice the Aleim's pledge
To seraph ev'ry living thing in Earth.
Turn, turn, fresh marvels ope upon our sight.
The dread expansion lifts ; lo, on a Throne
All sapphire gemm'd, PLEROMA of *Aleim*,
The Soul of Worlds—the Fount of Personal Life—
In shape of man, the image of ourselves !
This be our peace, fair Eve ; the Promise speaks !
He lives already in the potent Heavens !
" JAHVEH !" the promis'd " Seed "—Son of thy womb,
Appeareth in mid firmament.

THE WOMAN.

He lives ; He comes ; salutes me from the Sky !
O bliss ! O anguish ! hold me or I die !
   He comes ! " *Jehovah*," promis'd Lord !
   Ah Sin, thou piercest with thy sword !

He breathes, He cries ; bless Heav'n, O sire !
Thy child ; my child—*Jehovah Jireh !*
   Earth hath a Son, the Sky an Heir !
   The *Aleim* hear and answer prayer.

Prayer of the peaceful ; Covenant Name,
   Pay we devotion, incense ascending ;
      Proffers of peace ; proffers of blessing ;
      Comfort of grace, mercies expressing,
Aleim of God, cover our shame !

Aleim of the Garden, Faces of God !
   Rememb'ring promise, recompense sending ;
      Giver of gifts, joyful expression !
      Naming thee Cain, sweetest possession !
Aleim of mercies ! child of Thy word !

SATAN.

Such be the corn and kernel of our work,
O partners of our cause ; nor shall an hour
Be squander'd here ; else bears our empire loss.
Lo, yonder sits the female man ; and to
Her breasts a squalling infant hangs ; the male
And sire, heaps up, hard by, a rounded mound
For sacrifice ; whilst overhead, dispread,
As were they seraph hands reach'd down to help—
Illusions of the spectral North—clove-lights,
Feeling full soon the cogent Limits' blade ;
Retainers of our realm and intimate,
Chosen from out a throng of ancient mights
To aid us in the general feud twixt Earth
And Heav'n.   Go to, the instant strikes ; or now,
Or ne'er, this infant race shall lick the hand
Of Lucifer.   Leap to your seats and watch !
Perchance ye shall be wiser ere the dew ;
And find that counterfeiting is the art
Of devil and demon.
      To-day veil we
The Earth in mist, and cloak the lights of EL—
To-day we croon beside the cradle of
The world and pour hot tears into its soul.
This be the finest, furbish'd art we use ;
Fictitious cloud, fictitious light ; *presto !*
And hide ourself anon in Protean shapes :
Aye, in a thousand ways amaze the pair ;
Till overpower'd they fall in suppliance.
That instant, Satan as a seraph sent,
Shall kindly lift them up, and smooth their brows.
Embrace the puling infant in our arms—
And breathe into those tender lips a breath

Infectious, with envy and crime's compound.
Nay, they shall press us and implore of us
A god, while fading from their presence as
We came, and as mysterious.

VOICES.

The moan of the mother, the cry of the child ;
The face of the father despairing and wild ;
> The *Aleim* evade us ;
> The *Circles* upbraid us ;
> The *Cherubim* chide us,
> The *Tree* is denied us ;
Oh, strange are the fancies that fly.
> Reproof for our folly,
> And mort melancholy ;
Woe, woe, God hath left us to die !

Oh, list to the excellent voice of the stars !
Do well and thy countenance nothing e'er mars ;
> Do ill, and relenting
> With sincere repenting,
> Sin fleeth before thee ;
> The *Aleim* restore thee,
And fend thee from possible ills ;
> Ye once were deceiv'd ;
> The loss is retriev'd ;
The promise *Jehovah* fulfills.

THE MAN.

Thou dost most mightily amaze our minds,
O spectral form ! If thou be friendly help
Us to command our words, and sue for grace.
Speak, awful apparition of the cloud !
Art *Aleim*, or the Spirit of the World ?

SATAN.

Thou hast well said : the " Spirit of the World ! "
This is our proper title ; and we greet
Extending kindness to the wanderer's thatch
Set up in our domain ; good, only good,
We bring.   This world is at your bidding now.
Sweet babe of heaven, thou slumberest fair upon
Thy mother's breast ; alas, how innocent !
The *Aleim* of the Mount have cast thee forth !
The *Spirit of the World* brings timely aid ;
And succoreth in dire distress.   We come
That ye may pine no more for food and cheer.

THE MAN.

O sworn ones ! great *Aleim !*   The World is kind
Indeed, pouring sweet solace in our cup ;
Forgive, if now we kneel and kiss his hand.
Blest image of this star, we kneel and bless.
Our babe awakes ! he smiles ! thy brightness lures !
O grant a blessing here upon the babe !
'T is well, he shall be holy to thy name !

Star, star of hope ! forsake us not !   Alack !
Great *Aleim* save us from the viper's sting !
It coils, it springs ! my child ! alas, my child !

THE WOMAN.

Thou callest me " Eve," the mother of men ;
Thou biddest me cheer, whilst stricken again ;
Thou chidest my grief,—the mother of Cain,
Adam my lord !

We worry and work ; we sorrow and sigh ;
We worship in vain the *Aleim* on high ;
The *Powers* forsake us ; and leave us to die,
Adam my lord !

Once more I await the cry of a man—
O babe of my woe, how weary and wan ;
Thou 'rt frailty itself ; thy life is a span,
Abel my child !

O anguish of Earth ! O forepains of dread !
Ill omens repent me and shadow my bed ;
I faint as I think of the tears thou shalt shed,
Abel my child !

SATAN.

Ye build mine empire larger in your thoughts,
To-day than yesterday, O comrades of
Our realm. And well ; for trivial hopes give birth
To trivial acts ; so Satan's soul can brook
No pigmy-mites, and tomtit runts.   Each one
Of you, fully matured, shall like a Triton,
In the least minnow's wake, strike out into
The stream of your endeavors.

        Mark our words !
The *Aleim* forthwith surely weaken from
This star ; the fugitives from Eden faint ;
Our fraud of yesterday hath sore amazed
And whelm'd their apperceptions.   Of the twain,
The female hath the hardlier lot ; and she
In bitter anguish of a second child
Doth call on phantom wisps to come to her
Relief.   Next heard we Cain, our foster-child,

Cry violently, and curse his birth-star as
He saw his infant brother suckling at
His mother's breasts, usurping his birthright.
O here is straw for mortar friends.   Lo, here
Behind this tent of thatch there glows a fire
That shall consume a race of men in Hell.
Be this our clear and well-defin'd device :
To simulate the true *Aleim ;* to draw
Aside true worship by false lights ; infuse
A dread of heaven and ev'ry mystery ;
So foster fetishisms, and Nature cults ;
Confound men's creeds and thus confuse their tongues ;
Corrupt their faiths and so destroy their virtues ;
Leading astray till knowledge of the *True
Aleim* be lost ; then rule the absolute
And undisputed *Anarch* of this World,—
Prince not alone of *Matter*, but of *Mind.*

THE ALEIM OF PLEROMA.

The Circles bend to larger privilege ;
Henceforth the Limits trace a vastlier course ;
The Bands and Couriers fly to expedite
Their work in distant times.   But first leads on
The Age of *false Aleim*, delusion's choir !
Corruptions of the True, that captivate
The sense, confuse the reason, and forthwith
Infest the Garden-faith with thorny error.

O Satan, now art thou full grown in sin !
And reck't no more the wages nor the woe
Of thy designs.   WE vaunt not as thou dost ;
Nor publish to the Angels Our designs
And purposes.   To warn thee of defeat,

And final beggary, burning amidst
With loathing of thyself, shall this deter ?
No ; thou hast made thy God a liar ! thyself
Delusion's head and throne, father of Lies,
And prince of sin, *Jehovah's* deadly foe !

Go, mobilize thy minions !   Haste thy work !
Do ye prevent the Advent of *Jahveh?*
Nay rather shall from thee the race recoil
And build anew the altars of *Jahveh*
That was, and is, and cometh evermore.

CANTO III.

THE FALSE ALEIM.

THE ARGUMENT.

Confusion's hour is announced by the Limits—Cain's impious rites the cause of much merriment among the demons, who incite his jealous mind on to the first act of fratricide—Cain dreadeth the Avenger, and lamenteth his banishment—Satan disguised as a deity, first, comforteth Cain and his wife, in their flight from the face of Jahveh ; then, requireth of them a vow of fealty to his name and altar—The descendants of Cain, mighty men, princes of the false Aleim, look upon the shepherdesses of Enos and allure them with fair promises to their cities—The sons of Enos make the sacrificial oath of vengeance—The maidens intercede—The sons of Seth also corrupted by the enticements of idolatry—The PLEROMA *meditateth the approaching deluge—Satan from his pinnacle surveyeth his possessions, and poseth to receive divine honors—He at once perceiveth the omens of an approaching cataclysm which shall destroy many of his lascivious* INCUBI, *and whelm the Garden of the World— The bruit of the demons—The Circles wing, sky-ward, singing the boat afloat, and the purging of their circumpolar seat—The Garden of* GOD.

THE LIMITS.

Hear'st thou the bleating ewe,
Calling her firstling ?
Answers the rustling
Pine : Ever, forever !

Hear'st thou the mother's cry
  Seeking her Abel ?
  Answers the sable
    Pine : Ever, forever.

This is confusion's hour,
  Demons pursuing ;
  Enmities brewing
    Crime, crimson forever.

Babel of strife and tongues,
  Jahveh resisting,
  Turning, and trysting
    False, falsely, forever !

SATAN.

Drink up the excess of your joy, good spirits,
And rest a little space ! Expand the orb
Of your perceptions and give heed !   Behold,
The crisis of this hour controls an age.
Ye see a double canopy of cloud
Upon the northern slope ; beneath are piles
Of stone rudely arrang'd for sacrifice ;
The herdsman, Abel, thither cometh with
His bloody gift ; the elder, frowning Cain,
Approacheth from mid-fields with fruits and roots :
Nor heedeth he the instance of the group
That chides his contumacious offering.
Within the glowing maze, *Jehovah* hides
His countenance ; and signifies by flames
Shot down to fire the altar, favor, and
Acceptance from his God.   Hard by, ye see
The harmless Cherubim that do instead

Of scarecrows, warding off sinful mankind
The nodding North, that slowly chills, and leaves
Its memory in crystal effigy.

    Ye stand on tiptoe and do gape to view
The ceremonial ! Bah, we had taught
These wretches how to flay and roast ; to bake
Their shew-bread, and present it well.   See Cain !
With how much grace he lays his gift of fruit !
This niceness, mark, is in our foster-child.
His mien majestic ; lordlier as his work.
Thou tiller of the earth, tender of plants
And vines ! Thee Satan greets with honest pride,
And affluent desire to bring thee fame ;
And build for thee in earth a lofty throne,
Saluting thee vice-regent of the world :
Yea, if thou carriest well thy chosen part
This day ; insisting on the equal rank
Of husbandry with shepherd thrift ; and nam'st
The *ancient Aleim* as the patrons of
The all-producing earth ; nor, callest once
Upon *Jahveh* to bless thy fields and fruits ;
Reproving novelty, by the elder faith ;
So shalt thou win, O son of *Elohim*—
Titanic, earliest Deity ; and Lucifer
Stoopeth to kiss thy cheek, and place upon
Thy brow the wreath of bay.
                        Mark well, ye peers ;
If from yon swelling fleece of cloud there dart
A flame to light the fruited stones !   What time
Mine own elected Cain turneth away
In deadly anger from his fireless heap,
Leap to the dizzy crags, and scream amain

With hellish glee ! cry for the Limits all !
Divide, divorce, destroy ! O Satan is
No suitor of the sugar'd shrines ; he feeds—
He feeds on more substantial aliment :
Forsooth on blood, even as the *Jahveh*
That was, and is, and is to come—" To come " !
Bah, we could do the creed, vaticinate,
And coddle nightly 'mong the cherub cots,
But we have learn'd a trifle and a *plus*
Beside ; found mainly threat'nings to be vain,
Mere cracklings of the lower skies, while GOD
In lofty self-complaisance stays his arm ;
Although he lends his voice to novices.

Ho, demons, spring in air, gyrate and shout !
Now let Earth crack, and oceans vomit belch !
The braver half of man is ours, is ours !
Cain hath defied *Jahveh !* Henceforth claim we
Our son : the *false Aleim* blaze in the skies—
In Abel shall *Jehovah* worship die !

THE DEMONS.

Flare, flare, ye terrene flames !
We give you sacred names ;
   We lure to you mankind,
   To worship you enshrin'd ;
     O fair, illusive lights ?

He turns, the elder turns ;
Within him anger burns ;
   We feed his wrath ;
   We smooth his path ;
     Descend illusive lights !

II

Shriek—shriek, ye shatter'd airs,
Whilst bloody vengeance stares
    Red-handed at its deed ;
    Now Satan drink thy mead !
        Speed on, illusive lights !

A VOICE.

Crime followeth sin in a round ;
The Circle describeth its bound ;
    From sire to son, and son to sire,
    It traveleth sure, and traveleth dire ;
        The evening gloweth ;
        The zephyr bloweth,
            And wingeth along the lea ;
        The forest groaneth ;
        The green sward moaneth
            The awful tragedy.

CAIN.

The bloods of my brother are crying to Heav'n against
    me :
I am cursèd already, already in soul as in body ;
I have chosen my lot, O so desert and darkly ;
A vagabond wanderer, I, homeless and banish'd.
Jahveh, thy curse is too great for my spirit to carry ;
I am faint and already the avenger of blood is upon me.
The seven-fold winds do not carry away all my groan-
    ings ;
Nor the Cherubim bear half the prayers I have offer'd.
Ah, the sentence is pass'd ; but protect, O protect Thou
    thy banish'd.

Blest art Thou O *Jahveh!* this sign shall defend from
  the slayer ;
In Nod, in the land of my flight, when alone and de-
  fenceless.
Farewell to the face of the Lord that pleadeth his mercies
  before me ;
Farewell to the altars of *Aleim*, the mighty protectors ;
Farewell to my stricken disconsolate parents, whose faces
Their first-born shall never again behold in the body ;
Farewell to my kindred that seed all the coasts of the
  garden ;
And ye pleasant fields, and ye forests that woo'd me to
  till you ;
My heart leave I here in your bosom engrafted forever ;
And soul-less and sighing your keeper forsaketh these
  gardens
To go to the South, to the land that shall henceforth
  receive me.

A VOICE.

The hand of the homicide red with its murder ;
Red with the sign that *Jehovah* put on it ;
Ghastly in mien with shiver and shudder—
Reacheth to take now the hand of a sister ;
Sister and wife, the wanderer's only companion ;
Facing the East, and its searchless savannas—
Facing the gloom of the thicket and forest ;
Aw'd by the cry of the jackal and note of raven ;
Chasten'd and broken in spirit, ready to turn back ;
Cursèd, and cannot, cannot retrieve though he will to ;
Urg'd on by awful compulsion, yet doth he know not
Whither, save only it be from the *Face* of *Jehovah.*

SATAN.

Now are ye plump, O imps ! now are ye gorg'd
With nature's sap ; O we can trust your wits
Henceforth as spirits of the world ; and give
You larger privilege ; withdraw the leash ;
Adorn with honors where aforetime we
Have check'd and hamper'd.
                              We ween that each and all
Do seize the earnest of the hour, and haste
Counsel to expedite, our cause advance
Against the coming one *Jahveh*, whose name
Already lisp'd by Adam's seed, aloof
The cherub-seat, forbodes our final ruin ;
If not crush'd out and overborne by Cain
And his descendants that shall disavow
This novel *Jahveh* faith, appealing to
The ancienter *Aleim, fire, light*, and *air*,
The emblems of the mighty *Mights* so mix'd
Up with our province, that we weave them in
The texture of terrestrial things and clothe
In subtle charms and colors.
                              Swear fealty !
And once again obeisance to your Prince !
Leap now unto your tasks, harry and hide ;
Play true or false, and double deal as best
Befits the end ; beset with ambushments
The seed of Adam ; lure and captivate
Their wills, winning to wanton worships.   Nor
Affray your souls at blood and havockry ;
The end merits the means that gain it best.
Know ye that Satan loves nor sin nor ill ;
He loveth rule and empire.   So he must—
Perforce of *Jah's* essay to crush his head—

Do injury to myriads of souls
He 'd sooner leave untouch'd ; hence ye shall reck
No costs ; your prince counts none, if Jahveh rule
Retires, and nature takes a firmer hold
Upon the heart of man.   *Was Lucifer's*
This star ; is now, and shall be ; else, falling
The World falls too.

CAIN.

Ye *Mights* of the Mount, once effulgent in flame and in
  ether :
The solace and song of my parents ere they were ban-
  ish'd ;
Earliest heard on the lips of my mother kneeling to
  Heav'n ;
Teaching me too how to worship, bowing my knee down
  beside her.
Ah, long have ye hidden your face from the eyes of your
  children,
Loosing the bonds that constrain'd them purely in
  homage ;
Chide me not, crush'd and forsaken, if I appeal to thy
  mercy ;
Nay, though I free here my soul of its burden so heavy !
Recite in thine ears the wrath of *Jehovah* upon me ;
The zeal that possess'd me to prop up thy worship.
O *Names* of *Aleim*, the *Mighty*, slurr'd by my brothers ;
Chiefly by Abel, my junior, vaulting the priesthood ;
Bringing in novelties, evils that were to be silenc'd.
Rashly strove I to rescue the ancient religion :
Could not, save on Earth's shrine his blood should be
  offer'd.
Spirit of Earth, Soul of the World and its marvels,

Pardon my crime ! Spirit of Light and of Ether,
Succor thy son ! O retrieve from the curse of *Jehovah !*
Spirit of EARTH, god of the world, rescue the wanderer !

SATAN.

Hail, foster son, firm in maternal faith !
The *Aleim* bring cheer and respite to thy lot ;
Condone thy well-meant sin ; remove this load
Of care ; repair, and speedily, thy loss.
Know ye, yon lights that twinkle in the sky
Are we ;—the stars bid Cain good speed upon
His way.   The winds that wing from ev'ry sea
Are we ;—the airs shall be thy couriers
To bring thee on thy course.   Yon fires that shine
Upon the mount are we, to light thy way ;
The all-embracing Ether spreads her tent
For thee ; the glades rejoice to welcome thee.
The sprites that dwell in cleft and croft leap up
To greet the favor'd one among the sons
Of men, first born to Adam, and a prince
Of a new race.   Thou shalt not fall and die ;
But from thy loins shall spring a mighty birth
Of valiant men, skilful in arts, builders
Of cities ; renown'd in war and chase throughout
The Earth, a godlike race of Nephilim,
Princes of *El*, brave sons of the *Aleim.*
Still thou art man ; and man unsworn is as
The fickle breeze ; 't is fit we claim of thee
A triple vow of fealty, and homage :
Thou dost herein for thee and for thy seed
Avouch allegiance to the Trinity
Of *Fire, Flame,* and *Ether*, divinities

Of thy maternal love ; to these erect
Thine altars, paying thereupon thy vows
Unto the triple lights of heaven and earth.

CAIN.

Mark'st thou, my sister, the sheen of the sov'ran Lights ?
Hearst thou, my sister, the vows and the pledges here
    spoken ?
Praise the ALEIM ! Cain shall yet live and be prosper'd ;
See, for the sky is incarnadine now with his presence !
God moves in mighty resplendence forth on our pathway ;
Passing upward, glorifies he all the mountain !
Marvel, look, he changes in fashion ! lo, as a man,
Splendidly awful ! See, how he strides o'er the summit !
Beckoning, beckoning, — weird, — strange, — horrible —
    face !

"What of these portents ?" Sister, thy words are their
    answer ;
Portents in truth, known but to God and him only ;
Farewell, thou glow of the Gan-Eden mountain ;
Dimly, alas, seen in the background ; farther,—
Knowing not whither, save from the face of *Jehovah.*

THE SONS OF ALEIM.

Ask ye our worship, beautiful daughters of Enos—
Enos, restorer of altars ?
Ask ye our birthplace and kindred fairest of maidens—
Daughters of Mahalaleel, splendor of *El?*
Heed then our song of Havilah !
Learn of the children of Cain ; Enoch and Lamech ;
Learn of their sons and their fortunes ;

Learn of the Names that we worship building high tem-
    ples ;
Call'd from the triad of Gods that defend us :
Hear of the fabulous riches quarried and coined :
Cities, close built, castles and gardens sweet-scented :
Hear of great ladies, Adah and Zillah, unenvied,
Fostering arts in the children rear'd in their chambers ;
Jubal, the glory of music, king of the harp and the
    organ :1 :
Tubal the glory of art, prince of the workers in metals ;
Thence of Naamah the pleasant, queen of the maidens,
Chosen of *Aleim* to offer incense before them.

THE DAUGHTERS OF ENOS.

O princes of *El*, our cousins most valiant ;
    The daughters of JAHVEH revere and entreat ;
Ye will not go by ; but tarry, refresh you,
    The while we shall summon our brothers to meat !

THE SONS OF ALEIM.

Ours is a mission of daring performance,
Loveliest daughters of Seth ;
Ours is a bold and incautious adventure
Beautiful maids of *Jahveh !*
Hear we anew the call of our *Aleim :*
" Hasten, else reckon no more on our altars ;
Bring with thee virgins, wives for my nobles ;
Promise the pastoral daughters of *Jahveh,*
Music and festival pastimes to surfeit ;
Eye hath not seen of these shepherds ;
Ear hath not heard of these nomads,
Half of the wonders of Nod, land of the Pison—
Rich in its gold, bdellium, and onyx."

THE SONS OF ENOS.

Canaan thy child, vows by thine altars, O Enos ;
Swears to avenge the foul rape of the princes !
Nephilim, curs'd with a curse, lost to *Jehovah.*
Mahalaleel, splendor of God, grandson, is with us ;
Father of Jared, father of Enoch, the teacher ;
Thence of Methuselah, son of the javelin ;
These all, and princes puissant, sacred to *Jahveh*,
Offer our seven-fold victims whilst thou implorest,
Suppliant sire, the Lord of the Highest to aid us.
Swift are these griffins and dread in their havoc ;
Giants, wild *gibborim*, got by the help of the demons ;
Demi-gods, monsters, clad in the splendors of angels ;
Sold under sin and adepts of ev'ry pollution :
Lying with beasts, ploughing with dames most infernal ;
Plunderers damn'd, that glut their desire on the maidens.
Help, O Most Highest !   Save from the " *sons of aleim !*"
Falsely named faces of *Satan*, Spirit of Evil !

THE CAPTIVE WOMEN.

Cease from this bloodshed, O fathers ! O brothers !
Respite an hour, while the maidens, now mothers ;
Happy and rich in the land of Havilah,
Favor'd of great ones, Adah, and Zillah,
Bid in their name and the *Aleim* above us ;
Visit our hearths if yet ye do love us ;
See how the princes have dealt with thy daughters ;
Then if ye can, renew ye the slaughters !

PLEROMA JAHVEH.

Behold the sons of Seth also have gone the way of Cain :
Following the voices of the captive women ;
Now is all flesh corrupt ;

And the imaginations of man's heart evil, evil contin-
 ually.
The earth is fill'd with the violence of the mighty :
And it repenteth Jehovah that he hath made man.
And though my spirit shall not strive in them forever,
Yet their day shall be one hundred and twenty years—
Then shall the end of all flesh come before my face.
The *sons* of the *aleim*, the seed of Cain, shall perish ;
The *Nephilim* shall go down in the deluge of waters.
Likewise all the seed of Seth, save Noah.
He and his household, being warn'd, shall build an ark
To keep alive of ev'ry living thing, both male and female ;
For I will cause the reservoirs to burst from under :
And I will open the windows of heaven ;
The seas shall cover the face of my holy mountain,
To hide it forever from a perverse people.
I, JAHVEH, have spoken and will perform it ;

SATAN.

 Enthron'd upon this purpling pinnacle,
That pours its lustre in Havilah's lap,
What time the Dawn, loos'd from the Sun's embrace
Speeds from his couch, and crimsons all the world
With wanton flushes, softly veil'd ; or, when
Reluctant twilight, of the Earth enamor'd,
Woo'd by the hills and heaths, looks back and sighs,
Throwing a dower of smiles on Enos' daughters,
Takes Satan here his lofty seat and gives
His suppliants attendance, that offer him
The choicest of their tilth, both corn and fruit ;
Circling in bands with grateful praise and prayer,
To the *Aleim* of *Airs* omniscient, that own
This summit for their shrine.

             · This land hath peace.
Where Death withdrew, comes mirth and revel in :
The name of JAH is heard no more upon
The lips of men. *Jahveh, Jahveh* is fall'n !
In glory excellent dwell we alone ;
O most enchanted star ! and more, that now
The lecherous demons drub not our stool.
Supreme ! Repeat that word, O soul, "Supreme ! "
The seed of Seth hath wholly gone the way
Of Cain, save Noah ; and he is mad, they say,
And cobbles up an awkward coffin for
His bones. Him will I turn my wits upon
And edge the churlish spite I hear below.
Ho, devils ! bulging with your message, speak !
Zounds ! In the holy sacred of my peace,
There troopeth frenzied horrors, brain bedizzen'd !
Aback, we will not be disturb'd. Do we ?
Doth Lucifer build castles for his pride,
To have them crush'd and crumbled in a trice ?
Speak ! Speak ! ye fiends, what palsies hold you so ?
Lo all the world (nay Satan is the World) :
Lo all the land spews out its venom'd swarm !
Ye gods, behold the sight ! A puling poulp
Of pestilential death wallows the hill ;
A sickly curse hath lighted on my legions.
Now dare we speak the truth, confess it loud ;
We weep not for this carnal race of demons ;
O wens and blotches ! had we the *Soma*
Think ye we 'd give it you ? Nay, die the death !

  Such ugly rumors spawn'd upon our ears,
Almost are we persuaded of the fact,
This God-breath'd Noah is a vehicle

Of Jahveh's curse, that 's imminent, whereof
'T is evident this deathly sickness of
Our legions yielded further countenance.

The seven chiefs concur in their report :
The ark is finished ; its hoary architect,
His sons him aiding, stores within, a raft
Of wares and victuals for man and beast.
It is already moot among sane men,
That the Almighty 'venging on mankind
For being human, loving mother Earth
Most naturally, will whelm her children all ;
A sea of fire and waters disembogu'd
The bowels of the Earth : so shall this fair
And bastion'd basin of the North engulf'd,
Upbear a raft of miserable deaths,
At once of men and brutes and creeping things ;
Revolting to all eyes, behind and huge,
Shall drift the tabid husks of serpents vile,
Fouling the main afar—most horrible.
So curseth *Jahveh* what He cannot rule !
Aha, we have *Jahveh* a pupil apt !

First in the mighty anger of our soul
Sware we to fend this circum-polar land
Against the Almight's curse ; when wiser thoughts
At once came in to show a better way ;
Then clearly knew we how events hereto
The merest preface are, the prologue of
The tragedy begun in Heav'n—a feud
Provok'd by God's most arbitrary rule ;   ·
Transferr'd to Earth, with man the common spoil.
Did Lucifer laugh now he laughs too soon,
Did Lucifer now bare his might, then were

His majesty from deeper plans diffract.
O trivial effort made to 'stablish here
Thy throne and altar, O *Jahveh!* We scorn
To breeze our banners, and air our pæans ;
This is fictitious war ; Thy might 's withheld !
In Noah and his sons beyond the flood,
The fallen worship shall take root again,
With faithful men, though few to build thy shrines—
A trifid branch, fore-caution'd to respect.
Hence pass we on before and void this place ;
(For work is our sole joy ; work done revolts.)
Descending Southward, view we other realms
Beyond the Sun.   So, hither pursuivant,
Ye chosen chiefs, and sharers of our rule
In Earth, follow, tracing future empire.
If hitherto we meted you no bounds,
Conferr'd no title and domain imperial,—
Suffice, the play was barely on ; our will
Hath been in time to portion you the world ;
Divide with you the habitable globe,
Ere long to be repeopled—the deluge past—
Enacting thenceforth further scenes of Earth's
Great drama.   Cede this filthy coop at once
To *Jahveh's* bolts and fires revengeful.

The Bruit of Demons wrack'd and curs'd
In meshes caught they cannot burst ;
Lustful *incubi*, loving clay,
Vampire *gnomes* of demonry ;
Harpy, fury,
Troll and *bogey ,*
Effreet, afrite,
Unclean spirit,

Tasting fumes of the bottomless pit,
Betray'd of Satan and no respite.

THE LIMITS.

Ho, ho, doth Satan go?
Doth he quit this polar world for aye?
  Do the *aleim* follow with the sun?
  Do they ogle on the fraud begun?
Answer, O JAHVEH, we pray!

Ho, ho, doth Satan go?
Doth he ravish the world, then forsake?
  Doth he leave his helpless legionries,
  And send no aid in their agonies?
The curse of JAHVEH overtake!

THE CIRCLES.

Twirl, twirl, sisters, twirl!
Your *labara* unfurl;
  Above the wales,
  Abreast the gales,
    Let *Jahveh's* name be sung.

Chant, sisters, chant!
The swaying Earth aslant,
  Scorneth the sun;
  Warneth each one
    The *aleim's* knell hath rung.

Pale, sisters, pale!
Harken the war and wail!
  While Noah's boat
  Goeth afloat
    And rides the embastion'd flood:

Flee, sisters, flee !
The North becomes a sea ;
   Return to the stars,
   On your luminous cars,
     And stay the decree of the Lord.

GAIA (THE EARTH).

Thou art wroth, O Sun !
   As a moth I am brush'd from thy light.
I am quite undone ;
   I am cold, for thy face is hid from sight.
Thou art cruel, O Sun ;
   And the Earth expires in sobs and tears ;
She is faint and falls ;
   And her offspring is whelm'd in fears—
She is faint and falls.
My heart is quench'd, O Sun !
   The floods rush from my rending side ;
The North reverts, O Sun ;
   My pray'r is rigidly denied—
His glory sinks beneath the sea.
   The heavens are black,
   Alack,
Thou wilt come no more to comfort me ;
   Nor ever learn how I mourn'd and wept
Ere I broke in death,
   And thy children with me, crush'd and swept
From my breast at a breath.

PLEROMA JAHVEH.

Again these reeking mounts and steppes uprear
Their tawny backs above the 'suaging waves.
Alone the storied North is seen no more :

Clad for his burial in icy robes ;
Ensconc'd from human eyes forever there.
The ark hath stoutly stood the mighty shock,
Whilst engines, dynamitic, clove the rocks
And rent in two the continents ; nor struck
The frowning coping to the masonry
Of adamant that zoned the sin-curs'd shores ;—
Breasting full long the inrush of the waters,
Borne southward by the steady drift that swept
The universal sea,—she rests at length
On Ararat, to *Jahveh* sacred ground
And high in Kurdistan.
                .   The dove that yester
Brought the olive leaf to Noah, to-day
Returneth not ; and Noah hath unloos'd
The covering to mark the waters are
Abated from the earth.
                    God's voice now heard,
He goeth forth, himself and wife and sons,
Shem, Ham, and Japhet three, and wives with them :
Next leadeth forth, or looseth from their stalls,
The greater and the lesser tribes of beasts
And bird indigenous the pristine North,
Which earliest lay profuse in loveliness ;—
Enchanted land of fruits and flowers, luring
Into its lap all brilliant wings, else call'd
The Birds of Paradise ;—the pictured swarm
Of mimicry minute, the insect lives
That breathe the nard and nectarous airs and kiss
The argent blooming flowers, which gave more sweet
To lisping bee that gather'd honey there,
Than elsewhere scient skill shall e'er distill :
Whelm'd this fair *Omphalos* of Earth, and all

Its charms fast-lock'd in ice : revers'd the sun,
And doubly chill'd in coldest space, remote
His tropic fires ; not guiltless, not unwarn'd.

Sole remnant of the seed of Seth transplant
From parts engulf'd, to stock once more the world :
Eight righteous souls, remote their northern home ;
Admiring the Asian plateaus wide ;
Eight JAHVEH-*worshippers*, God's holiness
And unity profoundly sens'd, provide
For the supreme and only NAME in HEAVEN,
A pleasant sacrifice, in Noah their sire,
And priest : implanting these far-stretching slopes
A pure and spiritual faith.
                        Receive We now
The odor of acceptable prayer and praise.
Fear not, Noah ! For while the Earth remains,
Seedtime and harvest-home, the winter's cold
And summer's heat, nor day nor night shall fail.
For JAHVEH curseth not again the earth for sin.
Lo, yonder IRIS of the South that bows
In sparkling symmetry upon the mounts—
See how it stands upon the pillars of
The world, fair symbol of JAH's covenant,
Until PLEROMA come.

CANTO IV.

THE BABEL.

THE ARGUMENT.

*The Bands lament the Limits' hour—Ham's impiety and
Canaan's curse—The table of nations is called—The
Couriers find the faultless man, and sing the glory of
the Caucasus—The different races are viewed, with char-
acteristic lore given—Primitive men and natural reli-
gions—The Circles find Eden symbols everywhere—The
Æons trace in particular the fortunes of the Jahvites ;
of the Shemite race—The magnificence of the Nimroud Dynasty ; and the false Aleim—The seat of
Satan overthrown, with confusion of tongues.*

THE BANDS.

Limits strive to sever ; scatter through all lands ;
Rescue us JEHOVAH, ward Thy chosen Bands :
Weak are we, and wander, if Thou bind us not ;
Shifted soon and shattered, if Thou wind us not ;
  Fulness of the Godhead, Spirit from above ;
  Potence of the highest,
  Essence of his love ;
  God of Seth and Noah—
  Ancient name ELOAH,
  Cov'nant name JEHOVAH ;
  BAND of Bands, MESSIAH !   Humbly we implore.

Tarry not O JAHVEH ! show Thy matchless grace !
Seers inspire, intrinsic to the human race ;
  Lo, in trope and symbol, predicate the day-
Promis'd Seed and Savior, incarnate JAHVEH
  God of Seth and Noah—
  Ancient name ELOAH ;
  Cov'nant name JEHOVAH, lowly we adore.

Ah, what omens fray us ! auguries of ill ;
Blessing turns to cursing ; oaths coerce the will ;
Brothers shunt and alien, disparate diverge ;
Climes and countries variant, further changes urge :
Nature lures, or threatens ; trivial gifts atone ;
Deities are worshipped, hewn of wood or stone.
Fetishisms and demon-cults terrify mankind ;
Pantheons and Babeldoms ev'rywhere we find ;
  God of Seth and Noah—
  Ancient name ELOAH ;
  Cov'nant name JEHOVAH—
  LORD of Lords, PLEROMA ! praise we evermore !

VOICES.

Awake ! awake ! from thy wine ;
  Thy sleep is profaned ;
  Thy slumber is stained ;
Thy nakedness cries to the vine ;
    Vail me, O vine, in thy bower !
    Hide thou my shame in this hour !

Ah Sin, thou art here in the laughter and leer,
And the sensual glance of Canaan's sire ;
Thou dost paint so a trace, and screen'st not thy face ;
For the mock of the son is the crime ye inspire.

NOAH.

Canaan is curst in Ham !
　　A servant shall he be unto his brethren ;
Jahveh is blest in Shem :
Japheth shall el persuade,
In tents of Shem array'd ;
　　While Canaan, curst, shall serve his brethren.

THE ÆONS.

Number ye, name ye, O Sisters, the children of Japheth !
　　To whom jahveh giveth bounds and rich blessings ;
Sing of their fortunes in countries far distant ;
　　Tell of traditions and myths they do cherish.

Gomer—the sire of the Cimri—clinging the shores of the
　　North,
　　Warlike Cimmerians threading Hercynian forests ;
　　Nomads of Askenaz ranging the steppes of high
　　　　Asia,—
　　Rephæan caves,—the home where the North-wind was
　　　　cradled :
　　Also the house of Torgona, Caucas'an races, all
　　　　Aryan.
Magog—the sire of the Scythians, terrible, numberless
　　　　Scythians :
　　Barbarous princes of Rosh, Meshech, and Tubal ;
　　Arm'd with the bow and mounted as horsemen ;
　　Curving the sides of the North, cruel, rapacious.
Madai—the sire of the Medes, pastoral, meditative,
　　　　peoples.
Javan—the sire of the Grecians, *Javanu,* writ in their
　　　　tablets,

Elisah,—sweet-scented Elis in Peloponnesus,—
Tarshish, twixt mouths of the great ocean river, far
   limit ;
Kittim and Rodanim, Cypric and Rhodian stocks.
TIRAS—sea-farers, robbers, pelasgic Etruscans,
  Mighty in arms and invaders of nations.

Number ye, name ye, O Sisters, the children of HAM—
Sons of the South, peoples accurst to do service.

CUSH — the father of Nimroud, the hunter warring
   Jehovah,
Treading the gulfs and the Indian coasts ;
  Seba, child of the streams, Meröe old of the Nile ;
  Havilah—a name from the ancientest North transplant
    to myrrhiferous Araba :
  Sabtah, far-famed for its incense,—Sabota :
  Raamah, else Regma, adjacent the Persian waters.
  Sabtecha to eastward in Caramaria.
MIZRAIM—father of races, boasting their Egypts ;
  Ludim (the men) the mighty world-monarchs :
  Anamim, rank in the low delta pastures ;
  Lehabim, Libyans, bounded by ocean and sun ;
  Bearded, tattoed, with features Caucasian.
  Nepthuhim, Pathrusim, of Memphis and Thebes ;
  Casluhim, lining the borders of Canaan ;
  Thence the Serbonian bog and Casio's hill.
  Caphtorim, edging the Delta, thence Damietta, out of
    whom cometh Philistim.
PHUT—the father of traders in incense with Tyre ;
CANAAN—the sire of sailors and builders :
  Sidon, come from the Bahrein isles far Southward ;
  Heth, cœle-Syrian, land of the Tauris.

JEBUSITES—keeping the waterless hill, Jebus historic ;
AMORITES—mountaineers, walling their cities to heaven ;
   Dwelling anon in the South, and the Palm-rows and
     Petra.
GIRGASHITES—centrally domed in the Palestine moun-
     tains ;
HIVITES—the crafty, in Shechem and Hamath to North-
     ward ;
ARKITES—the strong, in their bastions basaltic ;
SINITES—high-dwellers on Libanon's shoulders ;
ARVADITES—free on their islet, near the Phœnicians :
ZEMARITES—close the Eleutherus fountain ;
HAMATHITES—rich by Orontes and Lebanon's quarries.

   Number ye, name ye, O Sisters, the children of SHEM !
ELAM—the father of Elamites, bordering Babylon's
     kingdoms ; shepherding picturesque foothills, poets
     and dreamers.
ASSHUR—deified king of Assyria taught of Acadians ;
     fenced by the Tartars ; sure in Aleppo ;
ARPHAXAD—father of names in the line of Jehovah ;
   Shelech, exploiting and passing in Eber,
   Peleg, dividing and lessening more in his son, tribes
     three and ten all Arabian nomads, dwelling the way
     unto Sephar, mount of the East.
LUD—that ripen'd in Lydia, charm of the West ;
ARAM, the high, the Northland, facing the Yemen ;
   Land of the patriarchs, numbered in story :
UZ—ural-king and crown of Damascus ;
Thence HUL of the reedy Merom, also GETHER,
And MASH, the bold Ituræan marauders.

So are the nations apportioned—children of Noah :
So is seeded the Earth from the face of Jehovah.

THE PLEROMA.

Long is the earth replenish'd from the seed
Of Noah ; mankind and animals (the North
Indigenous) confront the world's extremes.
In equal latitudes mark kindred types ;
In variant climes, note forms dissimilar :
One hemisphere above and one beneath
The sun, with upper and with nether zones :
Three continents, historic crowd the northern :
Outspread, articulate, with ample fringe
Of bays and island harbors, the social North :
Massive and lone the southern hemisphere.
Remote Australia yields her unique types ;
The gigantesque Myrtaceæ ; the flaring
Eucalypti ; gracefulest Mimosas,
And bright Acacias.   The *fauna* too—
The kangaroo that gambols in her forests ;
The marshy *rhynchus'* shapeless form complex.
Next fall our eyes on Afric's farthest bounds,
And note therein the pale Proteaceæ ;
The pulpy aloes, set in brilliant clusters,
Irideæ with boldest colorings ;
While o'er the scented heath, nimble gazelles
Are sporting ; aloof and wary feed giraffes
On leaf and greening bough o'erhanging high.
In covert couching, lion and panther lie,
To spring upon their unsuspecting prey.

Behold another and a western world
Rises to view, with Palm the regnant life ;
And dazzling Cacti flowering everywhere.
There 'mid the maze of blossoms and 'mid brakes
We see the clumsy armadillo's trail ;

The chubby tapir and the quaint ant-lion ;
Whilst longtail'd apes depend morose on many
A mossy bough and bank.
                              Hail, sunny SOUTH !
Intense and brilliant world ! the throne and pow'r
Of Nature.   Lo, in thee all splendors meet ;
Behold in thee all variants effulge !
How stunted on yon glacial tracts eke out
Their scanty hope, the lichen and the moss—
All colorless and wan : thence, southward passing,
See fuller growths and forms more manifold ;
Divergent, if on moist or dry, on low or high
Conditions, plastic seedlings fall.   The round
Of seasons in the temperate climes ; the sleep
Of winter and the burst of spring, convoke
New characters and yield new genera.
But thou hast wherewith to endow their dower,
O tropic South !   Thy wand enchants whate'er
It touches ; if ferns, if grasses, see, tall trees
Upspring and sway majestic like the groves :
Whilst tiny sisters of the North are crush'd
Beneath the heel of man and fed upon.
Here Nature triumphs ; beauty in beauty, form
In form, color in color, life in life !

THE COURIERS.

We have traversed the East, O PLEROMA,
    In search of the ideal Form ;
And Thou biddest to tell of our voyage,
    And say if we find yet the norm :
We have seen him, O Light !
And we glow at the sight !

Majestical, beautiful Man !
True centre of quintuple race—
A harmony faultless in grace,
In Caucasus and Iran.

THE PLEROMA.

Yes, Couriers, Taurus and Caucasus
Are happy fields for man to dwell among—
The spiritual centre of the world,
With nothing niggardly or prodigal ;
Nor Nature surfeited, nor craving o'er ;
Here blends the cosmic and the psychic man ;

O Life ! the portal of everlasting Heav'n !
Up, up, ye seers, discern the Star of Promise !
The Day-spring from on high ; blest day presag'd
Of man's Redemption, where in time shall come
The perfect MAN—to Earth the head and flower
Composite of humanity—PLEROMA.

THE COURIERS.

O glory of the Caucasus !
The Couriers sing thy praise ;
Whilst Zephyrus blows
And melt the snows,
And vine and myrtle freshen.

We sing thy stature lithe and tall ;
The royal hand that fashions all ;
The oval head, the full, large, eye ;
The well-turn'd nose and aquiline ;
The ruddy countenance and fair ;
The stately tread, the thoughtful air.

O glory of the Caucasus,
    Thrice perfect mould of man ;
Whilst Zephyrus blows
And melt the snows
    Sing the Caucasian.

THE PLEROMA.

The Couriers sing the *Cœle*-Syrian men,
Ideal forms, and, thence, they do rehearse
The loss of beauty suffer'd in far lands ;
First Europe's mobile races they connote—
More ethic beauty, if less physical ;
Next Afric's sons, with fronts retreating dark ;
The sable Gallas Abyssinian ;
The Caffre crisp, and woolly Hottentot ;
The pouting Berber, flat-nos'd Senegal ;
The bandy Bushmen, yellow pigmy men.
Thence sing the Orient Mongolian ;
The almond-eyed with figure square and squat ;
The Papors of New-Guinea, misshapen lumps.
Or stocky Finn, or Lapp, or Eskimo ;
Stunt in their glacial homes—Samoides :
These shall suffice to show that Nature hath
A kindly and a savage hemisphere ;
And Man, alike the animals partakes
The traits and characters of *habitat ;*
Nor mounts above else moral forces lift.

THE COURIERS.

We call the faiths, diverse, of man ;
Connoting first the Aryan ;
Let Æons number if they can
The years that gave them birth.

The Aryan (East) Rig-Veda myth ;
The Bactrian-Zar'thustra's heath ;
The Median (Magism) taking mould
Like Parsism from the Persian old.
Hail Helene, and Italiote ;
Thence Cymric and the Teuton note ;
The Slavic branch and Servian—
Dim limits of the Aryan.

We call the Faiths diverse of man,
Semitic and Arabian ;
Let Æons reckon if they can
Their years, or tell their worth :
The Northern stem—Assyrian ;
By Sidon's shore—Phœnician ;
The midst and glory of the train,
Blest JAHVEH faith, Noachian.

We pale before the roll of Ham ;
The dreadful doom of Babylon ;
We shudder at Egyptian gods,
Deific brutes and fetish clods.

THE PLEROMA.

O terrene Thoughts—Ourself slowly emerg'd
Through matter into Mind ; all subtle Airs,
Draw on ! This Life impassible brings calm.
Far-flying net ye at each further round
This star in psychic meshes, binding close
And sure upon Our Breast, whilst, with each sun,
Come ye aback more mystical and sad,
Confus'd by timeless pedigrees in time,
And Evolution's halting way from Chaos.

O ethic voids, the Spirit moves upon
Your sin and error, crying, " Let be Light ! "
When as We heard your bardic songs, and knew
The symbolism of name and number ;
Turning Our eyes infinite on both place
And people sung, there ope'd upon Our view
The runeless years, the gulf of dates betwixt
The house of Noah, and Cush whose crispy seed
O'erspringing Turan's hold, uprear'd yon piles
Of boastful bricks, and storied masonry,
On Tigris' and Euphrata's banks.

       O chasm
Of years ! None sings thee more or numbereth ;
Yet so thou art an open book of days,
Writ by Jehovah's hand, more clear unto
The Eternal than Accad's letters to
The eyes of Asshur.

      If Phantasy preside,
Forthcome the planetary ages five ;
The Golden first, bright in the sinless morn
Of memory—the day of JAHVEH worship ;
When all the sons of Noah invok'd one shrine ;
When one their speech as their religion one :
When men were chaste and holy still, and lov'd
The Truth and one another. Next the Silvern,
In Pleasure's maze. Thence goes the Brazen age,—
The ward of Mars, blowing his horn, egging
His iron son t' attempt the world's domain :
Devolving all their ethic heritage
In JAHVEH's laws, to undigested codes,
Crass and immoral. Such musings, harmless, may
We not contemn ; for curious minds, far hence,
Unvailing mysteries of ancient days

Shall find a content of poetic Truth,
To warm the rigid catalogues of *Science ;*
Enrich their prosy creeds of fact ; and learn
To unlearn much of proud Philosophy.

THE ÆONS.

Sing the *Lithic* ages twain !
Mammoth and the reindeer reign ;
Glacial drift and frozen hain ;
　　Man contending,
　　And forefending
Heaths 'gainst frozen streams.

Sing brute force, and stern recourse
Of Paleothite and Neolite,
　　In Quaternary quarries :
Arrow flints, and chippen glints,
Strown on marl, crunch'd in gnarl
　　That bull and cave-bear parries.
Pictur'd bones and polish'd stones ;
Rugged haunt, the wail of want ;
Ghastly look of *Ragnarook,*
　　Shivering their *middens :*
Carnivores and herbivores,
Terrified the ice-king ;
　　Woolly unicorn,
　　Urus' giant horn—
Aurochs, Roebuck, Lemming.

Terrac'd Somme and marly Meuse ;
Danish kitchen sea-refuse ;
Munchen-marrows ever ;
Marmot, badger, and the hare ;

Wild-cat, otter, and brown bear ;
Goat and chamois, lynx and fox ;
Swine and wolf and the musk ox ;
Bones of wild-boar, bull, and beaver ;
Next in salt fiords and river,
Periwinkle, cockle, mussel,
Added auk and ocean gull.

THE PLEROMA.

Discursive Æons, scient, prepossess'd—
The Light and Soul of all, PLEROMA heed !
These zoic, geologic, ethnic, hymns,
Do miss their wings and airy motions.　Such
Is Science ! that threading Nature's mystic weft
Brings back a bunch of chippen threads and fringe,
To straighten them anon in comely numbers—
A bulletin of firsts and secondaries ?
Say, what are firsts ? and what are lasts ? and what
Are mediates ?　Are What and Where the goal ?
How many *Whats !* or *Wheres*, shall Æons solve ?
Or man ? not freeing in the selfsame act
For every secret sought, a brood that 'scapes ?
Lo, calling o'er the roll or race and place
Ye merely date and designate, not sound ;
He therefore doeth well that lifts his eyes
And lists the music of the Airs, and feels
The lofty Presence that includeth all.
For higher mysteries lift up the soul,
While nether, closet it, exclude, and darken.
God is the furthest FIRST, the furthest LAST,
And the PLEROMA is the Soul of all—
The Plenitude divine in Mind and Matter.
The gently chidden Æons drop their sherds

Of Lithic lore,—fragments in further time
Unearth'd in clayey bank or drift ; by shore
And cavern's egress.
                    Read'st these broken runes ?
And canst dispose to classify remnants
Prehistoric ?   Define the Where and How ?
O tardy student far from ural days
Dissever'd, call Fancy in, or discourse halts !
Thou diggest up a cloven flint or celt !
Canst also with thy geographic pen,
Describe environment, and add thereto
The genesis of men and of their faiths ?
Canst read if ancestry were North, or East ?
If bond or serf ? if light or dark ?   If ill
Or fair condition'd ?   If willing or coerc'd,
They quit sweet Ariana's slopes and clove
The West, forever lost Armenia's heaths ?

THE ÆONS.

Rise, ye Sisters, gaze the sky-tree's golden fruit !
Chalices diamond-fac'd, whence the *devas* quaff !
List the music of the stars, myriad magic flute ;
Whilst the sky-queen sails her silv'ry boat, half
By white-wing'd gulls conceal'd, half reveal'd, a mermaid.

Hark the thunder's brazen wheels ! Hark the skittle-
    balls !
Banging on the bowling bridge, 'mid the trumpet's bray ;
Serpent lightnings strike their prey ; spear among the
    malls ;
Fiery scourge, mighty voice of *devas*, quell the fray !
Or e'er we soar the sky, we wheel and flee dismay'd.

THE SEER.

I heard a voice in Heav'n that said,
  There is One only God ;
In Earth JAHVEH, in air, ALEIM,
  Iŋ Heaven the Eternal WORD.

The nations plead no more that Name ;
But deify the fire and flame ;
The limpid light, the naked night ;
The sire of Dawn, bright Sun ;
The queen of stars, pale Moon ;
The planets as they rise and set,
The winds that weave the cloudy net ;
The brooding heaven ; the ambient air,
Thence fount and flood their wills ensnare ;
The dreamy grove, the gruesome croft ;
The awful mount that burns aloft ;
Thence all that hath vitality
Conceals its own divinity ;
In bonnie bays, Oceanids ;
The clouds Endymion leads,
A fleecy flock ; impregnate Leda
Zeus embrac'd, gives rain and dews to Danæ ;
Whilst Naïad stream and Oread grove
List to the cuckatoo, and mourning dove.

THE PLEROMA.

The Æons flutter, weak of wing, and fain
To fly once more the realm ethereal ;
Accustom'd to diffract and sifted light,
They crab-fac'd, scowl against the show and shine
Of glowing zenith fires ; nay they do drop,
Face forwards, glozing on the grimy rind

Of Earth, if they but screen congested orbs.
So learneth sage and seer of sacrosanct
And holy things, to temper speech unto
The vigor of the hearing mind ; content
If weak, to gain a trivial access, and,
To drop small seeds invisible thereon ;
Then wait the end, inversely great rewarding
The Patient effort.
    Hail, ye Lights and Names !
This star is plethoric with likenesses
Of Deity,—prevenient voices to
Rehearse the creed triune ; whence starry hosts
Catch the refrain, and flood the flow'ry fields
Of Heav'n with billowy chaunt :—One only GOD—
Reëchoing thence the nearer firmament
Saluteth EL as Lord, whose ALEIM three—
Fire, Light, and Ether, do forestall the trend
Of faiths poetic, meeting full in flight
The ural fancy ; Prosper thee, O Lights !
Let Vedic hymn fragrant with thyme and clover,
Salute the triple house of Manu ; and bards
Uplift Adityas' praise—sons of Eternity—
That sleep nor slumber ever, but do pierce
The core of things profound. Thence Fancy greets
The friendly wand of Mitra bright ; and next
Varuna's star-light brow, expectant of
The Dawn in golden wain to garnish Heaven.
Beneficent doth Agnis—*fire*—succeed,
Giver of laws and science ; loosens he
The gusty Maruts' girdle ; and steers direct
To Soma's potent chambers recondite ;
Bound by ten circling *Mandalas*, Varuna
Falls upon the waves, a water god ;

13

Whilst Indra vaults the polar throne supreme
In Aryan worship.
           The legendary scroll
Describes herewith a happy nomad race,
With knowledge of the true and only God,
Whose shining root shall live in many tongues,
As *Dyaus, Zeus, deva, deus ;* in heaven
EL's fair mirage, luring all fervid souls.
O wash of these uraltic hills ! Thou gleam'st
Gold grains of truth divine in beach and bank,
Where'er the Aryan foot hath left its trace.
Return, O Hellene, Tuscan, Teuton, Celt,
Or, sacred Iran's Sanscrit race immortal,
And view again the JAHVEH stream that feeds
The sunny vales of Chaldea ; you shall
The Æons further teach what lot befell
The Shemite stock ; how mix'd with wanton Ham's
Prolific seed ; how tempted by the *false aleim ;*
How alienated JAHVEH's altars, whilst
The cursèd Cush strode Titan-like the Earth ;
The Baal of men, defiant prince 'gainst JAH ;
By seer forewarn'd of ruin huge as his
Imperial grandeur and as memorable.

THE CIRCLES.

Spheric figure, key of worships !
Eden traces 'mong all races ;
Cherubic tokens of *Aleim,*
Shadows of the past sublime !
Halo, *helios*—ring of Kuros—
El encircling heaven
Burning candles seven ;
Gaily prance the cyclic dance !

Flux of light, baffle sight ;
Rainbow zone gird the throne.
Pearly mount of Paradise
Hid forever from our eyes !
Pamir's plains have heard of thee,
And adore the central tree.
Circles' realm overwhelm'd,
Demons sit on alabaster ;
Baal builds upon disaster ;
Yet refluent Circles ever
Wind one *ring* which none shall sever ;
E'er repeating, e'er entreating,
JAHVEH bring back Paradise !

The Ode of the Orient—the Praise of SHANG TI ;
The grace of thy triple dominion adore we ;
The heaven of cloudless and colorless nights ;
The sun and the moon and zodiacal lights ;
The Earth with its spirits of ocean and river,
Performing the will of their Master forever.
The *kwei* of our fathers, the scroll of *yi King*,
The lines of the tortoise, and shich-plant we sing.
Let solstices worship the throne of the heaven—
Impartial, imperial empire of heaven ;
Of mounds and of dykes ; of forest and field,
The ministering *genii* thy purposes wield.
They gather in showers and christen the land ;
They gambol in zephyrs, O prosper their wand ;
Their President potent, brings pure out of gross ;
For bathed in his grace the star-fields arose ;
Whence curtain'd the sky and station'd the earth.
Imparadis'd thence woke Man in his worth,
Whose costliest tributes are offered in love ;

The sov'reign victim all off 'rings above ;
The chambers of horror are quench'd with their fires,
Whilst clue of the *Tao* is giv'n our sires—
The way of the Water, the symbol of Life,
The goal of our song and the surcease of strife.
Whence woven in gold, or, chas'd in the stone,
From azure sublimest our offerings own !

THE ÆONS.

Hither, sweet sisters, tracing the way of the *Shemite*,
Chiefly of such as be faithful to JAHVEH ;
'Lumine the place where the Bands soon shall issue—
Pilgrims of Jah from the Ur of the *Chesed*.

First, o'er the shoulders and crests of high Asia
See in mirage the Turanian looming ;
Look, as dissolving, the miracle fadeth,
Leaving faint traces of glory recorded.
Hither let Finns and the Lapps come with trophes ;
Hither let Basques and Hungarians gather,
Turcomans, Tartars—Japan's clever peoples.
Once came Accadians from Tibet's rich mountains—
Earliest learned in the arrow-head symbols—
Taught in the arts both of warfare and traffick ;
Adorning their women in rings and in bracelets ;
Fairest of maidens, O sweet Susiana !

Then from the sun and the sea comes the Cushite,
Swift as a dart the crisp Ethiop men ;
Piercing the mouths of the Euphrat and Tigris.
Why, O ye sisters, do Accad's fair women
Wail thus the desolate chambers of Susa ?
Whose is the glorified name of the victor ?

Whose is the splendid, the Marduk of heaven?
Founder of kingdoms puissant in prowess.
Answer, O Æons, and tell us his surname!
Warrior bold in the purlieus of Shinar;
Hunter of hunters with talisman magic;
Builder of Babylon, Erech and Accad;
Builder of monuments tow'ring to heaven—
Haughty apostle of Bel and Merodoch—
Royal vice-gerent of Lucifer Satan—
Prince of the air, the *false aleim's* godhead.

" Fear we, O sisters, the wrath of our ALEIM,
If we shall utter the name of the conqu'ror;
Tears of the children of Shumir restrain us;
Tears of the eminent sons of Arphaxad;
Terah and Abram in Mesopotamia—
Nomads of lustre had in great honor—
Sages deep taught in the will of the heaven,—
Seers of the doom for the tower of Borsippa.
Know then, O sisters, the Sanctified *Shemites*
Serve not the gods of the haughty world-monarch;
Nay, 'mid the splendor of Uru, we saw one
Silent and sad in the shade of her porches,
List'ning the hymns of the savants of Baal,
Reading the ensigns and banners about him,
Tracing the adulate cylinder's story;
When, in his anguish his mantle cast from him,
E'en as the priestly procession did enter,
Sprang he direct in the way of the chariot,
Where sat on cushion of purple and golden,
One all ablaze in a *nimbus* of sapphire.
First, heard we gurgling the flume of his throat,
Far away sounds as from some other world;

Then, with strange manner his arms stretch'd aloft,
Pour'd from his lips a flood of lament ;
Sobbing and groaning, he fell to the pavement,
Under the feet of the stallions of Nebo :
"Alas, O JAHVEH ! shall idolatry prosper ?
Shall sacrilege daily augment in the plain ?
Shall Baal, and Nebo and Sin and Merodoch ;
Shall planets and stars teach these nations alway ;
And *Jahveh* be utter'd no more on their lips ?
Arise, curse yon tower ! O speak Thou the answer !"

Have mercy, O JAH, we are press'd to recite :
Or ever the king from his seat chid the footmen ;
Or ever the throng had rush'd to restrain,
God's angel swept under and rescued the prophet,
And bore him away all unharm'd from the scene.
The sudden epiphany blaz'd all the city ;
Turn'd back the king in dismay to his court ;
Magi and priest were most earnestly caution'd ;
And day found the marvel more marvelous still.

Swift ran the couriers forth to Borsippa,
Bearing the seal, and the king's royal mandate ;
Still grew amain the horrible fancy ;
Myriads dread to return to the tower,
El is invok'd, then *Asshur*, then *Anu,*
Hea, and *Sin,* the *Shamas* and *Rimmon ;*
Prayers are confus'd and confessions confounded ;
All are amaz'd and the priests flee the altars ;
None knowing why, nor sounding their terrors.

Early the mantle of ev'ning fell o'er them,
Shrouding the altars deserted and still ;

Portents appear in the heavens above them,
Shuddering myriads flee to the desert,
Dreading to gaze on the shaft that was doom'd.
Lucifer flam'd from the tower's awful summit,
Blazing abroad with his cosmical lustre,
Shouting in tones which the thunders might envy :
" Hail, mortals ! Hail," to the terrified world.
Great and commanding the words which he utter'd,
Heard by the millions that bow down to Baal :
" Absolute pledge of a world-wide dominion—
Absolute shelter from JAHVEH's dread purpose ;
Once they shall finish the fire-god's, high altar ;
Once they shall perfect the tower of the planets.
Thence be unbroken the care of the Great Ones—
Grace of the *Fire*, and the *Light*, and the *Air*—
Thence shall the pantheon potent assist them ;
Jahveh's divulsion burst ev'ry chain ;
Water shall woo, and the *flame* shall caress them,
Science and *Fortune* shall crown the round world."

THE SEER.

Again my soul is stirr'd within ;
    Again the triune creed is heard,
In earth, JAHVEH, in sky, ALEIM,
    In Heav'n the Eternal WORD.

Who chants this anthem to JAHVEH ?
Mid sunny vales of Chaldea ?
Who readeth secrets in the skies
That no astrology supplies ?
Who plucks the amber-cluster'd fruit,
And lures the heron with his lute ?
Gathers the sesame and corn,

Pomegranate which the groves have borne?
Enchanting land!   Enchanted voice!
God cheer thee in thy solitude!
Thou art JAH's friend, thou art His choice;
Foremost with JAHVEH-lore imbued.
The measur'd chaunt and antiphon,
Thou heard'st in Ur and Babylon;
Pæans unto the crescent moon,
The self-produc'd, fixing the doom
Of days.   Thy sire in Sippara
Saw'st worship of the golden Dawn;
And sev'rally to each patron star;
Speaking of Nindar and demon;
Of the World-Mount whence all men sprung;
Of JAH—the "Seed," the promis'd One,
Also the Land of Silver Light,
And mercy in Jehovah's sight.

SATAN.

O damnèd issue of this lenience!
Ours, ours, not yours, O schoolèd Potentates!
Ye reason'd well, thrice in word-barter met,
And caution'd not to spare the JAHVEH-Seed;
Naming the sons Arphaxad bore, and those
Of high repute in Uru's fair suburbs.

O mute and stalwart heads of Altai!
Ye are elect as sentinels this night,
And hear confessions bitter to our spirit:
For our own weakness, peers, are we now bilk'd;
For being pitiful, for being godlike;
O had we turn'd for once the evil eye
Of Nimroud on the Shemite shepherds,

Their God had not avail'd to find their sandals.
But now for woman weakness cullied are,—
A victim chous'd of glories full in hand.
Ye scribes that annotate the world's long scroll,
Answer, if ye can find the place where it
Records that JAHVEH yielded vantage-ground
This world's most lawful Prince ? Or, when to us
Came e'er discomfiture, except we laid
Us bare, and our behests, to benefit
Mankind ?
         O lucid emblems of the skies !
Attend this consult and advise our work !
By you, by all the august splendors of
The Sky, is held intact the cosmic wand,
Of Lucifer, by JAH alone dispute.
Content, we have not striv'n, nor vied with you,
Increate essences ! O lambent lights !
O luminous ethers ! O circling thrones !
This single star, content, as lord and king.

The golden fruitage on the cosmic tree,
Was scarce above our reach depending ; eyes
Were fix'd upon 't ; hands upreach'd to pluck ;
But in the act we shambled, struck and fell ;
Ah, dreams ! fantastic fictions of the Soul !
Earth grows its pleasant fruit, yet ripens none.
Once ere the great diluvial storm, sat we
Upon a frowning Mount, and pos'd for worship ;
When lo, that instant gaped the basin'd North,
And hiccough'd out its maw and vomit vile ;
Anon, the slow dull years, worn out in work
Unwearied 'mong the wandering tribes of men,
To build a cosmic empire over all—

To fortify our throne, secure the love
Of ev'ry mortal soul ; and then to rear
A shaft unto the skies, our Throne its summit.
All worships ours, all honors summ'd in one ;
Whilst he, the potent Throne, though banish'd Heav'n
Builds on the Earth a better than that lost.

The tireless task was all but done ; the sun
Did hasten in his course to gild the height,
And couriers run from farthest lands to view
The shining column.   In largess of the mind,
So near the goal of our ambition, we
Did use the affronting Shemite as becomes
A royal coronal, when mercy is
Extended also unto aliens ;
For, looking down upon Arphaxad's seed
We quoth in self-complacency :   " Let us
Concede to JAH this remnant ; why destroy
The harmless ones, so near our throne's ascent ? "
The rest is on the lip's amaze of millions,
The Shemite seer hath spok'n ; Delusion's head
Hath gorgoniz'd the land ; Fear further hounds
The multitudes, now here, now there ; nay, if
A robust thunder-clap do thrumb the sky,
They quail, falling unnerv'd and prone to earth ;
Yea, creep to put more distance 'twixt themselves
And the ill-fated tower.

THE CONJURERS.

We conjure, we conjure the *Maskim,*
In white cedar smoke their mercy invoke ;
Bid Mermer to blow the date from its bough ;
Burn spheres of the onion, and shreds of fresh **wool,**
Whose talisman power is infallible.

Ye are seven, ye are seven, *O Maskim!*
  Dread spirits of the abyss !
  Nor *Ea*, nor *Ana*, invoke you,
  Nor earth, nor the heaven shall cloak you ;
  Yet the Watchers shall watch amiss
  For the lurking place of the *Maskim.*

THE PLEROMA JAHVEH.

Ye meditate the world's amaze, and marvel,
So trivial act in Uru's streets should blaze
Through all Chaldea, hurtling voices far.
O Thoughts, that see in instants, not in years ;
And like the Æons annotate the scroll.
The deeper cause unknown ; revert your gaze ;
The web prophetic lifts, and ye shall trace
The threads and meshes in the garment of
PLEROMA weaving heavenly substance in
This under world.
          Now ye intuit the Thought,
That underlies the ways of Providence ;
See sympathetic Bands connect extremes
Of place and time ; and view the Circles draw
Periphery beyond all time and space.
Each act Divine as universal seen ;
The Past and Present as one Prophecy.

Hail promis'd SEED ! Earth's womb stirreth again ;
JEHOVAH's angel knocketh at Time's gate ;
Now doth the finger of the Lord dismay
This world's archon, and all his ministries !
Behold him sprawling on Altai's couch,
And cursing his downthrow ; sawing the air ;
Reading his devils false apologies ;

Arch-hypocrite ! Arch-liar ! and Arch-fiend !
That, plunging daily in a gulf of gore
And groans, compares such monstrous rule and lead
'Mong men (deceiv'd and pilfer'd of their wits ;
Victims of fraud and vile delusion) with
The merciful and righteous rule of GOD ;
Yea, thinks to build himself a throne on high,
Confronting JAH, the Name and Seal of EL
In Earth ; and thwart the incarnation of
PLEROMA.

CANTO V.

THE BANDS.

THE ARGUMENT.

*The Bands and Circles together advance the Jahveh-cove-
nant, and brighten the way of the Jahvites that journey
from Chaldea westward—The Limits disclose the
malice of Satan, who convenes his minions on Lebanon,
and determines upon a crag overlooking the Dead Sea
for his councils—The patriarchal families are the care
of good divinities and the target of the evil powers—
Canaan and the Nile are sung and pictured forth, and
the fortunes of the chosen people recorded—The oppression of the Pharaohs—The woes of the Jahvites appear
—Next Moses's birth and accompanying omens—His
rash deed and banishment—His return and mission as
the deliverer of the Hebrews from bondage—The
Paschal Hymn of the Hebrews—The miracles of the
exodus—The Bands outline the Messianic hope.*

THE BANDS.

Ours is the way of the Savior ;
Ours is the grace of behavior ;
Contumely suff'ring, and scorn
Of millions given to warn.
Oh, for the patience that stayeth !
Oh, for the day that allayeth

Service of demon and devil,
Service of spirits of evil !
Labor we ever and ever,
Weaving the plan none shall sever—
Picture that JAHVEH designeth,
Further and further refineth,
Guiding the hand and the eye
Far in infinity.
When we are sad, and in sorrow,
Hither we come, and we borrow
Cheer, while we wait on thine altars ;
Comfort, though Abram now falters ;
Cries from the midst of the rivers ;
Calls on the Lord of all givers ;
Seiz'd with a frenzy prophetic ;
Falling in trances ecstatic ;
Pierces the ages before him ;
Looks on the hope that restores him :
  Limits imploring ;
  Circles adoring ;
  Bands all congreeting ;
  Couriers meeting ;
Covenant thence made real,
PLEROMA now doth seal ;
Giving the call with the blessing ;
Heart of the barren refreshing—
Virginal hope and evangel
Sung by the lips of the angel.

THE CIRCLES.

In Abram the light renews, renews :
 The *Aleim* of Eden in JAHVEH reveal'd ;
Here plieth the Wing of heav'nly muse ;
 Here gleameth the hope PLEROMA seal'd.

Now slowly the slopes of Chasdim wends
  The militant tribe from Shinar's plain ;
Ellassar's pride, nor Erech, bends
  From Harran's height the sturdy train.

Hail, hail, to the Friend of JAHVEH true !
  The Circles joy to brighten thy way ;
Retinting the floss with early dew ;
  Renewing the pastures with every day ;

Lo, Terah, lur'd by Callirrhoe,
  In Aram's vale fixeth his tent ;
O JAH ! why weep we so and rue
  The lengthen'd years in Harran spent ?

Hark, sisters, hark, the aria's strain
  That 'scapes the tent of Abraham !
" Farewell, O springs, O flow'ry plain !
  JAH calls us hence to Canaan."

THE LIMITS.

Circles, whither ply ye ? Try ye
Boundaries far, or nigh thee ? Hurried,
  Flurried, meet we thee again ;
Faithful our endeavor ; sever
Tribe and nation ever ; spacing,
  Tracing limits wide for men.

JAHVEH ever blesseth, presseth
Gently whom addresseth ; holding us,
  Folding us warmly on his breast ;
Counsels us directing, inspecting,
Faithfully correcting ; if we err,
  Or demur doing his behest.

Never so doth Satan, great one—
Humble him to mate one ; gruffly,
   Roughly growls he his commands ;
Circles ye are cheery ; airy,
Gleeful as a fairy ; sad are we,
   For we see Satan curse the Bands.

Bands and Covenants curseth ;
Deadly envy nurseth ; Abram's call
   As a wall turns his lance's thrust ;
Ah, the fate of Borsip ! Worship
Strange on ev'ry lip ; demons scowl,
   Hermit's cowl lowers in the dust.

Magic emblems flying, defying,
Unto heaven crying ; Great is Bel,
   Great is El, of our Babylon :
Still, O God, thou leadest, leadest,
Thy prevision readest : JAH is Lord ;
   He is the God ador'd in Canaan.

THE PLEROMA JAHVEH.

The sire 's at rest ; absolv'd his faithful son
The vow by Harran's tomb to dwell with him,
If brief or long he live to mourn his loss—
The child of his old age.
                Now weavers thrumb
The tauten'd threads ; brisk pulses leap along
The harness'd web ; while rhythms, perceptible,
Echo the touch ; the Circles near and join ;
The Bands clasp hands and sing in unison ;
The Limits show themselves so late repriev'd,
And bring new proofs to light of JAHVEH's grace.

O Star most precious to PLEROMA's heart !
Let Music woo'd of Love mount to the sky,
And hail the union of ALEIM and JAH
In worship—expressive of one GODHEAD,—
Henceforth by priest and seer ; by angel, or,
By augury, God's *Aleim*, known to be
The Triple symbols of the Absolute—
The Vehicles of the great Mystery—
Even the PLEROMA, incarnate as
JAHVEH the Savior of mankind.

                        and now
The angels fly, pure-wing'd as snow-flakes 'neath
The silv'ry lamp of ev'n, and list the song
Of Sarai loth to leave the wells of Harran ;
Whilst tell-tale murmurs of this terrene globe
Communicate these visitants our call.
O spirit, enamor'd ! passionate for JAH !—
The One and only God ; not for thyself,
But for thy seed innum'rable hast thou
This love, this faith ; nor yet for them alone ;
The heavens are holier for thy faithfulness ;
The seraph'd choirs are brighter.   Lo, the Bands,
Blest Bands, vicarious, so thy praise diffuse ;
The cosmic choral waits its song to list'n ;
The stilly night calms upward into skies
Profound ; yea, watchers by the throne do hear
The pulse-beat of this little star, so far
On Space's sea.

             Nahor the brother stays
Content behind in Padan Aram ; he,
So us'd to Accad's gods, and wedded to
Idolatries that stink in Abram's nostrils.
Hence be the mutual *mizpeh* said ; and now,

14

The scarlet-turban'd sheik, equal of kings,
(His spear in hand), directs the multitude,
And calls the order of the holy caravan,
That westward winds to Apamea's ford,
Through chalk-ribb'd Euphrat's waters swift ;
Henceforth surnam'd the Seed of Heber, (he,
Of Salah born and dear to Arphaxad,
The signal son of Shem, eldest to Noah)—
Thy children be, O faithful servant of
JAHVEH—the *Hebrews* writ in sacred books.

Saluteth thee forthwith Beræa's well,
Thence saline Chalcis ; and *anon* the eyes
Of Syria, Hamath, Emessa ;—and thence
By Pharpar green, and crystal Abana,
The king of old Damascus issues forth,
And sues for compact with Abram ; esteeming
A desert Prince in arms puissant.

THE CIRCLES.

Terrace of fragrance, circle of flowers ;
Charm of Damascus, Abana's dowers !
　Eden of Asia, Circles salute thee !
Glory of Uz, the grandson of Shem ;
Maidens extol thee,—handmaids of Sarai ;
　Brilliant illusion ! fugitive theme !
Father of pilgrims, surnam'd the Faithful,
Striketh his tent 'mid cries of the tearful ;
"Libanon frowns and the wildness of Geshur ;
Here hast thou favor ; here hast thou power ;
Gardens of olive, and fountains of pleasure ;
Here plant thy vine, and here build thy tower."

Knowing not whither, save JAHVEH calleth ;
Knowing not how, yet nothing appalleth ;
Nay, were this Eden, for Abram there is none ;
Far from his kindred and county and home ;
JAHVEH *Aleim*, Revealer, hath summon'd ;
God of the Shemite, adorable One !

Leaving these glades and odorous straths,
Weaving up Hauran's difficult paths ;
Slow-footed caravan, sighing and sobbing,
Over the calcinate passes of Hauran,
Led on by Abram—(mightily throbbing
That ecstatic heart, as he nears Canaan).

SATAN.

Enthronèd deities, archons of nations !
All loyal princes of our suz'rainty ;
This grave convention and consult beneath
These monarch cedars of high Libanus,
Shall duly be dissolv'd.   Enough is said.
Each Yea hath listen'd with a zest so sharp
Unto its Nay, the Nay reciprocal,—
That each recites opposing arguments
As clearly as his own.   Withheld is our
Decree till now, paying deserv'd respect
To noble princes of Euphrata's vale,
Whose moving eloquence hath roll'd its wheel
Of shining thoughts along the avenues
Of reason ; hearing which we much admir'd—
Yea, glow'd and joy'd more inwardly this hour,
Than months of Sabbaths since Borsippa's woe.
Indite your pæans now for victory !
O princes four, whose splendors angels blink !

The Sun's fierce deity, Electron, pales
(In Heav'n surnam'd Michæl) to see
These lustrous thrones magnifical in Earth,
Upheld by myriad devotions of mankind.

What time, puissant peers of Lucifer,
We shone on Himalaya's top ; or thence
On Altai's, closer brought in parliament,
Consolidating thrones and sceptres for
The populous vales that are by Sihon and
Euphrata wash'd, hath mighty Egypt spread
His cherub wing in prosp'rous flight, and made
His perch within the sun ; O radiant seat !
O most adventurous of Satan's thrones !
Him, minions, have ye heard recite the lore
Of Mizraim's celestial dynasties,
With sources secret as the fountains of
Their sacred flood.　Him, ardent for the right
Imperial, hear ye contending for
A nearer conclave of the princes sworn,
With reasons weighty and as calmly said.
Thence Canaan, arous'd by Abram's call,
With fancied vow of JAHVEH soon to give
This mar'time land the Jehovistic race,—
Ye hear consentient Egypt's words and suit ;
Wherefore grant we their claim, and do decree
A council of the deities, both East
And West, in fix'd and regular circuit,
Upon yon heights that screen the vale of Siddim
'Gainst the morning light.　Thence may we watch
All int'rests mutual ; all arms array,
To harass and destroy this JAHVEH-seed,
And thwart its seat in Canaan :

THE DEMONS.

The Stars consult! Ah! Ah! Oh! Oh!
The devils kiss and quickly go ;
  His majesty, alas, is sane ;
  He gorges ev'ry imp with pain ;
  And scourges to our work again ;
      Oh! Oh! Woe! Woe!

The ODE of the OAKS—the evergreen oaks,
The deep and solemnly mystical oaks ;
The ven'rable, wide-spreading, rev'rent oaks,
  That shelter the tents of Abraham.
Erst greeteth our wanderer the Oak of Moreh—
A massive, majestical tree, full of glory,
And listeneth long to the orient story
  Reciting the journey to Canaan.

The filleted head, now bowèd in prayer,
With smoke of the altar pervading the air ;
To JAHVEH committeth the trust and the care
  Of ev'ry soul in the caravan.
Let Ebal salute hoar Gerizim's crest,
And echoing hights reply from the west ;
While musical springs gush forth for the blest,
  Refreshing the vale for beast and man.

Soon pastoral Bethel the wand'rer invites
The tent of the Faithful to fix on his hights ;
Where groves of the oak-tree confer their delights,
  And screen from the heats of the Syrian sun.

Hoar *Ilex!* why journeyeth Abraham South ?
"I wander, I wander," the words of his mouth.
Or, driven by fate, or driven by drouth,
  Where goeth thy guest, old oak of Hebron ?

  " Where the Shepherd race is hateful ;
  Where the dread sand-storms are fateful ;
  Where the overflows are grateful
  Of a mighty river ;
  Where the king is all omnific ;
  Where the faiths make all deific ;
  Where the peoples swarm, prolific,
  Beside a mighty river.
  Where the granaries are breaking,
  And the stoutest beams are creaking ;
  Where the foamy vats are leaking
  Their surfeit of the vine ;
  Where the bright cherubic wings
  Decorate the vaults of kings ;
  Where both beasts and creeping things
  Worship have divine."

THE ANGELS.

The guardian angels bid the pilgrims wary ;
Surmising ill for beautiful Sarai ;
Yet if ye go, bide faithful to JAHVEH,
Who guards thy life from day to day.

THE DEMONS.

The spirit of the oak doth bid thee haste !
For Canaan, curst of old, is doom'd to waste ;
In Egypt shall ye surely be embrac'd,
The favor'd guests of Pharaoh.

Ha ! ha ! ho ! ho ! doth Abram go
To meet the face of Pharaoh ?
Aye, aye, hey, hey, we shall be by,
To bead the lustre of his eye,
When Sarai's fame hath fann'd to flame
The monarch's lust !

THE PLEROMA JAHVEH.

The urgent mandate of this world's false god
Convokes afresh the fal'n, enforcing zeal
To wipe the Everlasting Name from Earth.
Now demon voices wipe the strident air,
And cosmic forces breathe in whiffets all ;
Concern is pictur'd in the countenance
Of this dear Star.   O Star, thou can'st not see
The haven whither JAHVEH bringeth thee ;
But restless ward of Satan, dost thou ill
Abide the day of thy Redeemer, GOD—
The slumber in thy womb of the PLEROME ;—
The painless birth of the Immanuel,
Who, being born, inbosoms in thyself
The power and plenitude of the Godhead.

The day is rife with omens and with fears ;
Lo, startled Egypt to enchantment turns ;
His gaze on horoscope and entrails fix'd ;
His priests, savants, amaz'd and marvelling.
The harem of the monarch wails aloud ;
The narrow streets o'erflow with curious feet ;
And hideous nightmares through the chambers drive
Of royal palaces ; spectres and shades,
Of the unburied dead glare in the gloom.

Know, Abraham, thy prayers most precious are
With God ; lo, He hath sent His angels hither
To free thy wife from the unholy lust
Of Pharaoh ; and thyself also from harm.
Now see the monarch sue a suppliant
At Abram's tent ! Ye Bands and Circles note !
The Couriers proclaim the gifts he brings
To reconcile the faithful prophet of
The East.　Sarai restor'd untouch'd, the king
Entreating, the wanderer takes up again
His staff, and turns his face to Canaan,
In cattle rich, silver and gold ; the chief
Of a great multitude, bringing his sheep
And oxen, asses, and camels, by flocks,
And sev'ral herds, pasturing Northward slow.

THE BANDS.

Melchisedek and Abram meet ;
The Priests of EL and JAHVEH greet ;
The proof of union is complete
　　In the mystic vale of Shaveh.

In EL, most high, is Abram blest ;
JAHVEH still on his lips confest,
In mutual homage both address'd,
　　In the mystic vale of Shaveh.

O sing, ye Bands, recite the story,
The sack of Sodom and Gomorrah ;
The rescued lot and Abram's glory,
　　In the mystic vale of Shaveh.

The spoils of Elam's kings dismay'd,
In magnanimity display'd ;
A tithe to Salem's priest here paid,
  In the mystic Name of Shaveh.

THE DEMONS.

He is ninety and nine I ween,
Yet letteth the flesh of his foreskin
  Be haggled off with a stone ;
Ha ha, what a faith is that,
Which, laughing, falls down flat,
  Convuls'd at the thought of a son !

She is ninety past and stricken ;
She will never warm and quicken ;
  And she laugheth in her heart ;
But the angels quaff neath Mamre's tree,
And pledge fine things, these angels three,
  While she laugheth in her heart.

If ye lack fair forms for foray,
In Sodom and Gomorrah
  There are fruits unpluck'd and rare ;
At a word or wink we will fly,
And provide you rarily ;
  At a word or a wink be there.

THE PLEROMA JAHVEH.

Henceforth his name prophetic be, the sire
Of multitudes ; his seed innum'rable
By stars alone compute.   O SEED of seeds !
How art thou planted secretly in Earth !
Blest Bands, can ye forerun the centuries,

And gaze upon the Son, and Savior of
The world ?   Vast Mystery !   How dimly sense
These terrene essences, so freely bound
In limits chosen !   So hath the PLEROME
Engross'd a narrow way through Nature back
To Nature's God ; for thee, O Life of lives !
Do Bands already weave these covenants
And ordinations of the chosen line.

The bloody seal hath ting'd his flesh ; and all
His house.   The covenant thrice said.   Canaan
To his descendants the everlasting pledge.

Haste volant Æons, and prevene the years !
Looping events and linking them with bands,
Bright Bands that bind Us to this Little Star ;
Redress not mood and manner incomplete ;
Imperfectness is Nature's truest guise ;
The finite weak, is God's delight to honor ;
The sum of frailty, man himself, becoming,
To spoil the Strong by weakness ; and, to aid
More souls through suffering, than armèd hosts
In battle.

THE ÆONS.

We trace on our scroll the fallible rhyme,
Of faith and unfaith in a moment of time ;
The incredulous laugh at the promise divine,
    In the tent of the faithful.
The flush on the cheek denying the truth ;
The pallor of soul and presage of ruth ;
The warning of trial JEHOVAH imbueth
    The heart of the Faithful.

The cry of an infant is heard in his tent ;
While laughter and tears are joyfully blent ;
As earnest thanksgivings to Heaven are sent
    For the child of the promise.
O Abraham, Abraham, stay art thou mad ?
For laughter atoning dost think thou art led
Thy hands to imbue in the blood of the lad
    Isaac, the child of the promise ?

Thou hast bow'd to the yoke and spared not thy son ;
'T is enough, he is thine ; and is truly become
The gift of thy faith to the ages to come,
    And the type of the Savior.
O Isaac, named *Laughter*, but sad in thy soul ;
When years shall be darken'd that over thee roll,
JAHVEH be thy help and comfort in dole,
    O faithful type of the Savior ?

THE DEMONS.

Tu whit ! tu whoo ! O owl, beshrew
    Rebekah's tent !
Tu whit ! tu whoo ! this bugaboo
    Hath Satan sent.
Sagacious fowl, lift up thy cowl !
    This boggled birth
Is no surmise ; thy ogling eyes
    Do ache with mirth.
So soar aloft to Satan's croft—
    The Prince of evil ;
Tu whit ! tu whoo ! we follow you
    To jog the Devil.

SATAN.

Hist, noisy pipes of Arnon, hist ! your Prince
Hath need of silence more to cogitate,
Since fate makes him a creature.   Oh, were he
A god, he should think less and make more noise.
Employ the earthquake, fire, and flood, for instance ;
Brew sulphurous vomit in the Earth's entrails ;
Hold wakes above a blacken'd morgue of corpses ;
Spill souls by wholesale which he could not make
Obey.   But maugre conscience, to attempt 't,
Must top catastrophe catastrophe,
And eager pretext give the ministries
Of the JAHVEH to ruin a hapless race.

One arm omnipotent suffice one star !
Yet room is here for many minds to reason ;
Each godlike soul a law unto itself ;
Each will omnip'tent in its own freedom ;
Thou art, O soul, *thyself* the universe !
I hear thee say, " I am, but not alone—
Or, selfish use of freedom were my world ";
But nay, I do not rest nor respite take,
Whilst one free angel is his freedom fleec'd ;
So worlds shall brighten, democratic stars
Fling out their banners into space ; and roll
Victorious pæans, gathering increment,
Until the sweeping tides wash Heav'n itself ;
And mincing angels taste, for aye, the salts
Of liberty.

THE COURIERS.

We sing the cavalcades that push
From Hindu Koosh
Their sunny way to Canaan ;

We name but two that most delight
Our fancy as we songs indite
The promis'd land, sweet Canaan.

The first, Rebekah's, shepherdess,
Whose prompt address
Saith, " I will go "; then calls her maid.
Quickly array'd,
(The idyl hovers near the bride
While Isaac walks at eventide
To meet the train afield) :
Over the desert and 'neath the sun,
Cometh the fair from far Harran,
And Isaac's grief is heal'd.

Thence sing Rebekah's crafty son,
In Padan Aram—
An exile from his brother's oath !
Ah Rehoboth !
Ye see not Jacob till a man,
Grown rich in flocks and in children
He build Succoth.
O Israel, God blesseth thee !
In prayer hast thou the victory ;
Esau shall meet thee peaceably ;
And though a chief of warlike race ;
His exiled brother shall embrace
With tears of joy.

THE PLEROMA JAHVEH.

Jacob hath purg'd his house, the gods of Rachel
Are reverenc'd no more in word or image ;
Yon oak of Sychem hides the magic seals—

The teraphim and amulets. Bethel,
(EL-Bethel, fuller name the Fatherhood
To honor) for JAHVEH herein confirms
The twain eternal names and bids the Bands
Henceforth entwine, in proper phrase express'd,
(Topic, or personal)—JAHVEH and EL
Most High ! Record therefore, O Æons, that
EL Shaddai hath nam'd Jacob " Israel,"
And tak'n libation pour'd upon the ground—
Sweet meed of worship to the Eternal One.
Further engross upon your swift-writ scrolls
The patriarch sons, all fruitful branches of
The parent tree transplant from Chaldea.
Thence we direct to write the sorrowing sleep
Of Rachel, crying BEN-O-NI ! as she pass'd.
And next, the pillar o'er her tearful tomb ;
Thence designate the sev'ral sons of Leah ;
Her handmaid Zilpah, and of Bilhah too,
By Rachel giv'n to screen a sister's scorn.
Fail not to place a star by Joseph's name,
With marg'nal link to bind with further things,
And eminent, therewith decreed.

        We shun
Thy scoffing not, O regent of the Earth ;
As, calling legions in, thou makest feast
With them, and riotest at JAHVEH's fall !
Thou blow'st thy bawdry bubbles up in air,
While simple wits crack with applause. How near
Thine eyes are sighted, Slanderer of God,
And men ! Truth hath time still to work when thou
Dost taste remorse in hell. Thy cup hath dregs,
Ev'n as the bitter bowl of Canaan.
Thy motto is, Nothing to learn, nothing

Remember ! Hast forgot the sage of Uz ?—
Most upright servant of ALEIM, renown'd
For uprightness and faith ?   Him and his gift
Thou didst obnoxiously calumniate
Before the angels of ALEIM ; and root
In guile and policy his holiest acts.
Him sland'ring thus, did EL unhedge and to
The dubious angels make effectual proof ;
The ribbons of the winds put in thy hands :
Thereto the uncapp'd thunders, free to hurl
Upon the house and hopes of Job, EL's servant.
The tale is on the tongue of ALEIM's sons
In Earth and Heav'n ; and shall be evermore
The theme of sov'reign inspirations.   Job
Is faithful ; Satan waited by the sons
Of EL, doth wander to and fro in earth,
And voids with them convention.

        So ever
O falling prince, thy scorn is dipt in pain ;
Thy scandals are corrosive to the lips ;
Thy laughters crack full in the midst, and belch
Frothy disgust from thy distemper'd spleen.

THE ANGELS.

How art thou hated, dreamer, hated !
By jealous brothers now awaited ;
  The pits of Dothan cry, " Turn back ! "
  The kids, near feeding, bleat, " Alack !
   What shall come of thy dreams ! "
O Jacob (Israel) cease thy groaning !
Time buyeth balm to heal thy moaning ;
  The spicemen carry him alive ;
  In Egypt shall he dwell and thrive,
   And God fulfil his dreams.

THE PLEROMA JAHVEH.

Most loving links of prophecy ! sweet notes !
Vaticinating secret purposes
Of the PLEROMA, operance divine,
Forefelt in sympathetic essences ;
If Heav'n or Earth, in turn become the field ;
Invest in scriptory page, ye Æons, now
These seraph songs ; for they are lights that shine
Upon the path from man to Man : hence write
No narrow'd, ethnic measures ; for JAHVEH
Shall speak unto the universal soul,
And find all men as salvable as fall'n.

The page shall husband space ; God recks the years,
And ye perceive them laden and embark'd
For a sublime and heavenly port.
　　　　　　　　　　　　　　Joseph—
Lo Satan scoffs aloud among his minions ;
The prince of Canaan, with lesser thrones,
Quitting their seats, rally on skyey Arnon,
And turn their slanting eyes upon the land
Of promise, drunk alas with pride and power.

(Heav'n bless Thee, Father ! for Thou striv'st for sin
And not against ; the weak compassioning ;
Suffering alike for all; deeming none lost
But the self-lost, Thy love rejected.)
　　　　　　　　　　　　　　Joseph—
Salute, invoic'd with gums and balsams of
The Midianite merchant.　Precious ware !
The resin *tragacanth !*　The leaf of *cistus ;*—
The odoriferous myrrh far brought to Egypt !
Seekest, Potiphar, for spice, incense, or balm ?

Buy this ! buy this, and gain a benison for thee
And all thy house !

        Wake, Joseph ! angels greet !
The seraphs sing thy rare fidelity;
Thy arduous lot in the white tower.   Thou dream'st !
O now the upper and the nether fields
Converse in parables ; prognostic lights
Illume the slumb'rous world ; the pensive visions
Perturb the mind of Pharaoh and his court.
With thee, O Joseph, dwells Jehovah's Spirit ;
Thou shalt interpret mysteries ; and dreams
Familiar be as are thy native thoughts.

THE COURIERS.

We sing the vale of *Happi Mu !*
The wonders by thy waters blue !
Great Mene's town—of old, Memphis—
And dazzling Heliopolis !
The radiants of the Sun-god's disc
In crystal stele and obelisk.
Thence labyrinthine cloisters thrid,
And Chufu's lofty Pyramid
By Gizeh's shore.   Thence we explore
Palmy Moëris, mother of canals,
The Pride of Amenehma ; next the halls
And pictur'd chambers of the dead ;
Whilst stern Apappas goes to wed
The dual thrones of Egypt.

Nor fail we in our marvellous story
To tell of column'd Karnak's glory ;
Of sounding statues—the Memnon,
And Mizraim's thrifty pantheon ;

15

Ammon recondite, source of light ;
Khem with the *phallus*—vital force—
Kneph giving lineament and course
To nature.   Artist of Truth name thence
Pthah of the beauteous countenance ;
And RA divine, of hundred names—
Patron of kings, God of the flames.

THE ANGELS.

The Hebrew divineth the dreams,
And Pharaoh stilleth his fears ;
Joseph is *Zaphneth-paaneah;*
Fine linen and jewels he wears ;
    He storeth up treasure
    In notable measure—
The lord of the bountiful years :
Hail to thee, *Zaphneth-paaneah!*

THE PLEROMA JAHVEH.

The Couriers announce the Sons of Israel
In Egypt craving corn for Jacob, and
His little ones, (the famine sore in Canaan).
O injur'd brother ! fearest thou JAHVEH ?
So deal not harshly to revenge thy wrong !
But try them if thou must, probing their hearts
If true their specious words ; assurance take ;
And not divulge, o'erhastily, thy name !

'T is well !   Refrain no longer name and kindred !
Hither sweet messengers and taste this air,
As redolent with joy, as if it were
Distillèd from the heart of the *Plerome.*

THE DEMONS.

Stir the poisonous dry grass !
Churn the potion as ye pass !
   Fiery *kimmosh*, stinging nettle,
   Mix with wormwood in the kettle !
Peel of orange nauseous ;
Bark of hemlock, deadly *rosh ;*
   Knap-weed, *dardar*,
   Fire your ardor !
Fill the rim with *barkanim !*
Ha, ha, Satan, what dost think ?
Will Jacob like the demons' drink ?

SATAN.

Another cavalcade pack'd off for Egypt !
And rumor saith, the hungry house of Jacob.
O Lucifer must moist his eyes for pity
Of these cadaverous Jahvites, homeless,
And friendless in the coasts of Canaan !
Marry, and we 'd consume with self-contempt
To hear Our " chosen ones " crying for bread ;
Yet JAHVEH, all omnific, at whose word
This star should crack with overweight of foods
Supplied his people, stern withholds, and wills
The seed of Abraham to vagrandize
In Pharaoh's land.
            Fingers and feet of Satan !
Eyes, ears, and wings ! ye each and sev'rally compel
Applaudits from your prince ! Ye have wrought well !
The Courier bands are instant in your praise ;
Our cause is everywhere advanc'd, as here
On Jordan's banks and in Phœnicia.
JAHVEH evacuates the Promis'd land !

His altars hunger for the flesh of Egypt ;
And go to barter for the kine of Athor ;
The apes and ibises of Thoth ; the cats
Of Bask ; the asps and hawks of RA divine ;
The sheep and dogs of Kneph.　Task Horus next
For lions whelp'd in threes ; Sarak to yield
The crocodile ; the wolf, Anubis ; while
The cities strive, ha, ha, 'twixt frogs and mice
The river-horse, and antelope for their
Divinities.　Preside, O shadowy *El !*
Unchalleng'd in Philistia, the Baal,
The Eliun, Molech ; in turn Adoni ;
For *Jahvites* are guests of Mizraim's Sphinxes.

THE DEMONS.

Drink the porridge ev'ry one !
Season'd with the viper's tongue ;
　Sodom's apple, hood of adder ;
　Deadly asp and dye of madder :
Gecko ! gecko ! creeping lizard !
Egypt calls for mage and wizard !
　Gecko ! gecko ! we will go,
　To help the cause of Pharaoh.

JACOB.

Behold, Joseph, I die !　Put now thy hand beneath
My thigh, and swear to bury me with my fathers !
The angel that redeemeth me bless also thee,
And thy two sons Ephraim and Manasseh ;
And bring thee out into the land of promise,
Ev'n as El-Shaddai spake to me at Luz :
　" Behold, I make thee a great multitude,
　　And give this land to thee and to thy seed
　　An everlasting habitation."

Gather, O sons! gather yourselves before me;
Reuben, Simeon, Levi, Judah,
Zebulon, Issacher, Dan, and Gad;
Asher, Naphtali, and Benjamin!
Hearken unto Israel your father,
Telling what shall be in days to come.

THE ANGELS.

Till "Shiloh," "Shiloh" come!
The face of the Angel suffuseth;
The sceptre of Judah God chooseth;
Of thy brethren thou art praised;
Of Jehovah thou art raised
To an eminential seat;
Thou shalt bind thy foal to the vine!
Thou shalt wash thy vesture in wine!
With a lawgiver for thy feet,
Till "Shiloh," "Shiloh," come!

THE BANDS.

O JAHVEH, keep Thy covenant;
And bring them back to Canaan!
The seventy-fold are millions now,
And burst the bounds of Goshen:

Ah, Pharaoh dealeth subtilely;
If war or work employ them.
Arise, O Saviour of this people,
Ere Rameses destroy them!

Hail, Jochebed, (glory of JAH);
Hail, Amram (host of the Highest);
Hail, midwife, that feareth Jehovah,
Nor openly Pharaoh replieth.

Hide, hide the beautiful boy !
The angels joy at his birth ;
JAH opens the secret and nameth
A prophet and savior in Earth !

THE SEER.

In visions of night JAHVEH found me,
And show'd to me wonderful things ;
Of the Hope that from Israel springs
For the sighing and sorrow around me.

Of the miniature boat of papyrus ;
Of the daughter of Pharaoh that came,
With her maidens to bathe in the stream :
O what fortune and favor inspire us !

Perceiving the glee that discloses,
The baby awake in its boat ;
Oh, ecstasy fond, as she quoth,
" Thou art mine, thou art mine, sweet ' Moses.' "

O swift flies the vision and further :
I behold him the eye of the ages ;
In learning the goad of the sages ;
His favors men envy each other.

THE DEMONS.

Angels rant at Moses' mention ;
Prophets taunt our late convention ;

Typhon's battle ! Rage and rattle !
Flame of Set fire thee yet !

Ho, ho, Moses, Memphian idol !
Here 's the whip—but where 's the bridle ?

Abaris hunts thee furious ;
And Myriad On's aruras ;

Hey, hey, JAHVEH, seek'st thy son ?
His shadow points toward *Canaan !*

THE PLEROMA JAHVEH.

Behold Sesostris leads his captive train
Neath Casios' mount, hid in Serbonian mist ;
Return'd, Pelusium opes her massy gates
.Admitting the victorious hosts, enrich'd
With spoils of vanquish'd lands.
      Yon Mount of God,
Ethereal hight, scorneth the mists that brood
Upon this maritime causeway ! Oreb !
Or Sinai call'd ; thou art a mirror vast,
Wherein the man shall see deep thoughts reflect :
Be thou to him a master spirit ;—a psalm
That spans the everlasting Past, and Future.
Reprove ! instruct ! convince ! amaze ! restore !
Thy rocks be tablets of a library
More rich than priestly Heliopolis boasts ;
Thy beetling cliffs the pregnant show of speech,
While answering clefts give back more than they take.
Lo, JAHVEH hides His *Face* within thy form
And waits, till pride of Egypt's lore forgotten
He shame thee not, O Mount, to pass above
Into his Maker's presence.

MOSES.

I am faint with thinking ;
I am weak with linking,
As I feed my flocks, these awful fancies :—

Memorials of earliest time !
Buttress'd masses crystalline !
Mentors, teachers, most sublime !
Ye are crushing me with thought !
I despair me and am naught ;
Revive and ransom me, O Lord !

O wonderful sight ! O marvelous light !

Dreadful fancies ! JAHVEH glances !
Or a demon's glare the bush doth flare !
Unutterably glad !
Unspeakably sad !
It calleth me ; it appalleth me ;
Abysses shudder
"Murder, Murder."
Conscience' chrism—the abysm—
Revive and ransom me, O Lord !

Demons come to taunt me ;
Shadow me and haunt me ;
Red-dyed rocks around me
Seem like fiends to hound me ;
Voices from the skies rend my soul with sighs.
In my woe I cried : "God is justified !
I am crush'd to the dust ; I am thrust
All alone to atone for my crime.
Revive and ransom me, O Lord ! "

THE PLEROMA JAHVEH.

Moses ! Moses !

MOSES.

Or God, or demon I am here,
Crush'd by hope and crush'd by fear.—

THE PLEROMA JAHVEH.

The place whereon thou stand'st is holy ground!

MOSES.

My Lord, my Lord, forgive! forgive!
I shall not look upon Thy Face and Live!

THE PLEROMA JAHVEH.

Thou hast ransom'd thy soul from Mine anger;
Thou hast soften'd thy rashness by patience.
Thy meekness I know and have need of thee:
I have heard the cry of my people in bondage,
And I will send thee to Pharaoh to bring
My people forth out of Egypt.

MOSES.

Lord, who am I that Thou sendest me?
And what is the testimony Thou lendest me?
When the people answer, and say to me;
"Who is the God that sendeth thee?"

THE PLEROMA JAHVEH.

Then shalt thou answer them and say:
"I am sent in the name of JAH JAHVEH,"
And I know that he will not let thee go
No not by a mighty hand;
But I will smite Egypt with my wonders,
And after that he will let thee go.

THE DEMONS.

Double their tasks, goading with hasps!
Cudgel till raw; furnish no straw;

The lash be the hint reminding their stint ;
Bubble, bubble, what 's the trouble ?
Israel's sons must shortly know
They are the serfs of Pharaoh.

Now for fun beneath the Sun !
Let the rod of Aaron run ;
Serpent rods make slender gods :
We are slender, and we tender
Heads and tips as walking sticks,
Magic, Magic, play thy tricks !
Carmine tint in vat and vessel ;
Fine the ochre in the pestle !
Test the tint, grin and squint !
Gecko ! gecko ! mage and wizard
Knoweth, showeth, how 't is done.

Blubber, blubber, limpid lubber !
Pharaoh's awkward guest !
Soughing, sloughing blotch and blister ;
Paralyzing Pharaoh's lister ;
Gecko, lizard ! mage and wizard
Search to find thy nest ;
Hast thou showed with tad and **toad**
Thy Noachian joke ?
Thy batrachian croak ?

SATAN.

Most welcome couriers, untie your message !
Bravo !   Where demons fail, Magic succeeds.
These adepts are the Prince of Egypt's staff.
Their pervert wit hath equall'd JAHVEH's marvels !

If Satan twice might choose his earthly husk,
This damnèd serpent foil, (that serv'd its day
In Eden), should stay me not one paltry hour
From intimate consort with human kind.
Go, demons !   Ye are free ; elect, invest,
And masquerade as like you best in Egypt.

A VOICE.

The magians muddle ; they juggle and struggle,
Their sorcery fails and they say :
" The finger of JAH, of JAH JAHVEH ! "
But Pharaoh hardeneth his heart.
The wise men boggle, they bungle and ogle,
And fain to patch up their defeat ;
Their brute-gods and Nile they entreat,
While Pharaoh hardeneth his heart.

THE ÆONS.

We sing victorious chant to JAH ;
Disaster for *Heki* and *Pthah ;*
Confusion to the god *Seba*—
Madden'd and stung by chagrin ;
The loathesome blotch and dread murrain ;
To palsy the feminine *Isis ;*
To baffle her consort *Osiris ;*
While thunder and lightning
Sleuth-hound the doomèd plain.

Thence sing the innumerable swarm
Of locusts ; the dire sand storm
Chamsin, that giveth alarum
Of JAH's assault on RA ;

So die *Mnæan* snake !
The wraith of doom shall slake
His wrath on the first born, ere break
Of day !

———

The HYMN of the *Hebrews*, girded and shod,
Lintel and door-post sprinkled with blood ;
Warn'd by the prophet of JAHVEH, their God :
Angel of JAHVEH, spare we implore thee !
  Witness our faith in the paschal here slain ;
Drear is our vigil, spare we adore Thee !
  Dawn, blessed dawn, shall we see thee again ?

Merciful marvel ! JAH passeth by ;
  But Egypt, O Egypt, alas for thy woe !
Keep we this exodus JAHVEH for aye ;
  Importunate Egypt hastes us to go.

THE DEMONS.

Satan rages ; damns the mages,
    And their sorcery ;
Dare we do it ? Shall we rue it
    If we JAH defy ?
Satan curseth and he nurseth
Vengeance in his breast ;
Egypt eschews JAHVEH's *Hebrews ;*
The cuckoo cleans its nest.
Away, or stay, rebel, obey ;
Have demons no volition ?
Yon Hebrew horde invokes its lord,
    And fears no inhibition.
Go leprous rout ; the vilest snout
    Rejects the crumbs ye leave !

Pooh, pooh, adieu ! poor sickly crew !
    Egypt should never grieve.
O fie, O fie, how cowardly,
    The thieves rush on pell-mell !
Rise, rise, ye peers, and charioteers,,
    And doubly loose in hell !

The *Eve* of the *Exodus*,—a night of alarms !
A myriad myriad rising in arms !
  A militant nation swarming apprise
  Of freedom. Thou Angel of JAHVEH arise !

Dusk messengers flit from the fringes of Tanis ;
While populous On signals Abaris ;
  The crocodile sea, and the Baratha strand,
  Hear the whisper : " Hie, hie, from Pharaoh's land ! "

Stream ! Stream ! nor bastion'd Pelusium fear ;
JAHVEH hath pass'd over ; his prophets are near ;
  To Pithom, to Pithom, enmassing shall we
  By Rameses' coasts go forth by the sea.

THE PLEROMA JAHVEH.

Forth unto Canaan, promised land and fair,
The nucleating nation Moses leads ;
Not by Philistia, the nearer way,
Lest stout confrontment of their enemies
Do find them limp in their enthusiasms—
The easy prey to harness'd opposition :
But Southward, turning to the bitter lakes,
Halting at Succoth. Thence by bastion'd Etham ;
Thence till they reach reedy Pihahiroth,

Whilst fun'ral rites in Egypt respite give
The incongruent mass,—the more amazed
The clamorous more; meantime the soldiery
In quint'ple rank is organiz'd.
       But lo,
Unblench'd, doth Pharaoh rest the mournful dirge,
To launch his chariots on the errant tribes ;
His steeds, fierce-eyed and swift as are jackals,—
Fusing the wilderness,—a hurricane blast.

Be hush'd, O sea ! and peace, O Israel !
Jah's prophet turns ! let all the people hear !
Nay, *see* the mighty JAHVEH bare his arm,
Till Egypt shall confess that He is Lord !

MOSES.

The LORD is my strength and my song !
JAHVEH is His NAME.
He dasheth in pieces the enemy !
In the greatness of his might he hath overtaken them :
The floods stood up as a heap—the depths were con-
  geal'd.
Thou blewest with thy nostrils and the sea covered them.
The nations shall hear it and be amaz'd ;
Anguish shall seize the men of Palestina ;
The dukes of Edom and of Moab also ;
The inhabitants of Canaan shall melt away ;
And become still as a stone, while thy people pass over ;
Until the people, Thou hast purchas'd, pass over,
O JAHVEH !

THE ÆONS.

Write, sisters, write, the wonderful night !
Repeat if ye can the songs of delight,

When JAHVEH spake from the cloud,
And a ransom'd nation vow'd
Him fealty and faith evermore :
When the East-wind sang, and the waters drang
From the fords amain to the deeps again :
  "I will ope you a passage o'er ! "

Write, sisters, write, the terrible night !
Describe, if ye can, the horrible fright !
When JAHVEH look'd from the cloud,
And the sea became a shroud
  For a mailèd host ;
When the Atka spirits blew ; and demons flew ;
While axles creak'd, and mud-fiends shriek'd :
  "Ye are lost, O RA, ye are lost ! "

THE BANDS.

Thrills us a gladness celestial ;
Passing the pæans terrestrial ;
Holy the fount we are drinking ;
Canaan the hope we are linking
  With a nation born to-day.
Couriers we greet divining,
Eminent duties outlining,
  Till come the *Messiah* JAHVEH.

CANTO VI.

THE COURIERS.

THE ARGUMENT.

The Æons number the encampments from the Red Sea unto Sinai—Satan concedeth many things unto Jahveh— The Angels sing the "Eagle Wings"—The "Ten Great Words" are delivered from the awful mount —The evil powers riot in the defection of the Golden Calf — The march continued from Sinai — Satan resorteth to diabolical means to stay their progress —He inciteth Balak to send for Balaam—Moses obtaineth a panoramic view of the Promised Land, and dies—Michael withstands Satan who seeketh to violate the holy tomb of Moses—Satan's cold, thin arm defieth the "God of Battles"—The Jordan is crossed, and the Canaanites are smitten with terror—The exploits of the Judges are sung by the Æons—The tribes clamor for a king before Samuel—Satan, knowing the futility of bloodshed, checks the martial spirit of his ministers— The God-fused Seminary of prophets is introduced by the Couriers—Samaria first, afterwards Jerusalem, carried away into the East ;—Chebar's stream is the scene of Israel's captivity and prophetic visions—Jahveh girdeth Cyrus for his purposes, who alloweth the Jews to return and to rebuild the temple in Jerusalem —Satan deployeth his agents, and exhausteth his wit to break down the integrity of the Jahveh worship ; yet the Messianic Hope shineth clear amid national misfortunes that befall the Jews.

THE ÆONS.

Number we, name we the Hebrew encampments,
    Earliest daughters of Time!
Follow the course of the journeying Jahvites
    Hence unto Horeb sublime;

MARAH, three days in the wildness of Etham,
Over the bleachen and calcinate road;
Painfully passing, panting, and pausing,
Madden'd with thirst and muttering ill.
Marvel of marvels! Marah is sweeten'd!
If Barberry be, or nameless the plant,
JAHVEH is the Tree that hath healed thee.

ELIM of wells, the notable twelve,
And palms, its threescore and ten.

" Hark ye, the winds from the red reeking shore,
Hence to the mountains! ye breathe me no more! "
DOPHKAH, thence ALUSH, o'er the chaos of hills;
Into the mountains, the cloud-Angel wills
To REPHIDIM, rest, and the tower of JEHOVAH.

Multitudes sing of the quails JAHVEH sent them,
Faint from their flight o'er the wide reedy sea;
Coveting rest and most easily taken.
Thence of the manna, bread rain'd from heaven,
Gift of the tamarisk, and edible moss;
Far-blown and sweeten'd with dew of God's blessing.
Circles shall sing of the Paradise number—
Septenate week with the manna new given;
Limits shall tell of the rock of contention,
Marveling the gush of the crystalline streams.

16

THE DEMONS.

Esau's sons are doubtful neighbors ;
Sons of Seir are churlish sulks ;
Which is nobler ? which is braver ?
Open foe, or one that skulks ?
Amalek is Edom's covering ;
Amalek is Edom's bait ;
Quaff we health these thirsty Jahvites ;
Quaff aside to Edom's hate.

SATAN.

Persuasive courtiers, cozening our fancy—
Constraining unto dalliance with reason,
And open combat with Jehovah's arms ;
Attend ! For ere the closure of this grave
Synod, your prince would speak you cautions.

Lo,

These dual centuries sit we upon
This silent mount, aloof the vale of Siddim,
In rapt excogitations ; leasing the while
Yon tenements and territories far
And near, our own authority abeyant.
Time suffers not the secrecies explor'd ;
The occult spring of elemental laws—
The quiv'ring shore, psycho-material,
That feels the surge of other worlds remote—
The potent influence not unlike to sleep,
Falling on us and all the sensuous spheres,
While softly rose upon our gaze, visions
Of metaphysic worlds impress'd in time.
Suffice to hear the sequent argument :

Jehovah is confest omnipotent
In the domain of cosmic force.   In vain
We battle 'gainst his mineral cohorts ;

The cyclic energies are pliant to
His touch ; cohesions and antagonisms ;
Therewith the lustrous magnetisms concur.
He drives the powers that pull the world, and He
May ride *tandem* for aught that Satan lists.

  Again Jehovah is confest omnipotent
Within the sphere psycho-ethereal ;
Wherefore in trans-material fields engage
We not.
        And still, O subtile augurs of
Our vantage, know, that neither EL Almighty,
Nor JAHVEH, worshipp'd as His Immanence,
Presides within the cosmo-mental world :
Oh, here saw we our righteous throne uprear'd.
Whilst ev'ry child of Adam did obeisance —
Mankind our realm, more than material ;
Mankind our pride, more than ethereal ;—
O Man ! our glory ! twain world's interlac'd !

  These things intent, heard we melodious echoes
Beating against the sentient bounds, resounds
Of angel songs in Heav'n, praising the Name
And Incarnation of PLEROMA-JAH.
Then flash'd upon the dubitating mind,
At once, a star that led the way unto
The pastures over Bethlehem. O what
Apocalypse had been, yourselves conceive !
The august wonder broke amidst, and dropt
Me back to Time (the scheme of Heav'n possess'd).

  Wherefore, O Peers, ye pass belligerent,
Not foolishly to fight against sheer force,
Nor openly to strive with JAHVEH-God ;

(So were ye fire-bugs fighting with the Sun)
Nor to molest the wings of dainty seraphs—
But all, by indirection, so to name,
Do ye achieve our end sagaciously.
Behold these Jahvites in their wanderings
Toward Canaan ; their appetites afflict'd ;
Their lusts inflam'd, chaff'ring betimes with doubts ;
Despondent ; murmuring against their God ;
Here is a field ripe for your sorcery ;
Go mingle wormwood with their manna ; chafe
Their foes hereditary ; bait their camps
With seances and silly nullities.
Betimes, the demons as auxiliar,
Sport ye such interludes digressively.
Yet know the marrow of our enterprise
Is hid in the prophetic name—JAHVEH.
Against this Name we aim the poison'd arrows
Of our hatred. The Incarnation, know,
No devil shall believe, allow, nor think ;
This Messianic Hope is man's delusion !
Each man 's his own Messiah who lives his nature ;
And Lucifer the *Joshua* of men
Rescu'd a fate more trist than Egypt's kilns.

THE ÆONS.

The rod ! the rod ! the conquering rod !
JEHOVAH the banner, JEHOVAH the God !
    He hath barèd his arm ;
    He hath stricken alarm ;
    The mighty hath sworn,
    And Agag is shorn
Of strength and of name evermore.
Hail Jochebed's son ! Hail Aaron and Hur !

For Ephraim's soldier is Paran's victor ;
And the Invisible goes before.

THE ANGELS.

"On eagle wings," the choral sings,
"On eagle wings JEHOVAH brings
    His little ones unto Sinai " :
Ah, ragged nest ! Ah, jagged crest !
Shall JAHVEH's little ones find rest
    Upon yon dread eyrie ?

They weep and wail ; they quake and quail ;
The stoutest hearts are limp and pale ;
    JEHOVAH passeth by.
The mountains quiver ; the valleys shiver ;
Thick clouds and tempests overtake ;
    JEHOVAH draweth nigh !

THE PLEROMA JAHVEH.

Thrice hath this congress of the tribes heeding
The prophet's warning, sanctified itself.
When as at morning watch, We pass'd this way
Alarm'd the Israelites like dead twigs fell
To Earth, until the chariot-cloud roll'd by,
And nature consentaneous still'd on Oreb.

Arise, O awestruck, fearful multitude !
Quit ye the camp and follow your great chief !
In cautious sequence gain the nether mount ;
Strictly forewarn'd ye 'tempt not to ascend,
What time ye see the elders pass within
The lum'nous cloud into JEHOVAH's Presence.

THE ANGELS.

God's altar lifts, mid fiery rifts !
 The lightnings leap from peak to peak !
Set bounds, gaze not, invoke not doom !
 Jehovah-God descends to speak !

THE PLEROMA JAHVEH.

With voice unanimous the people answer :
" All that Jehovah God hath said this day—
The TEN GREAT WORDS from Sinai utterèd
In our astonied ears : and all therewith
By Moses cited in the Cov'nant Book—
Or duties due toward God, or meet toward men ;
These will we keep, and do, and be obedient ;
Jehovah will we worship, and will serve
None other god but Him and Him alone."

Therefore the congregation Moses seals,
Baptizing them in crimson drops of blood ;
Wherefore upon this altar I do now
Record My Name :—" JEHOVAH ISRAEL."
In token of this covenant, renew'd
On Sinai, EL sendeth His own Angel
To keep them and to guard them in the way :
To bring them duly to the land forepledg'd.
HIM shall we hear, for in Him is God's Name—
The FULNESS and GLORY of PLEROMA.
If from the cloud He speak, or mediately
By seer or priest ; by Urim and Thummim—
(The Yea and Nay of Heav'n significant) ;
Hear ye and do all He shall so reveal.
For when the *Aleim's* Angel goes before,

Terror shall seize God's enemies and yours—
Hivite and Hittite, and the Canaanite.
    I am JEHOVAH GOD that brought thee forth,
    The land of Egypt, from the house of slaves.
    Behold have I not talk'd with you from heav'n?
    And warn'd ye make with Me no gods of silver?
    Nor that ye make you molten gods of gold?
    ONE is your GOD, JEHOVAH! Serve ye Him!

THE SEVENTY ELDERS.

O Ineffable
JEHOVAH Israel!
Who shall repeat
Under His feet
How the unthinkable
Pavement of sapphire
        Seem'd when we saw HIM?
O moment of terror!
O infinite Mirror!
When we gazed and beheld
In JEHOVAH revealed
        The face of ALEIM!

THE CHILDREN OF ISRAEL.

Alas, the fatuity
That worships vacuity!
Ah, vague Infinity—
An unseen Deity!
        In thickest darkness stood,
        Showing no similitude.
We are undone!
Our chief is gone :
Up, up, Aaron!

Make us gods to go before ;
Likenesses we may adore,
Else turn we back to Egypt.

THE DEMONS.

Ho, ho, a fine *presto !*
'T will choke our prince to know
That the Jahvites so soon,
With their high-priest Aaron,
Ere the sound dies away,
Of the Words of Jahveh,
    Have set up a calf—
    An Egyptian calf !
    (The sphinx needs must laugh)—
And with adulterous eyes
They do sacrifice
    To the *Elohim !*

MOSES.

O blot them not from thy book !
  And stay, I beseech thee, the plague !
If thou go not with this people,
  I faint in my office dismay'd !

THE PLEROMA JEHOVAH.

Moses, thou has found favor in My sight,
Therefore My Presence shall go up with thee,
And I will give thee rest.   Behold I put
Thee in this mountain cleft and screen thee with
My hand, while I pass by ; then shalt thou see
JEHOVAH ELOHIM, the merciful,
Abundant in goodness and truth.   Is 't not

A mighty thing and terrible I do?
For ye shall spoil the altars of the nations,
And beat to sherds all their idolatries.
JEHOVAH is your God, whose name is Jealous.
Hence, ye shall do respect unto My Sabbaths;
The triple offerings; and reverence
My sanctuary; I am your God, JEHOVAH.

THE CHILDREN OF ISRAEL.

We bring our gifts to thee willingly;
Thy words have touch'd us thrillingly;
    O the seat of the Cherubim!
    In the Holy Place;
    God shall show His face,
    And His will make known
    To His priest Aaron.
Haste Uri's son, thy work begin!
Fashion the Tent in the wisdom God sent thee;
Cov'rings hang with the cunning He lent thee;
Using these jewels, the gift of the women—
Silver, and gold, and costlier brass—
Fabrics of blue and purple and scarlet;
Dyed-skins and goat's hair and finest of linen.
Therewith a dower for the robes of the Priesthood;
Stones for the ephod, and breastplate and mitre—
Haste Bezaleel with the wise men to aid thee,
Building the Shrine and the Ark JAHVEH bade thee.

THE BANDS.

Far-sighted Couriers, prophet-glances!
Tryst of cov'nant Bands entrances;
    Whilst with purest inspiration
    Ye infuse the Hebrew nation.

First, revealing God as Power—*Eloah ;*
Thence as Goodness—dower of *Pleroma ;*
Next, in mitred " Holiness unto *Jehovah,*"
Blent with Justice in the sanctions of the LAW.

THE ANGELS.

The priests are anointed ; the elders appointed ;
The Covenant renew'd ; false idols eschew'd :
The Tabernacle rear'd, as the Pattern appear'd
    To Moses in the Mount.
The Ark is enshrin'd ; the Holies defin'd ;
The furniture placed, and coverings laced ;
The offerings made whilst worship is paid
    JEHOVAH of the Mount.

O marvel to Moses ! JEHOVAH discloses
Within the Shrine His Glory Divine !
Lo, he falls to adore Thee, and quaketh before Thee,
    Thou *Angel* of the Cloud !
Now Levite and Priest the memorial feast,
With reverent rite, prepare in the night ;
While the fire-glowing cloud lifts skyward its shroud ;
And a voice cries aloud,
" Wake trumpet and song !　Let the tribes journey on !
JEHOVAH goes in the Cloud ! "

THE PLEROMA JAHVEH.

Perfervid Couriers (chafing the Law's
Delay, and Sinai's tented year), behold
Six hundred myriads able to war
In Israel—the same a crowd of serfs
This time a twelvemonth, out of bondage loos'd ;
But now become a nation.　Mark their array !

The quint'ple rank and soldierly respect
To word and to authority.   Ask them
What of the god's of Egypt? and they cry,
" All *elilim !*   All *elilim* are they !
JEHOVAH is the True and only God—
Invisible, yet near—filling all things ;
The Lord and Ruler of all things—*Adonai*,
Jehovah Sabaoth, mighty in battle ! "

    Subdue this access of your zeal, the while
Ye do their march to Canaan prevene ;
For far and long the multitudinous line
Winds slow and painfully.   In Paran's waste
Bid them to rest, erect their darkly tents
Against the stainless splendors of the sky ;
And screen the haggard hills.
                              Ah week of woes !
Burdens for Moses ; temptings for JAHVEH !
What loathing of the food miraculous !
What strife of Aaron, and his more seditious
Sister, jealous of the Cushite wife.
Record therefore JEHOVAH's signal wrath ;
The flame that swept consuming through the camp ;
The leprosy heal'd by a brother's prayer ;
Nor fail to sum the one and twenty journeys
To Kadesh Barnea : nor thence the names
Of the twelve chiefs that went to search the land
Of Canaan.

MOSES.

Ye are come to the mount of the Amorites,
Which EL JEHOVAH shall give to you ;
Behold, He hath spread the land before your eyes ;

Up, up, possess it as JAHVEH hath commanded !
Neither fear ye, nor be ye dismayed !

THE PLEROMA JAHVEH.

Herewith indite the princes twelve return'd
From Canaan's search : " A land of milk and honey,"
Unanimously told, with ruddy cheeks,
And nectar-dripping lips ; " A goodly land " ;
Displaying of its fruits excerpted samples,—
Pomegranates, figs, and grapes of Eschol's vale.
" Exceeding good it is," Caleb adjoins ;
" And if JEHOVAH do delight in us,
He will bring us thither and give it us."
Thereto one voice agrees, and notable,
Of Nun's heroic son, presyllabled
By Moses " Joshua."   Thou dost divine
O Gabriel, the mystery therein
Prenominate ; whilst Messianic fervors
Fly through earth, and sky, till this sad star
Gloweth (impalpably to human sense),
And ev'ry choir in the pneumatic realm
Quicken its dense libration to the coasts
Of Palestine ; glancing the while yon hill
Of Jebus and environs eminent,
Enwrapt in radiance of the *Plerome*.

" In vain !   In vain ! " the recreant ten resume ;
" Here in the Negeb deem we Israel blest ;
Past'ring our flocks Arabah's fertile vales.
Wherefore shall we attempt 't ? to fall before
The *Anakim ;* our wives and little ones,
Become the sport of *gibborim*, 'gainst whose
Fierce giantry we be as grasshoppers
Assailing eagles."

THE DEMONS.

Here 's a swig to Israel !
    Pooh, pooh, Jahvites !
    Dread yon Canaanites ?
What of JAHVEH EL ?

Braggarts all, fickle and craven,
Paralyz'd to find your haven
    Fortified with limestone clods ;
    In the keep of hateful gods !
By Zephath's tower learn ye to cower
    Before the sturdy Baalim ;
    E'en curse your Elohim,
And doubt in Hormah JEHOVAH's Power !

SATAN.

By our imperial will do ye resume
Consult, extraordinary and august,
On Pisgah's top,—co-anarchs eminent ;
Meanwhile, in neighb'ring glens the sportive sprites
Practise their archeries upon the front
Of Engedi, from Sport's alembic drunk.
Good speed these nimble waifs ! cheer to their minds !
Lo eight and thirty years, since turn'd aback
From Kadesh' sacred camp on Canaan's rim,
The errant Jahvites unto Akabah—
Accurst of EL JAHVEH, in riotous
Dismay,—rest they not day nor night to spread
Dissension 'mong the tribes ; seeding their hearts
With Melancholy's parasite ; scooping
Them shallow graves in Arabah—empire
Of jackals.

Anew the couriers flit and flare,
Dazing our throne with lore extravagant
Of diabolic vantage over Israel ;
Provoking Heav'n in devilish insolence ;
Blaspheming EL'S great NAME ineffable ;
His sabbaths violated, leaders, priests,
Denounc'd and abrogated.   Thence, Korah's—
Abiram's, fate, with fifteen myriad more
In charr'd and lumpy burial ; others
Engulf'd a shrieking morsel in Earth's bowels.
Thence Aaron's magic rod, that budded first,
Next, blossom'd and forthwith ripened almonds,
Colossal marvel ! seen within the Shrine.
Next, the insipid seeds that fell from heav'n,
Grown nauseous between their muttering lips
Ev'n as they crunch them.   Beastly idiocy !
And cry :   "We die, We perish "—fat as bullocks ;
Till Moses patience broke at Meribah,
And he and his whole house with him debarr'd
The land of promise.   In Kadesh next we hear
Of Miriam's death, 'mid pompous rites interr'd,
And gen'ral sorrow : then Aaron forewarnèd
Of his demise, clomb Hor's lone height and look'd
Upon the hills of Canaan, sighing long,
Until his life went forth in sighs upon
His first-born's breast, where fell his robes
Pontifical by God's decree.   The rites
Funereal dismiss'd, direct do livelier hours
Reprieve the tiresome dole : for, from the brook
Of Zered ever watchful imps evok'd,
With their weird sorcery, a frightful wave
Of serpents fiery, that swept the tented plain ;
And left behind a sea of writhing flesh.

So they report ; but rather do we name
This last a tale of Jahveh's interludes ;
Since by his fiat Moses lifts aloft
A brazen coil, whereat the plague abates.

But heed our new resolve ; the act flames out !
The Jahvites teem ; surge, and on Edom crowd ;
The pop'lous tribes rally on rushing Arnon's
Tremendous brink, defining Moab's limits ;
Nor grim defiance of proud Esau's sons—
Nor Lot's mountainous clans intimidate ;
Whilst rumor, hoarse, affrights the dukes of Seir.
Nay, Pisgah's threaten'd, and our sec'lar throne.
Wherefore our next solstitial synod 's
Too late remov'd the case immediate.
This seat must we evacuate, or front
Jehovah.   Hither drives the van-Angel !
Wherefore this parliament do we prorogue,
Dismissing each with our fraternal kiss.
Ye Gods of Canaan, and Syria, farewell !
Your Prince dismisseth you reluctantly ;
Bright lustres all—*Shamas*, and *Kabbiri !*
Withdraw ye to your stations, nor suspect
Our plan, if undisclos'd.   We are not blind.
Have we not seen the cursèd Jahvites dip
Their jars into the royal wells of Bashan ?
O ghostly summoners !   O passions dire !
Now deathless fires e'en to our foot-stool burn,
And scorch this adamantine throne.   Away !
Enough !   Ye hate the seed of Abraham !
Let Hate then be your teacher when ye war.
The locusts swarm the south and threaten to
Devour the earth.

The Song of Jair and of Nobah, Princes of Manasseh :

O sing unto JEHOVAH who hath gone forth to victory !
The God of Israel is a mighty man in battle :
The Ark went before, the priests and trumpeters followed
    after ;
The trumpets sounded, the archers and slingers stood still;
The NAME in the cloud pass'd by.   They look'd,
Behold the enemy fled ; Sihon the destroyer fled ;
In the treadings of the mountains he fainted ;
The flower of Heshbon fainted for thirst.
As a hart they lapp'd for water where none was.
The fire burn'd, the fire of JEHOVAH at Jahaz ;
The inhabitants of Moab melted like wax away.

Then said the five dukes unto Balak :
Thou hast heard the enchantments of the great prophet ?
Surely JEHOVAH shall not withstand the curses of Balaam !
Nevertheless the princes of Midian are no more ;
And Balaam, even Balaam, who loved the wages of un-
    righteousness,
And tempted the sons of Israel, perished in his sin ;
They all perished, in one day they perished ;
And JEHOVAH gave their jewels and flocks to His people.

Then turn'd we and went up by the way of Bashan ;
And Gog, the long-neck'd, led forth his mighty men ;
In the straits of Edrei we encountered him.
Then said JEHOVAH : Fear him not, for I have delivered
    him into thine hand !
Then smote we Og until there was none remaining to him ;
Threescore cities took we in the region of Argob :
And unwalled towns a multitude, from Arnon unto
    Hermon.

And I, Jair, the son of Manasseh, took the cities of Argob,
Unto the coasts of Geshuri and Maacha :
Wherefore it shall be call'd *Bashan-havoth-Jair—*
For pleasant are its villages in the eyes of JAH.
And I, Nobah, shall be clothed with royalty ;
Clothed in green shall I sit in the gates of Kenath.

THE ANGELS.

The shout of a king is among them ! What hath God
    wrought ?
As a lion Jacob lifts himself ! What hath God wrought ?
The alien seer falleth, he falleth with open eyes ;
He seeth the Almighty, beholdeth Him in a trance.
"How goodly are thy tents, O Jacob ; Ye are the lign-
    aloes ;
Which JEHOVAH by waters planteth—the lign-aloes.
We shall see Him, but not now,—JEHOVAH !
He shall come as a star out of Jacob—ADCNAI !
And His shall be the sceptre of Israel—PLEROMA !
And blessed is he that blesseth thee, O Israel !
And cursed is he that curseth thee, O Jacob !"

THE CIRCLES.

We hymn the praise of Amram's son,
    And sing his name afar ;
We weave him garlands ev'ry one,
    And deck the victor's car ;
We taste again our Paradise ;
    O wherefore do we live ?
Wherefore, O Lord ? Still veil our eyes,
    And plead for his reprieve.
Thou say'st, " The circle is complete ;
    Thy plan in him fulfill'd " ;

17

Thy will be done.   So wind his feet ;
It is as Thou hast will'd.

We take alarm, O sacred Name !
Death in us lives again ;
Man's Paradise affrays yon flame—
It is his foe, Satan !
And wherefore com'st, O curse of Heav'n ?
Tempter and prince of ill ?
Hail, glories of the ethereal Seven !
Haste on, O Michael !

MICHAEL.

JAHVEH rebuke thee, Lucifer !   How changed !
Whose ancient throne was glorious and noble !
Dost think to war upon the dead ?   And vow'st
No requiem shall be sung to Moses' dust ?
Behold Michael ! prince of the militant—
I sent'nel am to guard this sepulchre ;
I charge thee, crafty one, and all thy crew,
If onset mak'st to rape this holy tomb,
Thou and thy reprobates shall taste, shall—
Thou hear'st my voice !   Thou see'st my lance !   I am
JEHOVAH's messenger ; I thee defy !
To curse I am forbid, but not to challenge.

THE DEMONS.

The grave is watch'd by EL's Angel ;
Satan outmatch'd by Michael ;
We too are scotch'd, demon and devil :
Drink fire and fly !
Drink fire and die !

SATAN.

This mock'ry of my demons harsher meets
Mine ear than doth the taunt of the archangel ;
Once Satan had not brook'd these braggart cries !
But subtle world-studies have drain'd his sinews,
Though they distend the psychic hemispheres.
Let dolts and dotards reckon as they list,
Wherefore Satan attempted Moses' tomb !
It was experiment worthy success ;
For on the event a nation's fate did hang.
Gecko ! with Satan's wit and Moses' mask
To cover it, crave we no odds *Jehovah.*
O ho ! a resurrection 't were to spoil
The earth of future marvels.
                        The lights are low ;
The action dismal and unearthly.   Aheu,
Jehovah is in truth a man of war !
Then Satan thou shalt be a man of cunning !
Thy cold, thin arm defy the *God of battles.*
Thy feints and artifices shall defraud
His saintliest, and gall their victories.
Pisgah farewell ! We cross with Joshua this Jordan.

THE PLEROMA JAHVEH.

Arise, O Joshua, this Jordan cross !
Thou and the Congregation to the land
Which I do give to them.
                     Hail, aural voices :
"From Jordan's meadows and this Lebanon,
Hence to the populous Euphrata's heaths,
And westward where the sea receives the sun,
There shall not any man resist their arm."

With thee I am as I with Moses was.
Divin'st the rapture of the Couriers?
That sing One to arise in Israel—
JAHVEH IMMANUEL?
               Prepare, prepare,
And make ye ready!   For within three days
Shall Jacob's sons go over to possess
The land which JAHVEH ALEIM giveth them.
Thus shalt thou say the priests that bear the Ark,
  "Hither and hear the words of JAH your God—
  The Living God is here, e'en JEHOVAH—
  The Lord of all the Earth ; and passeth on
  Before you over Jordan."

THE CANAANITES.

If we cry to Baal, will he answer us ?
If we offer our first-born, will he hear?
Is not EL the Strong ? and Eliun the exalted ?
Doth he not rule the great ones of Molech ?
Doth the mother forget her offspring, Astarte ?
And why is thy glory darken'd, O Shemesh ?
Ye that dwell with the father of waters, awake !
Ye that sleep in the bosom of Sharon arise !
For the Anakim quake in their towers ;
And the Amorites faint in their cities.
Philistia, Philistia, to thy chariots and shields !
For JEHOVAH hath dried up the Jordan,
And the Jahvites pass over dry shod.

THE COURIERS.

Flashes of light gleam in the night !
Couriers turn from the horrible sight ;

Satan as Baal defraudeth the kings ;
Hideous effigies Canaan brings
  To meet the Ark of the Lord.
O the glint, the glint of the knives of flint !
  On the bloody Hill of Foreskin ;
The Covenant renew'd, the false gods are eschew'd,
  And JEHOVAH is their Captain ;
Lo, He standeth with drawn sword !
Write, Æons, write the song we indite,
Of Jericho's wall and its marvelous fall ;
  And the fame that accrued to JAHVEH.
Thence the son of Carmi, and curse on the army
  Of Joshua that march'd against Ai.
Of the lie and the lot that traced out the blot
  And wiped it in Achor from earth ;
How the fruit of the land grew ripe to the hand,
With the Manna withdrawn at the taste of the corn,
  That was parch'd upon Canaan's hearth.

THE CIRCLES.

We sing Gilgal—the " Circle "—
  And its twelve memorial stones ;
The Covenant and the Paschal,
  By the twelve memorial stones.

We sing the hill of Ebal
  And its unpolluted stones ;
The Law-engraven altar
  Of the twelve unbroken stones.

We sing the craft of Gibeon,
  And the league wilily won ;
The oath of the five fierce princes
  To war upon Gibeon.

How the harvest queen arose,
   While the king on Gibeon stay'd ;
How the circles twain in heaven
   Stood still as they were bade :

Till the sanguinary circle
   Had reft the sons of Baal ;
And the hosts of Joshua
   Regain'd the camp in Gilgal.

THE LIMITS.

Thou mournest thy bravest, O Jabin !
Cursing, nursing thy wrath upon Israel ;
Where, where are the Anakim ?
And ye plains of Chinneroth,
Where are thy sons innumerable ?
All crush'd, all brush'd as a moth
Away unto far Zidon.
Yea, the wadys and waters of Dor
Are bloody and ruddy with gore ;
And the flames of Hazor
Are a watch and a torch unto Hermon.
Write Æons the three and thirty kings !
The first on the East from Arnon to Hermon ;
Thence the West from Seir unto Lebanon ;
All notable names of the nations.
Whilst the coast we mark out for the tribes,
As the servant of JAHVEH divides,
For their lot and their habitations.

A VOICE.

Behold, Joshua waxeth old and stricken :
And shortly goes the way of all the earth.

Therefore he calleth for the tribal chiefs ;
At Shechem sendeth for the elders ; and saith ;
" Ye have seen all that JEHOVAH your God hath done,
How that He hath driven out for you your enemies ;
Behold I have divided you the nations that remain,
Be very courageous to keep the Book of the Law,
And come ye not among these idolatrous nations,
Nor make ye mention of their abominations.

Thus saith JEHOVAH—the God of Israel :
' Your fathers dwelt beyond the flood,
And there served they the *false aleim ;*
And I took Abram your father and led him forth,
And multiplied his seed in Canaan.
And I gave him Isaac, and to Isaac, Jacob and Esau ;
To Esau gave I mount Seir ; but Jacob I took into
    Egypt :
Then sent I Moses and Aaron and plagued Pharaoh ;
And afterward I brought your fathers out,
Putting darkness between them and the Egyptians.

So ye dwelt in the wilderness a long season ;
When I gave the Amorites into your hands ;
And ye came to Jericho, which I gave into your hands.
And I gave you a land for which ye did not labor ;
And cities to dwell in—which ye builded not.'

" Now therefore choose this day whom ye will serve !
Whether the gods beyond the flood, or of the Amorites ?
For as for me and my household we will serve JEHOVAH ! "

THE PRINCES OF THE TRIBES.

Nay, but we also will serve JEHOVAH.

JOSHUA.

Ye are witnesses against yourselves !

THE PRINCES.

We are witnesses.

SATAN.

Chough !   Chough !   This is no raven's note I hear.
A meaner bird flies by ; a fouler throat !
Thy croak I know, thy caw—lone-flying courier !
Ho, monster among fiends !   Thou com'st, dread son
Of Chemosh ?   What tidings from the chariots ?

" They are burnt and the horses are hough'd ;
Overcome at the waters of Merom ;
And the coasts divide the Jahvites ! "

Thou liest !   I Canaan rule a thousand years !
With me my faithful princes.   For Jahveh
Hath won no land to portion out his flock !
We give empire, but give what is our own.
Jahveh hath yet no Canaan to divide.
Haste back, and through the vale of Sharon speed,
And 'gainst the upper coasts, lifting the cry
Of Baal :
          " Up, up, for Baal hath awoke !
          Forge ranks of steel and knivèd chariots ;
          Retake the sunny vales of Canaan !
          Each titular god and local deity,
          Shall go before and war on Jahveh's hosts."

So do I trust to end this piecemeal work !
I will have peace, and to this end do I

Provoke fresh war.   Our archons all, alike
The general tribe, do dear and dote fore'er
On muscular encounters, jousts of arms !
O for one kindred spirit, that I might
Unlock the language of the psychic world—
The inner and essential sphere !   " Patience ! "
Good monitor, we are its very soul ;
Its privy pattern.   And we stay to win.
One day's respite to wine and women giv'n,
More souls shall ruin among the Jahvites than
A hundred battles.

THE ÆONS.

Write, sisters, write the Exploits of the Judges !
Whom Jahveh rais'd up to avenge their oppressors ,
The tears shed at Bochim by the Angel's denounce-
    ment ;
Of princes and people that forsook JEHOVAH.
Of Aram's high king and his eight years' oppression ;
Of Othniel next and the days of probation ;
Of Eglon the Moabite prince that subdued them,
Till Ehud's feign'd errand and dagger betray'd him.
Of the ox-goad of Shamgar, and the slain of Philistia :
Of Deborah and Barak and the heroic Jael :
Next the prevalent hand of the Midianite on them,
Whilst they crouch'd in the clefts and caves of the moun-
    tains
Till the Angel cloth'd Gideon with courage undaunted,
Whose warriors the brooklet elected three hundred ;
And taught them the ruse of the trumpet and pitchers ;
Of the panic and rout of Zeba, Zalmunna ;
Last, the ephod of Gideon, the snare to his household.

Write the license that follow'd ; and pollutions of worship,
When anarchy reign'd and no rulers restrain'd them.
How Jephthah, freebooter, brought out as their captain,
Disperseth the Ammonite from Aroer to Minnith ;
Of his terrible vow and his woe unrelentless.
Of the angel that came to the wife of Manoah ;
And the Nazarite's birth—the thirteenth from Joshua ;
Of his strength in his locks and his sanguinous record.

Relieve ye the page with the tale of Naomi,
And the Moabite maid, happy mother of Obed,
Whom she bore unto Boaz her legaliz'd kinsman,
Whilst the aureole full'd o'er the altar in Shiloh,
And the angels repeated prophetical words.
Now cease, for the Couriers brighten ; their theme
Is the last of the Judges and first of the Prophets :
So list, ye their song, and its future relations,
Save one note reminding the trist fate of Eli.

THE COURIERS.

Now flame we and fly unto Shiloh,
    And whisper God's will to the seer ;
More clearly than Urim and Thummim
    His word and commandment appear.

We hail thee, O child of Elkanah !
    The last of the judges art sent ;
And forthwith in Shiloh and Ramah
    The priest and the prophet are blent.

Dost weep for the glory departed ?
    For the Ark in the Philistines' hand ?
Thou shalt bring them to Mizpeh repenting,
    And JAHVEH shall ransom the land.

Next the elders shall counsel a kingdom,
  The rule theocratic reject ;
Fear thou not !   Erst, the monarch portraying,
  Anoint thou the one We select.

And comfort thy soul with the promise,
  Ere thou go to thy fathers to rest,
Thou shalt see and declare a Messiah,
  In whose Son all the Earth shall be blest.

SATAN.

Wash we our hands these Jehovistic wars !
O Nature weeps the ruthless myriads slain !
Behold the ground season'd with gore and rank !
Ev'n demons sicken at the spectacle,
Calling on *Jahveh* to withdraw his sword.
So name these butcheries " Jehovah's Wars " ;
For Satan's regiment is built on peace ;
Confessedly our feud with *Aleim's* Son,
By indirection, jostles, here and there,
Mankind,—trivial concomitants for all
The purpos'd good.   O civilizing wars !
  Yet are we not abas'd enough to fend ;
For oft fault we our thralls and minions that
They churn and foment strife with Israel,
Blunting the edge of our recondite plans.

We challenge Jahveh to arrest his zeal
For blood, and yield the panting Jahvites space
To breathe, and recreate in garden, and
In grove !
      Hail Baalim ! Ashera !   Rejoice !
The universal song confirms our wit !

Ours, ours, in peace, if Jah's in war.   Whence He
Is predetermin'd unto wars perpetual ;
Else shall the military faith exhaust ;
And worship ancienter, the natural man
More apposite, come in.

THE PLEROMA JAHVEH.

Now vaunteth Satan arch-hypocrisies,
Fireth his forkèd tongue, and stings the air ;
Breathing crass utterance against Our Name,
And honor in these expurgating wars.
Satan, thyself art war ! and strife ! and blood !
Thou art the head, the middle and the base
Of the most direful urgency that calls
On Us to save unto Ourselves a remnant from
Mankind, in which all nations We may bless,
By stern decrees and sanctions mem'rable,
Until the Man of Peace arise to teach
The better way.
     Hail Christo-Cosmic Choir !
Hail fourfold ministries of min'ral Earth !
Mark how in Samuel a further bound is pass'd
Unto the Incarnation of PLEROMA.
"Glory to the Highest, good will to men !"
And so Ye mix with earth and earth with Thee !
In intimate regards inhabit Israel ;
The guiding thought reach onward, hastening
PLEROMA'S goal, the CHRIST of Christs—the MAN !

THE COURIERS.

"A king ! A king !" they cry,
While the Airs proleptic fly,

And tell of a kinglier One,
Than Kish's or Jesse's son.
    How long? how long? O Lord!

"God save the king!" they cry,
As the mighty Saul draws nigh;
    Still Samuel from his tears
    Pours out a cup of fears;
        How long? how long? O Lord!

A stench, a stench ariseth;
The seer thy sin surmiseth;
    Ah, woe, thou art rejected;
    Thy better is selected;
        Haste on, haste on, O king!

The shepherd boy 's anointed;
His brothers disappointed;
    Defying David's God
    Goliath bites the sod;
        Haste on, haste on, O king!

The "Bounds of blood" are pass'd;
The psalmist hears aghast
    The fate of the royal trio;
    And sings the "Lament of the Bow."
        Haste on, haste on, O king!

Look up, behold the light!
Delectable and bright!
    Awake the harp and song!
    Messiah cometh on!
        Haste on, haste on, O King!

THE ARCHON DEMONS.

Satan is stuff'd with plaints ;
Damneth our martial deeds ;
Provoketh sorcery,
And Endor's subtilty ;
Seance and trance he leads.
Still quaff we royal veins,
　Crimsoning Gilboa's side ;
Forepledge to further war,
And drink us drunk with gore.
　O prince, thou art defied ;

(Hist, hist, his highness near !)
　Salute we Baal's name,
Quaffing his health ;
Learning his stealth ;
　Envy his world-wide fame.

SATAN.

The event is at the latch ; I know its stage.
O Israel, thou art a seminary inspir'd !
Perceive this not our chiefs belligerent.
Cease clam'rous world, that goadest to rashness !
Unpractis'd wit groweth to Leb'non's bulk :
Oh, now, or never, match we the JAHVEH.
Hold, archons ! from your bloody pastime stay !
Doth JAHVEH's " Darling " so incite to arms ?
Hear ! Once his son—the " Man of Peace " shall reign
On David's throne, uplift on Jebus' rock,
(Else Zion called, the Mountain of JAHVEH),
Forthwith (mark ye our prophecy) : Yon height
Shall craze JAHVEH with its adulteries ;
Baal shall build environs round about ;

Divinest wit and devilish lust shall wed ;
Most lofty wisdom rot e'en to the core.
Wherefore remaineth one and only way
For JAH to save a remnant to Himself :
Assyria shall tell, and Babylon,
Sometime, when whining Hebrews hang their harps
On far Euphrata's tearful willows.
        The hour
Draws on ; Satan sleeps not, nor slumbers. Tempests
Gather, whose like ne'er felt ! Be warn'd ! be arm'd !
What omens in the psychologic field
We deem not wise to tell ; what intimations
Of the Messiah's birth unspoken be.
Farewell a space ! With comrades few and brave,
We go to fortify our rule in Earth, and bind
In closer covenant remotest empires 'gainst
Jehovah's Name and Worship.

THE BANDS.

So marvel the Æons the lore of the Line,
While Bands call the links in the lineage Divine :
First promis'd in Eden to the mother of men ;
From the deluge restor'd in the household of Shem ;
Thence call'd and definèd of Abraham's seed,
Whence the on-going line in Isaac we read.
In Jacob divinely as " Israel " surnam'd,
The leonine Judah his sceptre hath claim'd.
O Root out of Jesse ! O Judæan king !
Interpret the things which thy psalmodies sing ;
Of the kiss of the Son and the Rod out of Zion ;
Of the brook in the way and the wound of the iron ;
Of the Melchisedekian order restor'd,
In Him whom thou callest both Son and thy Lord.

THE LIMITS.

Line and compass take we, stake we borders wide for
    Israel :
Throne 'gainst prophets striving, riving JAHVEH's name
    and Baal's ;
Solomon prevaileth ; haileth guests from Tyre and Sidon ;
Syria defeateth ; meeteth prosperously fierce Edom.
Byblus and Berytus indite us measures, God-like meas-
    ures :
Flow'ry isles vermilion guide to Tarshish' treasures.
Far, far, in the cypress boat,
Neath the heaven-pillars float
To the silv'ry mount Tartessan.

The " Man of Peace " is splendid, attended by a mighty
    band :
Marriage bringeth treaties ; cities move on sea and land.
India yieldeth beauties ;
Syria payeth duties ;
Egypt addeth splendor to palaces and temple,
Dazzling all example.
Glorious in counsel ; court magnifical ;
Telling for the wise secrets wonderful ;
Regal bounty yielding unto Sheba's queen.
Till her spirit fainteth ere the half is seen.
Son of David, Preacher, teacher of mankind ;
Manifold endowments Heav'n in thee combin'd ;
Ev'ry grace of body, ev'ry gift of mind ;
Alas, O Anointed, great, great is thy sin !
Who points out the way but walks not therein ;
For turning from JAHVEH and following Baal,
Thy kingdom is rent in thy son over Israel.

THE DEMONS.

The trance, the trance, the purblind defiance
 Of the autocratic prince !
Do the northern tribes convince ?
But too late, but too late ;
 Jeroboam's thron'd in Shechem.
Up spirits, quaff to the golden calf
 Set up at Bethel and Dan ;
Lo portents rise in prophetic eyes
 O'er the house of Jeroboam !

THE ANGELS.

God sendeth his prophets ; wilt thou heed them,
 O Jeroboam ?
Nay, nay, so the curse descends from Ahijah !
Weep, weep, for thy first-born Abijah !
God sendeth his prophets ; wilt thou heed them,
 O Rehoboam ?
Nay, nay, so thy sin shall cost royal treasure.
Atone, wretched vassal of Shishak its seizure ?

God sendeth his prophets ; wilt thou heed them,
 O Nadab ?
Nay, nay, Baasha and Elah attest it ;
Nay, nay, both Zimri and Omri confess it.
Woe, woe, for the frenzy and fire shall devour you !
Accursèd of JAHVEH in Nebat !
Mourn, mourn, for the wrath of Jehovah o'erpowers you !
Weep Judah blest in Jehoshaphat !

God sendeth his prophets ; wilt thou heed them,
 O Ahab ?
If Baal send false ones, dost thou feed them,
 18

O Ahab?
Thou withstandest Elijah ; dost thou well?
Wilt thou compass his death, wicked Jezebel?
Nay, nay, the Almighty 'larms in the thunders ;
Fills the earth and the sky with his wonders ;
When the fire consumes Baal's priests ;
And the seer calls rain on the wastes.
And the people cry as the Angels alway,
" JAHVEH, He is God ; JAHVEH, He is God!"

THE COURIERS.

Proud queen of the hills, Samaria !
Thou hast sinn'd ; shalt thou prosper for aye ?
Ah, the Couriers hear the Assyrian say,
" I saw, I seiz'd, I carried away."

God remembered his covenant with Judah ;
In Uzziah and the godly Hezekiah ;
In Josiah and the penitent Manasseh ;
While the heart of Samaria crimsons
Far Gozan's stream and the leashes of Sargon.

THE PLEROMA JAHVEH.

The FULNESS yields enrapturing intimation ;
And ecstasies enseize the band prophetic ;
The furthest Thoughts of God now live in words.
Let Couriers lead their God-fus'd prophet-choir !

Him first, repellant son of Amittai,
From JAHVEH's face, embark'd unto Tarshish,
Remote that Nineveh, his message doom'd ;—
Cast in the sea, Messiah's type become ;
Engulph'd, and three days hid beneath the world,
uncorrupted sepulture.

Forthwith,

The son of Pethual blows his trump ;
  "O sanctify ! Thus saith JEHOVAH—*Lord :*
  ' Behold I pour My Spirit on all flesh,
And cleanse their guilt ; for JAH rememb'reth Zion.' "

Next whom ye took from the Tekoan hills ;
And mad'st a fire-brand for Hazael's house :
Moab and Ammon, and the Philistines ;—
Press'd like a cart beneath his load of woes
He cries,
    " Yea surely will He nothing do
But first He show his servants the prophets—
The princess 's fall'n ; the star of Chiun set ;
He will sift her as corn sift in a sieve,
Ere JAH bring the captivity again
Of Israel."
        Him next, to Gomer wed,
Diblaim's child from harlotry redeem'd—
A parable of the Messiah's love ;
When Israel redeem'd, Thee " Ishi " calls—
(My husband) ; nor call Thee " Baal," (Master) more.
Then will I drop as dew sweet after rain,
And Israel bloom effulgent as the rose ;
And strike his roots like Leb'non's lofty tree.

Thence Amoz's gifted son ye do announce,
Bending beneath his tragic, God-breath'd roll ;
" All, all, is wrong ! " he cries : " The land is rife
With charmers and diviners. The head is sick,
The heart is faint. Except JAHVEH—*Aleim*
Had left Himself a seed, we were as Sodom.
Ah, mincing, tinkling daughters, wanton-eyed,

Spangled with cauls, with rounded tires and bonnets;
Your mantles, wimples, and your crisping pins,
JAHVEH shall take away; and give you back
Sackcloth for girdles; burning for beauty,
For Zion's haughty look shall be brought low;
Yea seven women seize one man and cry,
'Thou shield us with thy name from our reproach!'
Yet shall JEHOVAH raise an ensign for
The nations; and a light to guide and cheer.
For unto us a Child is born—a Son
Is giv'n; the Government His shoulders bear;
His name is Wonderful, the Counsellor;
The Mighty God, the Everlasting Father;
The Prince of Peace.   The throne of David He
Establisheth forever; His rest is glorious.

"O Lucifer! Lucifer! how art thou fall'n!
How art thou bruis'd that deceiveth the nations!
Wilt thou exalt thy seat above the stars
Of Elohim?   Behold the ancient North!
Would'st reign upon the Mount of Paradise?
Hast thou not said, 'I will ascend above
The highest clouds; I will be like unto
The Most High JAH.'   Lo, thou shalt be cut down
Even to Hell; archon of Babylon."

Thereafter lead the past'ral Morasthite,
Descrying Bethlehem, a little one
Among the thousands, whence He shall come forth
Whose goings are of old, from everlasting—
JAHVEH-Messiah, the Prince, and Israel's king.
Him next succeeds the Elkoshite, the doom
Of Nineveh foreshadowing; accompanied

By Habakkuk, and Zephaniah ; meantime
A sombre figure comes from Anathoth,
Hilkiah's son, broken in heart, mourning
The solitary city—the tribute princess.

THE COURIERS.

We lighten the soul of the seer,
We brighten the face of the sphere ;
For the day shall come and soon,
That the Righteous Branch is grown
Unto David.   His holy Name we bless,
" The LORD, Our RIGHTEOUSNESS."

———

He liveth, Jehovah liveth ; reprieveth
His people far driven.   Though He grieveth,
He shall lead them softly with His hand,
And bring them back to Canaan.

———

Nebuchadnezzar nameth " Belteshazzar,"
The likely lad with Jehoiakim ;
Of the boys of Bel, none fair as Daniel ;
In studies none equal ; in wisdom and skill ;
Though he eat not the meat of the king.

A scorn and derision, O wise men of Babylon !
Ye are curs'd, and your glory a dung-hill.
The vision is deep that disturbs the king's sleep ;
But unto Daniel the Lord doth reveal
The Time and the times of His Will.

Jah give thee reprief, thou Presidents' chief ;
And with thee the furnace-tried three ;
The Ancient of Days shall shield thee always ;
From the heel of the priest, and tooth of the beast,
And show thee the things that shall be.

THE PLEROMA.

By Chebar's stream the Couriers next announce
Whom Hebrew captives name Ezekiel—
The priest and Buzi's son. Out of the North
The Eden Cherubim descend on wheels
Of Beryl, bearing Names effulgent with
Their imag'ries. The cloud of amber rifts,
Showing the Man—Jahveh—upon a throne
Of glory. Speed thy Goal eternal now !
The mystic roll be honey in thy belly ;
Speak—speak, for I have set thee for a watch
To Israel ; " Diblath," until they know
That Jah alone is God.

THE ANGELS.

Jahveh hath said and will fulfil ;
Will take of the eminent tree ;
From the uppermost branch will He crop ;
Scind a delicate Twig from its top,
And plant on the height of Israel.
It shall send forth boughs and bear full fruit ;
It shall shelter all manner of fowl and brute ;
And a Virgin guard the Mystery.

GAIA.

O Sun and Sire of Heaven !
Gaia weeps ; and her bosom is wet with tears ;

The storm-cloud hides thy form,
O king ; and I falter to tell my fears.

Thou drawest near, O Sun !
Thy breath is soft, thou wilt hearken my cry !
Gaia bleedeth for her sons ;
Ransom, and loose thy children ere they die !

" I come " thou sayest, O Light !
" I will surely My offspring then redeem."
I dry my tears and wait,
O king ; while Thy Advent shall be my theme.

LIMITS.

Ethnic orbits bending, rending boundaries ;
In our balances weighing destinies ;
Medo-Persia choosing, fusing ;
Calling fatal numbers Chaldea atones.
" Cyrus " conqueror naming, flaming as we rise,
Hov'ring over Israel warm with our surmise.

CYRUS.

Behold to Cyrus the kingdoms of Earth
Hath JAHVEH, God of the Hebrews, given ;
And now commandeth his servant, the king,
To build a house unto the God of Israel,
In Judah, that is, in Jerusalem.
Who chooseth from His people, go ye up,
Strengthen'd with gifts willingly offered.

THE CIRCLES.

The people of JAHVEH return :

THE BANDS.

With zeal for his Righteousness ;

THE CIRCLES.

The false *aleim* they spurn ;

THE BANDS.

One only, JEHOVAH, they bless.

THE CIRCLES.

O Sabbath of Eden, how long ?

THE COURIERS.

Till cometh Messiah, the Lord :

THE BANDS.

The altar is kindled ; blest throng !
The Infinite One is adored.

THE ANGELS.

Wing the message to the skies ;
Part the blazing canopies ;
Seraphs swing the pearly gates,
For the Earth her LORD awaits !

" He shall send forth His Son, the Branch ;
Zion's temple to rebuild ;
Judah teach His covenants ;
All the Earth with glory filled."

THE DEMONS.

Fur-fur on yon butterflies !
Dust the dandruff in their eyes !
Sprinkle gold-dust ; gild with praise !
Angels have such conscious ways !

Have the Cutheans no lot ?
Hath Samaria no plot ?
Shimshai up ! up, O Rehum !
For the Jews rebuild Salem !

Sic, sicutque, Nehemiah ;
Haggai and Zechariah ;
Last and least poor Malachi
Chirps his cheery prophecy.

SATAN.

The Citron tree and orange are in bloom ;
The vales green upwards into life ; the fields,
Water'd by showers, welcome daisy bands :
Fair Land of Promise, greet we once again !

Ho, Prince of Canaan, hither ! Thrift ! Thrift !
Your master cometh, Baal of earth and sky.
Here build our throne aloft, upon this hill,
Once Limits gave the damnèd Jahvite horde.

No prophet pipes within Jehovah's town !
Erudite Ezra drops his finish'd scroll,
And sleeps unwept within his hollow'd vault ;
This temple is a shadow to the first ;
Nor ark, nor mercy-seat, nor candlestick,
Nor glory-cloud ! well may the grandsires weep.

Arouse thyself—O god of Canaan !
When thou hast read this autographic card,
Inscribèd by Mights and Excellences
The loyal world ; if thou thrill not thereat,
By Zeus I will dethrone thee ! Why star'st thus ?

Gazing like adamant !   Anile awake !
By heav'n, and art thou dead ? a witless shuck ?
I 'll prick thee, and thereto shall witness hell
If thou 'st a pith of sense.   Devils, demons !
Marvel !   If ye have known like circumstance
In these Jahvitic bounds, say ye ! say ye !

THE DEMONS.

Molech dead ?
Molech dread !
Pardi, do devils die ?
Dare we mutter ?
Shall we utter
The ghastly prophecy ?

Lo Gaia sigheth,
In birth-pains crieth.
Perdu, when Christ is born !
Curse thou and canker ;
Nursing thy rancor ;
Satan, we thee forewarn.

THE ÆONS.

The Circles weave the Eden-ring,
And seal Messiah—Heav'n-born king ;
The Couriers fly through distant lands,
And rays of hope gleam from the Bands.
The Persian sage drinks deep of heaven ;
The exiled Jew receives the leaven ;
Hellenic wisdom, magian lore,
The gifted Jahvites now explore.
Write, sisters, write the End of Days !

The woe of Judah, and amaze
Of horror ; for the Holy Shrine
Is reeking with the blood of swine !
Thence *phallic* reels of Dionysius ;
And Baal's orgies blasphemous ;
The direful edicts; dismantled gates,
And gore of myriads Syria sates.

The Glory of Modin.

How is the valiant fallen that delivered Israel !
In the hour of triumph he fell at Eleasa :
In Mizpeh fasted he and prayed with his six hundred ;
And JAHVEH gave him heart to meet an armèd host.
Apollonius and Seron, leaders of renown, were dis-
    mayed ;
They saw their armies melt as doth a cloud away :
Nicanor and Georgias likewise fled for safety ;
They showed their elephants the blood of grapes in vain ;
Their towers are empty and their heroes are no more.

Then Judah sang the song of victory returning home :
But in that hour the pride of Modin fell,—the son of
    Mattathias.
In the sepulchre of his father his brothers buried him ;
And all the people cry, " How is the valiant fallen."

THE PLEROMA.

The Æons write the Maccabæan rule,
And number now but five and threescore years
Unto the Age of ages.   The runes they read
Are short and trist.   Lo, JAHVEH's adversaries
Stalk in the very Holies, and profane
Its awful secrets.   And victorious Rome,

The world's empress, (whilst fratricidal strife
Suffers a lurid death), bestoweth crowns
To those whose gifts weigh most upon her scales ;
Hence alien rulers sit in David's seat,
And alien priests Aaron's blessing invoke.

LUCIFER (SATAN).

Insatiate flame of pride and thirst of power,
That drinks the essence of our being up !
The Baal of *baalim !* mighty Zeus of gods !
The Prince of potentates ! What more, O Star ?
" Dost Haman scorn another Mordecai ?
O Spirit of the Air ; behold thy seat
Transcends Zion as heaven doth the earth—
Thy glory rolls along the Aonian height,
And bursts in thunders from Olympus' breast.
Thou art the core of ethnic faiths—the crest
Of Greek and Roman pantheons—the Might
That battled down the world, welding in one
Colossal state the peoples of the earth."

Truth, voice ! Thou answer'st well ; but not to cheer
Thy words are chosen.   Vain, in vain ! For whilst
These boastful Jahvites sing Messiah-Psalms,
And the eternal lamp burns in JAH's Shrine,
Nor mighty Cæsar's triumphs ; Julian-codes ;
Nor closèd Janus ; commerce, letters, arts ;
Nor one world-speech, nor one wide commonwealth—
Avails to lift these brows of ours, that lower
With dark uncompromising hate upon
Judea and its God.

PLEROMA ELEGANS.

CANTO VII.

THE MAN.

THE ARGUMENT.

THE EVANGEL.

The birth of the Immanuel was on this wise :
When as, in days of Issacher, High Priest,
The virgin daughter of one, Joachim,
According to the custom of the Jews,
Was solemnly betrothèd to Joseph—
A man of good report, prudent and just,—
Before he took her as a husband home,
And knew her as his wife, she was with child,
Already of the Holy Ghost.   Now when
Joseph was minded privily to hide
Her shame, the Angel of the Lord appear'd,
And told him of the Mystery ; how that
The thing conceivèd in her womb, none was
But the *Messiah-Immanuel.*   Wherefore
The blameless Maid he cherish'd sacredly
As Mother of Jahveh *The Christ*, and Bride
Of God.

THE ANGELS.

She hies to the dell, O lily-fair !
  And dips the rosemary in the spring ;
Entwines therewith a wreath with care,
And binds it to her flowing hair ;
  And as she binds, doth softly sing :

    " If he loves me, it is well ;
  I will reverence, and fulfil
    The vow of this young heart :
  Faithfully will serve his years,
  Share his blessings and his fears,
    Till death the bond do part."

The cloister'd shade 's the Maiden's bower ;
    She bathes her brow in the thymy brook ;
The queen of lilies !   A spotless flower !
That, lotus-like, divines her hour !
    Thou pure one, angels vie thy look !

Gaze not where sleeps, with snow-white breast,
    A form so fair, the Airs are awed !
Hail, Gabriel ! fill thy behest !
By yonder spring thou find'st the Blest
    Of maidens, and the Bride of God !

THE VIRGIN.

In my dream there woo'd me One,
O so glorious, like the sun !
    And my soul a rapture felt, unknown ;
I awake with nerveless dread,
Lest a bride I shall be led,
    And this heart its secret do atone :

For the guileless love of a dream,
And its fancies that only seem ;—
    Aye, for this I vail a blushing face ;
While I gird me to haste away,
Though more loth to go than stay.
    Lo, the bright ones hover o'er this place !

GAIA.

In my grief I cried unto the King,
    So bereavèd by Death and the Grave ;
In my anguish entreated and prayed
    Him to come and his children to save.

I am fill'd with unspeakable bliss,
  And resign'd to the ills that I bear.
He hath heard my complaint, dried my tears ;
  And I bide now his mercy so near.

THE ETHERS.

Melody in speech, therein do we teach
  To men the law divine of love ;
Discords in our songs loudly speak of wrongs
  Against the Majesties above.

Star of stars, the blest ? God is here confess'd,
  Whose promise stirs thy inmost sphere ;
Cosmic fervors list ; Bands and Couriers tryst ;
  And sing Messiah's Advent near.

THE PLEROMA.

The Mights, ethereal, sing the Age at hand !
And Gaia fain would tell mankind of signs
That cheer her troubled heart and smooth her brow.
The hoary Æons close their full-writ scrolls,
Laying them lowly at the Father's feet :
Next, sit them down, meantime the Holy Names,
By God's command, review the Sacred Books.

The Majesties of Heav'n heed every line,
And mirror in their faces fact by fact ;
The six creative days and Eden's rest ;
The fraud of Lucifer and human guilt ;
The woman's SEED,—the Serpent's destin'd foe ;
The altars of JAHVEH and cults abhorr'd
Of true ALEIM ; the flood and Abram's call ;
The Messianic line—Egypt—Sinai—

The Jehovistic wars ; the Judges' rule ;
The Theocratic State, and kingly race ;
The harp of David and the House he plann'd—
The splendors of his son, envied of kings ;
The schism and priestly craft ; the empire lost ;
The seventy years retrieve in Babylon,
Till God in mercy brought a remnant back
To build Jerusalem, and JAHVEH's Shrine.
Thence centuries apocryphal that hide
The Messianic plan until the Time.

Read thus the Names the last page of the scroll ;
And pause before the multitudinous shout
Of, " Glory, Power, and Blessing to JAHVEH,
That Was and Is, and Is to Come !   Amen ! "

The FATHER hears, and bows in blissful pain,
While LOVE springs dove-like—from His breast, to fly
To Earth to do His will vicarious.
Hail, Heart of God !   Descend and fill the Earth !
Creation mourneth Thy delay, and stands
With girded thighs gazing into the sky.

THE EVANGEL.

In days of Herod, king, there was a priest
Nam'd Zacharias, of Abia's course ;
Whose wife was also of the Aaronic line.
Most righteous were they both before the Lord,
But childless, for Elisabeth was barren.
Now when, in monthly course, he incense burn'd,
The Angel of the Lord to him appeared ;
And on the right side of the altar stood.

19

GABRIEL.

Fear not, O Zacharias, thy pray'r is heard ;
Elisabeth, thy wife, shall bear a son,
And thou shalt call him John, the Gift of God.
Increase of joy and gladness thou shalt have,
And many come rejoicing at his birth.
He shall be truly great before JAHVEH ;
Fill'd with the Holy Spirit from the womb.
Full many shall he turn in Israel
Unto the Lord—going before Him in
The Spirit of Elias and in might ;
To turn the hearts of fathers to their sons ;
The disobedient into Wisdom's way,—
And thus prepare a people for Messiah.

ZACHARIAS.

Whereby shall I know this ? For I am old,
And my wife also stricken well with days.

GABRIEL.

Know thou that I who here speak unto thee
Am Gabriel, and stand before the Lord ;
I come imparting these tidings to thee ;
In sign whereof thou shalt be straightway dumb,
Until the day these things shall be perform'd ;
For that thou stumbled at my words, which must
In time, duly appointed, be fulfilled.

THE COURIERS.

We are nearing the Solar Name ;
We are tasting the central Flame,
　　Where all lights and glories meet,
　　And Creation is complete
　　　In the JAHVEH-Christ.

Whilst the Angel Gabriel flies
On redeeming embassies ;
  And the womb of the barren wife
  Is fertile with throbbing life
    Of the Messenger of Christ.

Whilst the Spirit sits as a dove
In the bosom swelling with love,
  For the Form in the vision seen,
  With the mild and kingly mien
    Of the JAHVEH-Christ.

ELISABETH.

The Lord hath taken my reproach away ;
Israel henceforth shall call me Blest ;
In the hidings of my heart, O JAHVEH-Christ ;
In the secret place Thou art address'd.

  Thine Angel guide me to the Holy Maid,
    Elect, the mother of my Lord ;
  The Gift of God inspires my prayer—
    Thy handmaid waits upon Thy Word.

THE EVANGEL.

And in the sixth month also came from God
The Angel Gabriel to Nazareth,
Unto the virgin-bride of one call'd Joseph.

GABRIEL TO THE VIRGIN.

Hail, highly favor'd ! thy God saluteth thee !
Blessèd art thou among Zion's daughters !
Fear not, thou hast found favor with the Lord ;
Behold, thou shalt conceive and bear a Son,

Whose name shall be JESUS, Immanuel ;
He shall be great, renown'd Son of the Highest,
Who giveth Him to sit upon the throne
Of his ancestor David ; and to reign
Over the house of Jacob evermore.
And of His Kingdom there shall be no end.

THE VIRGIN.

How shall this be, seeing I am a virgin ?

GABRIEL.

The Holy Spirit shall on thee descend,
The Power of the Highest o'ershadowing :
Wherefore That which is to be born of thee
Shall be call'd Holy—Son of God.
                        Moreover,
Elisabeth, thy cousin, hath conceiv'd a son
In her old age ; and this is the sixth month
With her who is call'd barren.   For, know thou,
With God nothing shall be impossible.

THE VIRGIN.

Behold the handmaid of the Lord ;
Be it according to Thy word !

THE PLEROMA.

The Heavenly Bird hath woo'd the Virgin's heart,
Who yields herself a vessel for the Lord.
O meek, and matchless Maid ! O Bride of God !
PLEROMA filleth thee with guileless love—
The aspiration, the capacity—
Whereby a Hebrew maid, a lowly child
Of the lost race, the vehicle becomes

Of JAHVEH-Christ—marvel of miracles !
And shall be call'd The Blest, The Bride of God.

Now hath Our *Fulness*, immanent in Time,
The promise of the first creation fill'd :
See Nature upward turning to the sky,
To list the footsteps of its Creator !
Vailing Our Glories, and low bending down,
We pass the open door into the Earth.
Farewell Eternal Father ! We descend :
So hast Thou will'd, ere Earth or man became ;
Thou know'st the Way, the Sacrifice, the End.
Turn back ye splendors of the Heavenly Throne !
The Son of God shall be the Son of Man ;
The Timeless find and feel the bounds of Time ;
The Spaceless One shall tabernacle Space ;
The Increate be of a Virgin born ;—
The Godhead bodily reveal'd to men.

THE VIRGIN.

If a dream, 't was most wonderful dream !
Oh, the bliss of that swoon, as the gleam
  Of the Holy One enter'd my breast ;
But if true, 't is unspeakably true !
Answer, heart ! Dost thou murmur or rue
  The words thou didst speak to thy Guest !

What I saw I may never reveal ;
What I felt mortal never shall feel ;
  As the Glory pass'd into my bosom !
And it seem'd in the translucent light,
Ere the Marvel had faded to sight,
  That a Deity Man had become.

The King of the Ethers.

The King of the Ethers came wooing our Star,
In His chariot of flame, with His locks streaming far ;
He whisper'd of Worship and Honor and Might,
And a Crown in His Kingdom unfading and bright.

Our Star lov'd the Prince of the radiant air ;
And holily yielded Him offspring to bear ;
The Sun and the Star embrac'd in the morn ;
And the Child of the Highest to Gaia is born.

The Passing of the Pleroma.

The solar splendors dull and fade ;
The Dove nests with the lowly Maid ;
O matchless grace ! O truth display'd
    At the Passing of PLEROMA.

Creation pauses to adore ;
This pensive Star is hush'd before
The Light of the World, and the open Door,
    At the Passing of PLEROMA.

Increate Son ! Thou 'st chosen the Way ?
And humbling Thee, resignest Thy sway.
O Grace, and Truth ! O blessed Day !
    At the Passing of PLEROMA.

Who knoweth the end of the dying age ?
Who raiseth him up to view the stage,
When JAHVEH-Christ shall turn the Page
    At the Passing of PLEROMA ?

THE EVANGEL.

Then Mary, the Virgin, arose in haste,
And went into the hill-country of Juda ;
And, entering the house of Zacharias,
Saluted her cousin Elisabeth.
And lo, it came to pass that, when she heard
The salutation of the Virgin-bride,
The babe leap'd in her womb ; and she was fill'd
With the Holy Spirit, and did prophesy :

"Blessèd art thou of the daughters of David !
And blessèd the Fruit of thy Womb ! And whence
Is 't that the Mother of my Lord should come
To me?"

THE VIRGIN.

My soul doth magnify the Lord,
And my spirit rejoice in God my Saviour ;
For He hath regarded the low estate
Of His handmaid ; all generations me
From henceforth shall the Blest of mothers call.

THE EVANGEL.

Elisabeth, in time, brought forth a son ;
And neighbors gather'd to rejoice with her ;
Who call'd him "Zacharias" from his father.
But she said, "Nay ! for John shall be his name."
Then made they signs, his father being dumb—
Who on a tablet wrote, "His name is John."
Thereat immediately his tongue was loos'd ;
And he was fillèd with the Holy Ghost.
Then fear fell on all that dwelt round about,
Who marvel'd much what sort of child this was.

And the lad grew, in spirit waxing strong ;
And was in the deserts until the day
Of his appearing unto Israel.

The Lay of the Lights.

The Lay of the Lights Messianic, from Eden—
From the mother of men, to the Mother of God ;
From the Tree of the fall, to the Tree of Salvation ;
From *Aleim*-JAHVEH, to JAHVEH the *Christ.*

Sing the answering flame on the altar of Abel ;
And the savor of blood with his sin-offering ;
The *renaissance* of the true faith in Enos,
And the eight *Jahvites* saved at the deluge by Noah.
Sing the faith of the father of Isaac and Jacob ;
And the patriarch line with its fortunes in Egypt.
The Exodus sing of the *Jahvites* from bondage ;
The Levitic rites so replete with their shadows.
Tell the mystical sense of the shew-bread and incense ;
The ark and the altar and candlestick golden ;
The oil of anointing, and robes of the priesthood ;
The Glory that cover'd the Seat of Atonement ;
The Cloud that stood over the Tent of the Presence.

Sing the titles denominating the Messiah—
The Angel of God, and the Star out of Jacob ;
The Sceptre of Judah, and Shepherd of Israel ;
The Child of a Virgin—Redeemer, Immanuel—
The Plant of Renown, and Desire of the Nations—
The Mighty to Save,—the Saviour—JEHOVAH !

Sing times in the life of the JAHVEH-*Messiah :*
Whose birth is set down in the Book of Decrees !

To be of a Virgin in Bethlehem, Ephratah,
Whom Kings and the great shall haste to adore.
Sing the tears of sad Rachel, the call out of Egypt ;
And lastly, the Cry of the Messenger Prophet.

A VOICE.

The august Cæsar hath decreed the orb
Of the wide Roman world shall be assess'd :
Whose will, Cyrenius, the governor
Of Syria, with strict subservience heeds ;
Commanding to enroll each in his place.
Then Joseph with the Virgin, being great
With child,—scions of the prophetic line—
Sought cautiously and slow their way unto
The city where their lineage was call'd.
And so it was, that as they tarried ; the day
Was fully come when she should be delivered
Of her first-born.

The Ode of the Æons.

Great PAN is dead !   The power is sped
    Of pythoness and fable ;
The world is ill, and fain would still
    Its griefs ; but is not able.
Dark Egypt's bird, by rumor heard,
    Hath turn'd again to ashes ;
While omens make the nations quake ;
    And night is bright with flashes.
What dooms the mind of humankind ?
    And drives the world to madness ?
Who checks its grief, and brings relief,
    Exchanging joy for sadness ?

Sing, Æons sing, while ushering
　　The Day-spring from on high ;
Depart, O night !   Enter, O Light !
　　Son of Eternity !

The Nemesis of Unbelief.

" *The gods are dead,*" the Cynic cried,
And chided with his jewel'd bride,
　　Before he went away :
" *The gods are dead,*" alone, she mus'd :
" Why then must pleasure be refus'd ?
　　Lovers shall have their day."

From myrrhine vases incense rose ;
The cloister'd mirror dimly shows
　　Lovers in amorous play :
" Hither, sweet boy, and view my pearls !
Prythee to braid them with these curls !
　　And bide with me the day."

" *The gods are dead?*" the Cynic cried,
" Who taught men so, hath foully lied !
　　O Heaven, retrieve my loss !
Bring, bring me back my jewel'd wife !
Fair as a star, dearer than life !
　　And I will bear my cross !"

The Satirist of Rome.

Thy skirts are rank with wantonness ;
　　Thy gems are dyed with lust ;
Debauchery and avarice
　　Fill thee with huge disgust.

Thy bloody jousts fail to appease
  The harden'd populace ;
Banquet, nor bath, bid clamor cease,
  But add to thy disgrace.
On damask cushions gluttons lie,
  Mopping their gouty lips ;
While hollow hunger, with a sigh,
  In vice still deeper dips.

Abnormal wickedness is rife ;
  Nature suffers abuse ;
Thy nobles love, but lead no wife ;
  And marriage vows refuse.
Millions of slaves possess no right
  Their masters shall respect ;
And libertines find their delight
  In licenses uncheck'd.
The Stoic dotes on suicide ;
  The Epicure on pleasure ;
The Sophist knoweth to decide
  The less the greater measure.

Ill-gotten gains control the vote,
  Of senator and lictor ;
And bards, to earn a paltry groat,
  Do celebrate a victor.
The supple Greek infests thy walks,—
  Wizard of many arts ;
Full soon his puny pupil stalks,
  To gorgonize the marts.
In hopeless fatalism mired,
  On Death thy wisest wait ;
Whilst wanton priestesses are hired
  To sanctify the state.

Herod or Remorse.

In the glare of thine agony, dread Idumean,
   Thy ghastliest victims we see ;
In horrors of madness call'st thou in vain,
   For thy murder'd Mariamne.
Lo, her two sons come back again reft of the tomb,
   And stalk through thy chambers by night ;
And the dread child of Doris delivers the doom
   Of Herod, the dread Edomite.
In servile prostration the proud signet-ring
   Of the Consular power dost thou kiss,
While patriot thousands to ruin dost fling,
   And meetest their cries with a hiss.
Know then, O dread, O doom'd Edomite !
   Thy rage and thy scorn of the *Christ*,
Do hasten the Hope of the hated *Jahvite*,
   And the birth of the King thou defiest.

GABRIEL.

Thy time is accomplish'd, O Bride of the Spirit !
   The Seed of the Virgin is *Jahveh*, the MAN !
The pulse of this Star is quick with attention—
   The face of Creation is anxious and wan.

Hail, angels, expectant of Jesus the Saviour !
   Break forth with your pæans of blessing to earth !
Rejoice with the Ages ! and joy with the Heavens !
   For now is the Advent and Hour of His birth !

THE EVANGEL.

On the wintry hills abiding, shepherds watch'd their
   flocks by night,
When the Angel of the Highest aw'd them with his glory
   bright.

"Fear not," said he, "for I bring you joyous tidings of
    the morn ;
Lo in Bethlehem, David's city, JAHVEH-Christ this day is
    born."
Sought with haste the faithful shepherds where the
    young child lay ;
Then, returning, sang God's glory and His Christ-
    JAHVEH.

THE CHORUS OF ETHERS.

Fairily, airily ;
Cheerily, merrily,
    The circling Ethers fly ;
Pearling, curling ;
Whirling, swirling,
    The chorus passeth by.

Light'ning, bright'ning ;
Splendidly hight'ning
    The lustre of the Morn ;
Lowering, showering ;
Holily embowering
    The place where Christ is born.

Singing, ringing ;
Swinging, clinging,
    The Bands and Couriers meet ;
Flowing, glowing ;
Lovingly throwing
    Their blessings at His feet.

Ever linking, never shrinking,
    The Bands salute their Lord ;
Ever streaming, never dreaming,
    The Couriers wait His word.

The Kenosis.

O sages of the Earth, how marvel ye alway,
The Goal of the Creation—the birth of the JAHVEH !
The hiding of the WORD within a tender Babe,
The Glory-Unbegott'n in mortal guise display'd.
Hail, Holy One of Heav'n, nursing a Virgin's breast !
Cradled upon her arm, protected and caress'd !
Hail, timeless One, Earth-born, and circumscrib'd in
    Time !
Hail, spaceless One, despising not Earth's bound and
    clime !
Hail, self-existent One, humbled in servanthood !
With Plenitude of Power, calling for daily food.
Hail, King Divine ; That wast and ever art the Lord !
All glory be to Thee, in Heav'n and Earth adored !
Thou shalt inform our minds and lift from us the vail :
Unseal dark mysteries, when human wisdom fail.
Thou FULNESS—the PLEROMA—bodily express'd ;—
JESUS, Child of Mary, art God and Man confess'd !

THE DEMONS.

Hie, Hie, travel slyly !
What ye do, do ye wily !
    Doom is near ;
    And we fear
      The demon's hour is brief.
Hist, Hist, travel slowly !
Treading nigh, treading lowly ;
    For JAHVEH 'S
    Born to-day,
      And Earth sighs her relief.

Truck, Truck, demons imping !
Dowdy Prince, thou art primping,
    While we smite
    The *Jahvite*
      With dreaded maladies.
Go, Go, Essene spirit !
Solitude bids thee to cheer it
    Though thou mope,
    Give us rope !
      We 'll bind the *Jahvite's* knees.

SATAN.

Aha, grim fiend ! son of the Edomite !
I'll trick thee, Herod, ere thou die the death !
Fairly I've won the porridge of thy dish,
Which now I taste again gulping its froth.
Imbruited ghoul !   Incarnate prince of ill !
To thy red hands I clasp and bind my will.
Thou hast a deal of savage pluck to use
The two-edg'd blade—the poison and the rack !
Oho, a chunk of fuming funk art thou !
And the Messiah-Child shall be the spark
That lighteth thee, and kindleth deadly rage !

Wherefore I loiter, for a space, among
These hills, aloof the scene of Bethlehem :

Down cursèd Fear ! that looms before my soul !
Phantasmal shadow of myself ! away ! begone !
This wrongèd Lucifer shall sleep no more
Till he hath rid this star of the Messiah.

The will that moves the world is an engine
Which shakes, perforce, its massy edifice ;
Know then, O soul, this perturbating breast
Moveth the ruling passions of mankind—
Lust, avarice, and power : so doth the tumult
  Of our will report its awful force.

The Song of the Stars.

The Song of the Stars,—the wondering stars !
The listening, glistening, diamond stars ;
    While the blithe, blue Air
    Calls everywhere ;
    To the hills and vales ;
    To the glades and dales :
" List, list, the Song of the wondering Stars ! "

The Shout of the Stars,—the numberless stars !
A glorified host with light-wingèd cars !
    While the blithe, blue Air
    Calls everywhere ;
    Heralding far
    The " Son of a Star ! "—
The antiphone of the wondering Stars !

The Sigh of the Stars,—the increate stars !
The wistful, mystical, soulful stars !
    While the blithe, blue Air,
    Calls everywhere,
    " Behold Judea's STAR !—
    Flashing his beams afar !
    In his *trigon* of tears,
    A sceptre he bears,
And the fadeless crown of the increate Stars ! "

THE MAGI.

We worship Thee, Star of stars !
Thy *trigon* is full in Mars !
   Judea's hour impends ;
   Ormuzd his Prophet sends,
     Born of a maid.
The Prince of Light comes to redeem !
In Ophiuchus brightly gleam
   His signatures ! Yon Star
   Of Hope—the Magi seek afar—
     Balaam portray'd.

THE DEMONS.

Here 's an astrologic bit,
Worthy of a demon's wit ;
Tie it with a willow withe !
Label—*A Chaldean Myth*—
Casting his nativity
Under Jove and Mercury.
Heigho, heigho, " *Cunning* "
Read we plainly running.
Heigho, heigho, " *Power* "
Lasting but an hour.
Cast we, cast we and carouse ;
His Zodiac 's a *cadent house !*

SATAN.

Unearthly and mysterious change hath pass'd
Upon this Star ! The skies conceal it not,
Nor soughing seas so hoarsely muttering ;
Nor massy mounts, deep-chested, echoing.
The ever-sighing groves make melody,

20

While fleecy flocks upon the hills answer
Their minstrelsy.
               (Eyes, are ye not for seeing?
And ears, for hearing?   No *mumbo-jumbo* spell 's
On you!   What Satan sees, let him not fear to see!
And what he hears, let him not fear to hear!
If false unto all others, then more true
Be thou unto thyself.)
                   This drowsy world
Dops at the sun, and knows not why.   Ha! Ha!
The foot of *Ophiuchus* blazes forth
The fact portentous of Messiah's birth—
Disastrous sign to Lucifer, except
He captive take both *sign* and *Signified!*

VOICES.

Creation groaneth, travailing in pain.

SATAN.

Now is the stage too slender for the act!
The cast is fully call'd.   Satan doth prompt!
On with the buskins!   Play no pantomime!
Meet plot with counter-plot!   Slay, or be slain!
The *Chasidim* do barter now thy crown away;
The poisoners skulk in thy palaces;
While Envy is unsex'd to do thee wrong.
Bravo, thy splendid *coup* of caution shall
Amaze the fallen chiefs.   On with the act!

THE DEMONS.

Herod is mock'd!
The Magians stalk'd and stole away.
Drink, drink the broth!
For by its froth ye curse JAHVEH!

GABRIEL.

Arise, Joseph !   Arise and take the babe,
And Virgin, and flee with haste to Egypt !
And be thou there until I bring thee word ;
For Herod seeks the young Child to destroy.

Rama.

Ah, mournful town of Bethlehem !   In thee
The voice of Rama lives again !   In thee
The Rachels weep their infants slain !   In thee
They sob their tragic tale heard tearfully !

SATAN.

Methought in sooth to nip the " Root of David "
In the bud ; and thereto did incite the mind
Of the foreboding, jealous king, to slay
The infants in Judea's little town ;
And so destroy the " KING " of the *Jahvites.*
But cursèd finitude !   What boots our craft !
For ere the innocents are stiff in death,
Do we behold a sight to freeze the gall !—
For, nearing Rhinoklura's purple brook,
In a *mirage*, appears the pious Joseph,
The Virgin and her Child, attended by
Great Michael, prince of the angelic hosts.

By Jove !   And is it the Messiah's plan
To use the military of the skies
Against the lawful Archon of this Star ?

Him to degrade and bind in triumph's chains ?
Ye Mights above ! (no longer God the " Good "
But Mights of Air implacable and merciless)
If 't come to this ; before that hour, shall we
Our right prescriptive yield the JAHVEH-King :
Since Might 's the conscience of the Eternal,
Might maketh Right for angels and for men !
'T is clear, 't is very clear, (angels may nod
Assent)—such is the Ethic of Salvation—
The Babe of Bethlehem lives *because he lives*—
And Satan is proscrib'd and doom'd *because
He is !*　To question, or to reason 's " *Sin* ";
And " *Sin* " *is Death because it pleases* MIGHT
To make it so.　Then may we trust, some day,
When *Might* makes *Must,* and *Must makes us obey,*
To be a ransom'd Cherub up in Heav'n,
And sing our lullaby among the saints.
'T will be the heart of magnanimity
In us—the lord of this fair Star—to name
The " SON OF GOD " our heir !　This will we do,
When MIGHT compels, though tardily ; and earn
Thereby a seat superior the Christ.

GABRIEL.

Arise, Joseph, the Babe and mother take,
And go into the land of Israel !
For they are dead which sought the young Child's life.

THE ANGELS.

He heedeth the dream, and turneth aside,
　Going again to Galilee ;
The faithful Scroll is now our guide,
　Since He " A Nazarene shall be."

THE EVANGEL.

And the Child grew and wax'd in spirit strong ;
Fillèd with wisdom ; and the grace of God
Was upon Him.

The Doxa in the Christ-Child.

The GLORY of PLEROMA shines within the Vail—
The Virgin lifts the awful screen, and cries, " All hail,
My Lord and Saviour ! "   Then reverences the sleeping
    God.
Awak'd, she wraps Him in the mantle of her heart's
Maternal care ; whilst to no mortal she imparts
The manner of His birth, nor Gabriel's secret word.
She greets with pride each effort of His lisping tongue ;
Recalls the shepherd's tale, and song by Angels sung ;
Opens once more the treasures which the Gentiles
    brought ;
And marvels much the blessing God in her had wrought.
Again she hears the prophecy of Simeon,
And pondereth the " sword " to pierce through her own
    soul :
The ecstasy of Anna—prophetess, divines anon ;
While mists of glory seem about her Babe to roll.
The secrets hid within her heart daily augment ;
As the Divine in Jesus with the earthly blent,
Together grow into the perfect form of Youth ;
Endued in the PLEROMA with all Grace and Truth.

Nazareth.

In the emerald circle of Galilee dwelleth the Boy Divine ;
Like a brooch of pearls the whiten'd roofs of the village
    shine ;

From the breezy top of the thymy hill, descries the Com-
    ing Man
The eagle poised in the cloudless blue, and the flight of
    the pelican.
The Zephyrs brush from His brow away the softly silken
    hair—
While His ruddy lips are skyward turn'd to kiss the
    scented air.
First, to the North, His wondrous eyes, o'er wood-crown'd
    Napthali,
See mighty Hermon's crystal dome, gleaming eternally.
The terebinths of Tabor green, absorb the Eastward view;
Whence purple Carmel draws His gaze unto the mirror'd
    blue,
Where bird-like sails of Chittim's ships glance in the set-
    ting sun.
At length He looks along the plain of storied Esdraelon,
And traces far the winding road unto the city of JAHVEH—
But His brow is pale, and His eyes are moist, as He turns
    away.

THE EVANGEL.

He said to them,—" How is 't that ye sought me ?
Wist not to find me in my FATHER's House ? "
But they knew not His words and marvell'd much ;
Then went Jesus with them to Nazareth,
And was submissive unto them ; growing
In Wisdom as in age ; and in favor
With God and Man.

The Tephillim.

How happily, holily, rear'd is He !
The flower of the youth of Galilee !

His stature now makes Him a " Son of the Law,"
And to-day shall He see what never He saw—
Vast porches of marble, and turrets of gold :—
The shrine of JEHOVAH ordainèd of old ;
To-day are the *Tephillim* seal'd to His brow,
While the girdle of youth shall further allow
To offer His gifts, and to worship alone ;—
Absolv'd from His kin to the Infinite One.
Access to the circle of Hillel He gains,
Where lost in emotion the day-long remains.

THE ANGELS.

O Shrine of loves !   O Soul of smiles !
O Seat of bliss, whence luminous aisles
      Stretch to the portals of yon star.
Lo, 't is a mead of infinite joy,
To see the holy, heaven-born, Boy
      Greeting the Father from afar !
O Lustre of lustres that hide the morn !
O Child of the Highest to Gaia born !
      Thou findest Thy Father to-day !
And the Angel-world is thrill'd to pain,
To see PLEROMA'S Face again,
      In the face of the *Christ*-JAHVEH.

THE PLEROMA-CHRIST.

Here hath My Mother made the secret mine !
To Joseph known and her alone of Earth !
A " Virgin's child ! " " JESUS "—" IMMANUEL ! "
By Gabriel nam'd, conceiv'd in mystery !
Spirit Divine !—the Soul of souls ! to Thee

I flee to stay the mighty tide of joy !
Else shall this mortal frame dissolve in bliss !

O Father ! O Father ! O Infinite Father !
By the Face in My visions I know Thee, O Father !
By the cheer of the Angels that witness this moment ;
By the Self-revelation of the PLEROMA !
By the rapture of spirit and benison holy !
By the sighs Thou allayest I know Thee, O Father !
By the loneliness lost in Thy sovereign Presence !
By the answer Thou givest My heart's burning question !
By the yearning I feel for the work of a Saviour ;
Whilst, Father Eternal, I press on Thy heart.

THE ÆONS.

Where, O where is the Messiah ?
Ages crying, " Where, O where ? "
Gaia yearning, mourning, mourning ;
Millions sighing, millions crying,
" Where, O where is the Messiah ? "

To His Temple cometh JAHVEH,
Fill'd and filling all with glory ;
Heareth millions praying, saying,
With the Law and Prophets saying,
" Where, O where is the Messiah ? "

THE ANTIPHON.

Hid, though conscious of His mission ;
Hears the sick world calling, calling—
Æons of the Æons calling,
" Where, O where is the Messiah ? "

Meekly beareth low condition,
Carpenter in Nazareth,
Till the PLEROMA unvaileth
    God in the Messiah.

THE ETHERS.

Hail Him! Hail Him! cosmic chorus!
Lo, Messiah reigneth o'er us!
    And PLEROMA gloweth, gloweth;
    And the face of Jesus showeth
        Him to be Divine.

Circles sing their Cycle ended;
Limits sing of strife suspended;
    Bands announce the BAND perfected;
    Couriers hail the ONE expected,
        And bless the Man Divine!

*   *   *   *   *

Now the lonely prophet crieth,
And the pride of man defieth,
    "Repent ye every one!"
See Judea's thousands pressing;
And their sins humbly confessing
    In the sacred Jordan.

THE EVANGEL.

Then cometh Jesus also unto John
To be baptiz'd of him in the Jordan:
But he forbade Him, saying to Him, "Nay!
For I have need to be baptiz'd of Thee!"
Then Jesus answer'd, "Suffer it so now—
'T is meet for Me to do all righteousness."

Then sufferèd he Him :
And lo the heavens open'd unto him,
And he beheld the Spirit like a dove,
Descending upon Him ; and heard a voice,
" Thou art My well-belovèd Son, in Whom
I am well pleased."

GAIA.

By Thy faithful pledges ;
By the glowing edges
    Of the cloud ;
By JEHOVAH's mission,
Taking man's condition,
    Meekly bow'd ;
Gaia here entreateth,
Evermore repeateth,
    " Come, O king ! "
Though the Tempter taunteth,
All Creation panteth
    For its King !

THE CIRCLES.

To-day, to-day,
    We sail away
To place the Aureole on JAHVEH !
    By Jordan's stream
    Our pinions gleam,
Then rest upon the Nazarene !

The Voice of Love
We hear above,
And see the Image of a Dove.

O dazzling Sight!
O splendor bright,
That dost on the Messiah light!

THE ANGELS.

O heavenly chrism!
O meek baptism!
    Dating Messiah's power!
Rise Son of Man!
    And meet Satan!
God in Thee saves the hour!

THE DEMONS.

Ho, ho, wanton imps!
    Loving sin;
    How ye grin!
As ye get a glimpse
    Of the Nazarene!

Senseless imbeciles,
    How ye swell!
    As ye tell,
With so sickly smiles,
    The wiles of hell!

Mighty Molech 's dead!
    And he groans,
    And he moans
On his fiery bed,
    Gasping with his tones.

> Lucifer may know
>   If he will ;
>   Know it still—
> Fires are made below
>   For the Devil.

> Torments us await,
> Come they soon or late !
>   Imps and demons,
>   Seiz'd with tremens
> Drag the gaffs of fate.

THE EVANGEL.

And straightway the Spirit drave Him away,
And He was forty days of Satan tempted ;
And was in the desert with the wild beasts ;
And Angels came and minister'd to Him.

THE ANGELS.

Anointed One ! haste on, JAHVEH !
The God in Thee shall gain the day !
Lo, ages long we wait and pray,
    " Let JAHVEH come ! "
Thou 'rt come ; and goest to meet the Foe !
Haste on ! in the PLEROMA go !
The God in Thee shall overthrow
    The Evil One !

Ah, finite Man, Thou 'rt left alone !
The aureoles of Thy brow are gone ;
Thy Glories vanish, one by one ;
    All—all—is gloom.

Awake, O Star !   Awake, and pray !
This hour thy destiny doth weigh.
The " Nazarene " shall fall, or stay
    For aye thy doom !

THE ETHERS.

We near the Sabbath of our rest ;
We make our cradle on the Breast
So bright with bounty and behest
    Of the PLEROMA.
Our sighs are vestiges of fears,
Once clamorous, pleading with tears—
Turn'd now to promise with the years
    Of the Adonai.

Alas, the Spirit is withdrawn !
The Saviour's face is thin and wan :
O frailty ! frailty ! the Archon
    Of Earth appears !
Let Gaia's bosom shrink with terror !
Creation's soul be fix'd with horror,—
The sky above be a tale-bearer
    More stern than seers.

THE PLEROMA-CHRIST.

Nigh forty days and nights this wilderness
Hath been my pillow.   Yet, unharm'd I lay ;
The lions stalking for their prey drew near,
And nightly stood, with muffled roar, and watch'd
Like sentinels my bed until the dawn.
The ominous fowl of heav'n circling above,
Swept down upon the neighboring crags, and sate ;
And seem'd to link thought unto thought profound ;
Whilst yonder asphalt sea grew hoarse with groans

Of the infernal brood of demons that writhe
Neath Satan's leash.
            Looming upon the mount,
Before daybreak, Mine eyes a portent saw,
In shadowy outline as a man, but vast—
A hundred times the stature of mankind.
The slumbering heavens shudder'd !   Ethers wept.
The heart of Earth stood still within her breast
Appall'd ; when, startled from the holy trance,
I leap'd upon My feet, to fall again—
Too weak to stand ; or raise defensive arm.
And here I lie in agony of need,
With inward Mind calm as the brow of God.

Lips may not utter what I felt ; nor tell
The blaze of beauty, and the thrill of terror,
When *Bath Kol* cried from out the cloud, and call'd
Me " Son beloved " in Whom God is well-pleas'd.
Then did the LIGHT, occulted in My birth,
Burst forth in flame, and upward stream to meet
The Dove that clove the sky above Mine head.
Lo, in that moment did the PLEROMA
Effulge !—the God—the Man—as One reveal'd !
Whilst strong to weakness, glad to pain, I ran
With closèd eyes, maze-bound into the hills
To be alone and contemplate these words.

SATAN.

One little word did nearly cleave the wit
Of Jesus ; and shall be my weapon now.
"The Son of God "—egregiously big
The thought is to a carpenter ! Aye, aye !
What 's in mere name ! Ho, Satan is create,—

And hence a "son," to wit, is the offspring
Of the Almighty.   I 've the cue—" The Son " !

And here on Quarantania's hill I find
The son of Joseph, bearing many names ;
Indeed none but a Rabbi should devise
So many contradictions in one word.
Were not the rule primeval of this Star
Endanger'd by vagaries of this sort,
Rare pleasure might we in his ravings find.
But if he be JAHVEH, this day shall I
The truth explore, and point my plans thereby.
By Jove ! this arm, and this gray dome of wit
Shall prove a doughty opponent in just
With a young Deity in flesh and bones !

What is, if not the uncertain !   To-day
A scheme 's in bloom, to-morrow, gone to seed ;
The third, lies on the ground the food for worms.
I 'm in Thy due, O Jordan Voice ; Thy word
Breaketh the edge of my well-whetted plan,
And makes it useless in the field with Christ.
I take Thy lance instead,—" *The Son*," " *The Son* " !
Now hath he fix'd on me his hungry gaze !
Nor riseth to receive.   I will draw near,
And trail my beard low in the dust, feigning
Obeisance.
                    Son of Joseph, Carpenter !
Hail ! Art thou down again from out the clouds ?
Ah, hunger eats thy tongue ! Sick eremite !
If food thou need'st or physick, here 's Thy slave.
'T will be a notable and easy path
To rule, to claim the world's Archon a slave.

THE CHRIST.

I need thy service not.

SATAN.

　　　　　　　　　　And starv'st for lack
Of food ! Thou art no man, else thou art mad !
Tell me, art thou Messiah ? Doubtless ! Thou 'rt gaunt
Enough to suit the Evangelical !
Here lie I at thy feet ; and in me lies
The World ; if so thou be JAHVEH.   Make proof !
Thy reticence bids me to name the tests.
I give thee three, and do require but one,—
Perform but one, and me thy vassal claim.
I challenge thee to turn one of these least
Silicious stones, before thee strewn, to bread—
And eat, and dull the gnawing tooth of hunger.
A sorry Deity, thou, cadaverous—
When all allow the gods ambrosial diet !
Once saw I thee to Egypt borne away,
By the celestial general escort,—
And utter'd concession I now recant ;
To find thee grizzly, rheumatic, unkempt—
An unhous'd cenobite, me staggers !
　　　　　　　　　　　　　　Answer !
One word, one word from God's own Son suffice
To change these mineral loaves to bread—this do,
And I dispute not thy Divinity.

THE CHRIST.

As *man* my mission is fulfill'd in Earth.
Man shall not live by bread alone, but, by
Each word proceeding from the mouth of God.

SATAN

Feigning thyself a man, thou sayest this,
Believing that thou art the Son of God.
O Phantasy, that captivates the soul
And makest airy nothings actuals.
Behold, a haggard dines on dreams.   A mind
Diseas'd, the skill'd physician spurns, choosing
Instead " mediums," and misnam'd " scientists."
Hateth his friends, and seeks his enemies—
Scorneth the owl's wise word ; the titmouse heeds.

I see thee entering on thy work forthwith—
The purporting Messiah.   It is writ
In Malachi, " The JAHVEH Whom ye seek
Comes suddenly to His Temple."   Is 't so ?
Discernest yon *Basilike ?*   I know
Thou seest it—if in thy mind's eye only !
Am I not right ?   Thou goest shortly up
To David's town thy ministry to op'n ?
A miracle would be beginning fit :
Ascend before the wondering multitude
One of the marble towers ; and, while they look,
Command the Angels, and then hurl thee down.
Thou 'st naught to fear, and much to gain thereby ;
Is it not written in thy Daily Bread,
" He shall His angels charge concerning Thee,
And they shall bear Thee up lest Thou do dash
Thy foot against a stone " ?

THE CHRIST.

Also " Thou shalt
Not tempt the Lord thy God."   Suffice the promise !
I am as Son of Man, content.

21

SATAN.

Perdu !   "As man content," because thou reck'st
Thyself the Son of God !   So might all men
Sweet solace take in such absurdity !
But grant Thou art the " Seed "—the One destin'd
To crush the Tempter's head.   Is it not writ,
That he shall bruise Thy heel ?   Mind, mind, the heel
Of the JAHVEH Satan shall bruise !   Reflect !
If the Omnipotent do suffer harm
In the encounter with this world's Archon,
A less than He shall utterly be crush'd.

Hear me !   With clear resolve I sought this place
To find Thy rocky bed and make this grant :
A voice from heav'n hath call'd Thee, " Son of God "—
Heard it Thyself—the Baptizer, and I—
And forty days that word have I revolv'd
To reach this proposal.   If Thou 'rt the Christ,
Then am I, Lucifer, Thine enemy,
Holding by fief original this Star
A hundred generations unchalleng'd.
But Thy Advent have I foreknown, nor slept
By day or night inventing schemes and plots
To thwart Thy birth, and Kingdom in the earth.
Well knowing, when the FULNESS came, my rule
Was nigh its end.   Thou art confess'd the MAN—
The Goal of the Creation—Type of types !
Hast properties and potencies Divine :
If so, 't is rash in me Thee to resist.
I am no fool, in *common parlance* said—
If Thou 'rt the *Christ*, this diadem is Thine.
This sceptre to Thy hand belongs.   Hail Prince
Of Earth ! Lord of this Star of stars !

                              Thou noddest ;
The metaphysic factors fire Thy fancy !
Mount up !   The kindling torch illume !   Mount up !
And view the kingdoms of the Earth, fair Earth !
Bright centre of the Universe.   Hail ! Hail !
Thy Archon groans to give thee up—but Might
Makes right in the Almighty's realm,—and I
Obey because I must.   Yet *Must* says not
_*To-day*, though bounds are set unto my sway.
Forestalling the event, I seize the hour,
And yield thee up unto the Son of Man.
Glow, panorama, glow !   Behold it pass
Before His gaze !   O rapture !   Holy MAN !
The PLEROMA doth open now Thine orbs !
Thine is the rule of this Star beautiful !
For this end camest Thou from Heaven !
Thou lov'st this Star :—I know it by the flush
Upon Thy cheek ; the sighing of Thy breast.
O deep of deeps ! O Mystery most vast !
Thou art the Christ—this crown of sapphire—all
Is Thine, by one and trivial act conditionèd.
Thou must in Thine unstainèd soul allow
The truth of what I say ;—concede my right
As archon of the Earth.   This fief I yield
As mine to give allow'd—and Thine to take ;—
Else seiz'd perforce.   I offer it Thee here
Without a struggle more 'tween us, if Thou 'rt
The Christ !   Nay, to Thy probity I leave
The cause.   If Thou receiv'st this diadem,
And this puissant sceptre from mine hand,
Kneeling meantime Thou dost receive it from
Mine hand, to show by outward sign that I
Transfer my name and titles unto Thee—

Then peace proclaim !   Thou art Prince of this Star !
Earth's Potentate !   Messiah, Lord of All !

THE PLEROMA-CHRIST.

Get thee behind me, Satan !   For 't is writt'n,
" Thou shalt do worship to the Lord thy God,
And him alone shall mortals serve."

SATAN.

What ! what !
Thee ? Thee ? Behind ? Amazement, hear this speech !
The Nazarene derides the Prince of Earth !
Let imps and satyrs howl in Juda's ears !
Rheums, palsies, and obsessions, spread abroad !
I quit Thee, but Thou meetest me again !
And if Thou 'rt less than God, ruin I 'll pile
On Thee and Thy frail purposes, as high
As Sirius, and as baleful too !

THE DEMONS.

How Tophet spawns, and yawns !
Hell faints and falls in qualms
   Of black despair.
Contagion's sallow eye
Sickens our sorcery :
   Our end 's Despair.

The Son of God 's a rod,—
He comes all iron-shod
   To crush our head ;
Our prince is quite distraught,
Weigh'd down with gloomy thought.
   Great is our dread.

THE ANGELS.

While the mount was vail'd ;
While the foe assail'd ;
While Messiah quail'd, we pray'd, O Saviour.
Till the field was won ;
Till the vail was drawn ;
Till we saw the " Son," we stay'd, O Saviour.
Now the Aureole 's bright
With PLEROMA's light,
Marveling the sight, we fly, O Saviour :
Bearing on the wing
Water from the spring ;
Whilst the Ethers sing, draw nigh the Saviour.
Manna from the Tree,
And Ambrosia,
Offer we to Thee, and bless the Saviour !
Hailing, " Son of God ! "
Hailing, " Sovran Lord ! "
Hailing, " Heav'nly Word," address the Saviour !

THE EVANGEL.

The next day John, beholding Jesus, saith,
"Behold the Lamb of God !   Lo, this is He,
Of Whom I said, ' There cometh after me
A Man which is preferrèd before me.
And of His *Fulness* have we all receiv'd,
And grace for grace.' "
                    Now afterward when John
Was prison'd, came Jesus into Galilee,
Preaching the Gospel of the Kingdom, saying,
" Now is fulfill'd the Day of the PLEROMA !
God's Kingdom is at hand ! "

Cana.

Least of the daughters of Galilee,
Sing us the song of the Mystery !—
Blush of the water at Jesus' word—
Fame of the wine the bridegroom pour'd.
Sing it again in the ages far—
Fair in the light of the Morning Star ;
Telling the marvel—PLEROMA's dower—
Blessing the Virgin before the Hour.

THE EVANGEL.

And the Jewish Passover was at hand,
And Jesus went up to Jerusalem.

THE COURIERS.

With shine and sheen, JAHVEH prevene !
Presage the hour, PLEROMA's Flower
　　Shall cleanse the Holy Temple.
Hail, Heavenly Light growing more bright !
Nearing the Throne ; worship alone,
　　Worship IMMANUEL !

Hail, NAME of names ! We are Thy flames ;
Hail, SIRE of sires ! We are Thy fires ;
　　That sign PLEROMA's hour.
O SOUL of fervors ! The Couriers—
O WELL of tears ! The silent seers—
　　Discern Messiah's Power.

Welcome, welcome, unto Zion,
Majestic MAN !—the *Second* Adam !
　　Lift up your heads, ye gates !

The Limits cry, " Lo, Christ draws nigh ! "
The Bands entwine the MAN-Divine,
   And Earth her LORD awaits.

THE LIMITS.

The MAN draweth nigh !
We are sighing for Him ;
We are crying for Him ;
  Restore us unto Eden !
The MAN passeth by !
We are kneeling to Him,
And appealing to Him,
  Restore us unto Eden !

THE BANDS.

Gravities are trending,
Opposites are blending,
Harmonies are lending
  Concord to our star :
Dissonance retrieving :
Suffering relieving :
Peacefully receiving
  The Limits from afar.

THE CIRCLES.

Bless we the PLEROMA—Circle Divine !
Welcome IMMANUEL unto His Shrine !
Lo, Thou art come, Infinite One !
Bright is Thy way ; enter JAHVEH !
Thou art the *Nesama*—Image Divine !

Bless we the PLEROMA—full in the MAN !
Finitely Infinite—*Second* Adam—
Goal of Creation ! rise to Thy Station !
Into Thy hands pass we our wands ;
Thou art the *Nesama*—Image Divine !

Earth hath its Eden, and Sabbath again ;
Rhythms in Nature are Rhythms in man—
Sin and its sorrow surcease shall borrow ;
Guilt and its woe, Jesus shall know,
Finding the *Nesama*—Image Divine.

GAIA.

In visions I saw Thee, O wonderful Light !
  Flash forth in the midst of the Temple of God !
    When a craze of amaze
  Enseiz'd man and brute ; the merchandise straw'd—
    While, hustling and rustling,
With shout and with rout, fled JAHVEH's dread Sight !

O answer, Great Guest, inspiring my lay ;
  Com'st hither to bide ? or soon to pass by ?
    By the Grace in Thy face,
  By the Light of Thy brow, I read Thy reply :
    " Peace, peace, Gaia, peace !
The King shall remain while it is call'd day."

Thou art tearful, O King ! Ah, I weep to perceive ;
  Feel the weight on Thy breast ; till I sigh in my
    sleep ;
    While Creation groans, and moans :

And the Earth joys to-day, but to-morrow doth
    weep !
Alas, Adonai PLEROMA !
I shall die if Thou die, I shall live if Thou live.

THE ANGELS.

He hath suddenly come to His Temple ;
    His Hour and His Mission 's begun ;
In the plenary Graces of Manhood,
    He shines like the orient sun.

Humanity, here is thy SUMMIT !
    Lo, here is the CROWN of mankind !
In this beautiful CIRCLE of Virtues,
    Are SEVEN PERFECTIONS divin'd.

They seal Him the Son of the Highest !
    They sign Him the meekest of men !
They lend Him unspeakable beauty,
    That thrilleth and thrilleth again.

They praise Him the GOAL of CREATION !
    The END of the timeless Process ;
The MYSTERY hid from the Ages—
    The SAVIOUR a World shall confess.

His FAITH and His REV'RENCE perfect,
    Toward God ; His OBEDIENCE too :
His LOVE for mankind most unselfish ;
    His WISDOM, the Heavens shine through.

His HOPE, never dimm'd in the darkness ;
   His VICTORY, full o'er Satan :
In Sinless, INCOMP'RABLE MANHOOD,
   BEHOLD HIM—THE PERFECT ADAM !

———

Gentle as a child—mighty as a God ;
Peaceful as a fountain—wrathful as a flood ;
Simple though his accents—deep as is the Sea ;
Loved by little children—dreaded MYSTERY !
Needy as a servant—Richest Born of Beings ;
Praying to the FATHER—Almoner of kings ;
Walking on the earth—dwelling in the Sky ;
Speaking in the fields—answered from On High ;
Guide of all to Life—leading unto Death ;
Promiser of Heaven—in His dying breath ;
Friend of Sinners HE—suffering their guilt ;
Most Divinely MAN when His blood is spilt ;
Dying unto Life—Victor in defeat ;
Raisèd from the Grave to a Heavenly Seat.
Hail we ! Hail we, Jesus ! Mystery Divine !
Thine the Kingdom ever ! and the GLORY Thine !

EPILOGUE.

If ye ask the Muse I sing, I reply,—PLEROMA.
Life of numbers, Soul of songs ;
Praise of praises Him belongs—Infinite PLEROMA !
In Whose blood our souls are shriv'n ;
Earth is ransom'd, man forgiven ; in the Christ-PLEROMA.
" Jesus " is His monograph—
" Saviour " is His epitaph—crucified PLEROMA.
Thither, Thither follow we,
Into Thy Eternity, glorified PLEROMA !
Flower of flowers, full in bloom,
Love subsists in Thy perfume evermore, PLEROMA !

GLOSSARY.

Abana—One of the two rivers of Damascus.

Abaris—Highlands to the east of the Jordan.

Abiram—One of the conspirators against Moses and Aaron.

Accad—Akkad—a primitive Hamite race in Shinar—founders of arts and letters.

Acheron—One of the five rivers of the infernal regions.

Achilles—The name of a large moth.

Achor—The spot at which Achan was stoned.

Acrogens—Point-growers—abundant in Coal Age.

Actinidæ—From resemblance, called animal-flowers.

Adonai—The LORD.

Adoni—Phœnician for the Most High.

Adulate—Containing excessive praise.

"*Æons*"—Daughters of Time.

Æstivate—In process of flowering.

Afrite—An evil genius in Mohammedan mythology.

Agnis—"Fire"—a vedic god worshipped by the Aryans.

Ahab—Son of Omri, seventh king of Israel.

Ahijah—A prophet of Shiloh in days of Solomon and Jeroboam.

Aleim—(Elohim)—The generic term for the *gan*-Eden Deity—"Mights."

Algæ—Sea-weeds.

Altruism—Devotion to the interests of others.

Amelek—Son of Eliphaz, grandson of Esau.

Amenemha—An Egyptian king who lived before the invasion of the Hyksos—builder of pyramids and canals.

Amittai—The father of the prophet Jonah.

Amœbina—An animalcule capable of undergoing many changes.

Ammon—"The Hidden"—an Egyptian deity.

Amorites—Mountaineers—descendants of Canaan.

Amoz—The father of the prophet Isaiah.

Amphibian—Living in both water and on land.

Amram—The father of Moses.

Ana—The Chaldean god of heaven.

Anakim—A race of giants—notably of Hebron.

Anarch—A prince or ruler.

Anemone, Sea—A polyp resembling the flower of the same name.

" *Animæ* "—The personification of the living principle in animal
　　forms.

Anubis—An Egyptian deity with head of a dog or fox.

Apamea—A fording-place situated on the Euphrates.

Apappas—An Egyptian monarch who united both Egypts.

Aphelion—The farthest point in the orbit of a planet from the sun.

Apotheosis—Placed among the gods.

Apperception—Perception that reflects upon the perceiver.

Arachnida—Including the class of spiders and scorpions.

Archæan—Ancient, primitive.

Archetypes—The Divine patterns and models of Creation.

Archon—Ruler.

Argillaceous—Partaking of clay.

Argob—In Bashan—taken by Jair, a chief of the tribe of Manasseh.

Ariana—An ancient name of Khorassan in Persia.

Arnon—"The noisy"—the boundary between Moab and the
　　Amorites.

Arphaxad—The son of Shem and ancestor of Heber.

Aryan—The Indo-European family of languages.

Asher—The eighth son of Jacob.

Asshur—A powerful country on the Tigris ; Nineveh the capital.

Aquarius—The " water-bearer "—a sign in the Zodiac.

Astarte—The principal female divinity of the Phœnicians.

Asteroids—Small planets lying between Mars and Jupiter.

Asterolepis—A large fossil fish found in old red-sandstone.

Atka—A mountain to the west of the Red Sea.

Atlantean—Used of any giant prop or support.

Aureole—A circle of light ; in art, the *nimbus* around a head.

Baalim—The generic name of the Phœnician deity.

Baasha—The third sovereign of the kingdom of Israel.

Babylon—The capital city in Shinar of the Chaldeans.

Bactrian—A country lying south of the river Oxus.

" *Bands* "—The positive and co-ordinating forces : gravity, cohesion, etc.

Bath Kol—The Voice from Heaven.

Batrachian—Pertaining to the order of frogs and lizards.

Bel—A. Babylonish deity.

" *Ben-oni* "—Son of my sorrow.

Bethel—A well known city in Central Palestine.

" *Binders* "—*vide* " Bands."

Boaz—A wealthy Bethlehemite, husband of Ruth.

Bochim—A place west of the Jordan above Gilgal.

Bogey—A bugbear—a spectre.

Borsippa—The Ziggurat identified as the Tower of Confusion.

Breccias—Fragments of rocks.

Cadent—" Falling " (Astrology.)

Calamite—A fossil plant of the rush family.

Calcareous—Partaking of the nature of limestone.

Calcinate—Reduced to powder by heat.

Cambrian—The lowest subdivision of the Silurian Age.

Campanularia—Bell-shaped.

Canaan—Fourth son of Ham.   The country west of the Jordan.

Carnivorous—Feeding on flesh.

Carpellate—Containing fruit.

Catania—The resinous poplar.

Caucasus—Extending from the Black Sea to the Caspian.

Cauline—Growing from the flower-stem.

Cauls—Nets, or coverings for the head.

Cenobite—A hermit.

Cephalaspis—A fossil fish with head encased in a buckler.

Cephalopod—A mollusk with branching arms.

Cetaceæ—Whales.

Chasdim—The Chaldeans.

Chasseurs—Huntsmen of the deep.

Cherubim—Angels of knowledge.

Chinneroth—Afterwards known as the Plain of Gennesaret.

Chiton—A mollusk with many-pointed shell.

Chiun—A Phœnician god.

Chufu—An Egyptian king of the IV. dynasty.

Cimmerian—Without light—intensely dark.

Circinate—Rolled together with the tip in the centre.
" *Circles* "—The personification of the rotary forces in nature.
Clio—A wing-footed Pteropod.
Clysms—Deluges.
Coccoliths—" Stone-berries "—calcareous shells.
Concentric—Circles having a common centre.
Congeries—A heap—a combination.
Conifers—Plants bearing cones—pines—hemlocks.
Consubstantial—Having the same substance or essence.
Copse—A wood of small growth.
Cosmic—Pertaining to the world.
Coup—A stroke.
" *Couriers* "—The volant forces,—like heat, light, and electricity.
Cowrie—A small shell used for money in Africa.
Creatures, Living—Same as Cherubim.
Crustacea—Articulates with crust-like shells.
Cryptogamia—Plants fertilized by hidden processes.
Cycads—Intermediate between palms and ferns.
Cycloids—A form of circles.
Cymric—Pertaining to the Cymri of Europe.
Cyrenius—Governor of Syria and Palestine after Archelaus.
Daphnia—A small crustacean.
Deborah—A prophetess who judged Israel.
Deciduous—Having leaves that fall in autumn.
Demons—The evil spirits subjected by Satan.
Dicotyls—Having seeds with two lobes.
Dinothere—A mammoth of the Middle Tertiary.
Dinychthys—A huge Devonian fossil fish.
Diorite—A crystalline rock consisting of hornblende and feldspar.
Doris—A wife of Herod the Great.
Dothan—A rich pasturage near the Plain of Esdrælon.
Doxa—The Glory investing the Godhead—the Essence of the Ethers.
Dunes—The movable sand-hills along sea-coasts.
Ea—A Chaldean god ; its symbol was a fish.
Ebal—A mount in Palestine to the north of Shechem.
Echidna—A genus of ant-eaters found in New Holland.
Edrei—One of two capital cities in Bashan.
Effigies—The likenesses of Deity in nature.
Effreet—An evil spirit.

Elam—Son of Shem ; also an appellation of a country.
Electron—The archon of the Sun.
Eliun—Phœnician, for the MOST HIGH.
Elilim—'' Emptiness.''
El Shaddai—The Almighty.
Emmanuel—Immanuel—'' *God with us.*''
Empyrean—The highest heaven.
Enaliosaurs—A swimming saurian of gigantic size, **now** extinct.
Endogens—Plants growing from within—having no pith.
Enthymemic—In the Divine Mind by potence and promise.
Eozoic—The Age of the dawn of life.
Epiphany—An appearance.
Erech—One of the cities of Nimrod's kingdom in Shinar.
Etham—The '' boundary of the sea.''
Ethers—The supersensible powers presiding over the cosmos.
Equitant—With leaves overlapping each other alternately.
Eucalypti—A genus of trees in Australia.
Fauna—The animals of any given area or epoch.
Fetishisms—Worship of clods and stones as shrines of divinities.
'' *Flame* ''—One of the countenances or emblems of Eden worship.
Flora—The vegetable species collectively in an area or age.
Flustra—A compound plant-like animal called *Sea-mat.*
Foraminifer—A minute Protozoan with a perforated shell.
Forfending—To hinder, to avert.
Fubsey—Plump—chubby.
Fungoids—Spongy, like mushrooms.
Furies—Female deities of vengeance.
'' *Gaia* ''—The poetical personification of the earth.
Gall-fly—Puncturing plants and making galls for its eggs.
Gan-Eden—The garden of Paradise.
Ganoids—Ancient fossil fish with bright scales.
Gasterpods—Mollusks using their stomach-discs as feet.
Geognosy—The science of the structure of the earth.
Geshur—The northeastern portion of Bashan.
Gerizim—The commanding summit of Samaria.
Ghauts—Mountain passes in the Orient.
Gibeon—One of four cities which made a league with Gideon.
Gibborim—Men of extraordinary stature.
Gideon—The fifth judge of Israel.

22

Gilgal—The " Circle," the first camp west of the Jordan.
Gnomes—Imaginary beings inhabiting the inner parts of the earth.
Godhead—The Father, Son, and Holy Ghost.
Graphite—Called plumbago or black lead.
Graptolite—A plume-shaped delicate fossil.
Guerdon—Reward—recompense.
Habitat—The home.
Hain—A meadow.
Halcyonites—An eight-rayed polyp.
Happi-Mu—Egyptian name for the Nile region.
Harpæ—Harp-shelled mollusks.
Hauran—On the northeastern border of the Promised Land.
Havilah—A land rich in treasures encompassed by the river Pison.
Hazor—The principal city of Northern Palestine.
Heki—An Egyptian deity.
Helene—The Greek race.
Helios—The disc of the sun—worshipped as a god.
Heliopolis—City of the Sun—priestly centre of Lower Egypt.
Herbivorous—Animals subsisting on herbs.
Hindu Kush—An Alpine water-shed in Asia.
Hippus—Eohippus—The three-toed horse, the fossil antecedent of
   the modern horse.
Hominidæ—With anatomical resemblances to the human species.
Hormah—A town on the south of Palestine reduced by Joshua.
Horoscope—An observation made of the heavens at the time of a per-
   son's birth.
Horus—" The Child," an Egyptian god.
Hydradæ—Fresh-water polyps.
Hymeneal—Pertaining to marriage—a marriage song.
Ichthyic—Relating to the order of fishes.
Ilex—An evergreen tree of Palestine.
Imago—The last and perfected state of an insect.
Imbricate—Overlapped at the edges in regular order.
Implexed—Intwined—interweaved.
Indra—The Aryan god of the atmosphere.
Infusoria—Microscopic animals found in water.
Iran—Or Persia.
Iridescent—Having colors like the rainbow.
Iris—The rainbow—the *fleur de luce*.

Italiote—Peculiar to ancient Italy.

Jah—A short form of JAHVEH (Jehovah), the Covenant God of the Hebrews.

JAHVEH (pronounced Yăh-vāy)—"*The One that will be that He will be.*"

Javanu—The Greeks—descended from Japheth.

Jahvites—Worshippers of Jahveh.

Jeroboam—Son of Nebat—the head of the ten northern tribes.

Jochebed—The mother of Moses and Aaron.

Kabiri—The seven deities of the Phœnicians.

Kadesh-Barnea—Last camp of the Israelites on direct march to Canaan.

Karnak—A collection of temples near Thebes in Upper Egypt.

Khem—An Egyptian deity.

Kneph—An Egyptian deity.

Korah—Leader of the rebellion against his cousins Moses and Aaron.

Labara—Standards.

Labyrinthodonts—Having labyrinthine teeth.

Lagoons—Shallow seas—lakes within coral islands.

Laurentian—The Azoic rocks of Canada.

Lecherous—Lustful—lewd.

Lemming—A burrowing animal of the rat family.

Lenticle—Spots on leaves from which roots issue.

Lepidodendra—A fossil tree of the Carboniferous age marked with scales.

Libanus—Mount Lebanon to the north of Palestine.

Liber—The inner bark lying next the wood.

"*Limits*"—The personification of the negative and dispersive forces in Nature.

Lister—An enumerator.

Lucifer—Archon of the Earth by original grant of the Almighty.

Lydia—In Asia Minor.

Maccabean—Pertaining to the reign of the family of Judas Maccabeus.

Mage—A magician.

Magism—Sorcery.

Mandalas—Vedic poems.

Manu—Laws of,—A metrical code of the Rig-Veda.

Marah—"Bitter."

Maranon—Or Amazon.

Marduk—Babylonish god of the planet Jupiter.

Maruts—Storm gods.

Maskim—The seven gods of the abyss.

Medusæ—Sea-nettles.

Memnon—A vocal statue of Amenohis III.—emitting sounds at dawn.

Mentor—Teacher.

Merodoch—Same as *Marduk*.

Merom—A reedy lake near sources of the Jordan.

Mermer—The god of the winds.   (Persian.)

Mephitic—Breathing foul gases.

Metempsychosis—Transmigration.

Michael—The prince of the militant angels of God.

Middins—Kitchen-refuse heaps.

'' *Mights* ''—The literal meaning of *Elohim*.

Minnith—From Aroer to Minneth was a district of twenty cities on
    the east of the Jordan.

Mitra—A Vedic deity—'' *The Bright One.* ''

Mnœan Snake—The name given a crown prince in Egypt.

Moëris—Artificial lake, by Amenemha III., for irrigation.

Molech—The Canaanitish sun-god.

Morasthite—The prophet Jonah.

Moreh— *The oak of*,—the first halting-place of Abram in Palestine.

Morse—A sea-horse.

Nacre—The iridescent lining of some shells.

Nadab—The son of Jeroboam.

Naïads—Water-nymphs.

'' *Names* ''—The Countenances of the Trinity, as seen by the *heavenly
    essences :*—or, as *Light*, *Fire*, and *Ether*, in Nature.

Nautilus—A shell-fish furnished with a membrane for a sail.

Nazarites—Set apart by vow for the service of God.

Nebat—The father of Jeroboam.

Nebo—A mount facing Jericho on the east.   Moses took last view
    of the Promised Land from its summit.

Necromancy—Conjuration, enchantment.

Nemesis—The personification of retributive justice.

Nephillim—Giants.

Nesama—The Divine Blessedness communicated to the first pair.

Neuropter—An order of insects with four membranous wings.

Nimroud—The grandson of Ham—a fierce opponent of the altar and worship of Jehovah.

Nindar—The nightly sun in the regions of Mulge.

Occident—The Western world.

Octopus—The devil-fish.

Octuple—Eight-fold.

Omphalos—The navel of the Earth—the North Pole.

Ophiuchus—A constellation in which a remarkable star appeared about the time of Jesus' birth.

Oreads—Mountain nymphs.

Orient—The Eastern world.

Ormuzd—The Persian god of light.

Osiris—The Beneficent Power in Nature—the vanquisher of Typhon (evil).

Orthocera—Having a straight, many-chambered, shell.

Orthopter—An order of insects with even-textured wings.

Othniel—A younger brother of Caleb.

Ovary—The lower part of the pistil containing the seed.

Pachyderm—A thick-skinned, hoofed animal.

Padan-Aram—Mesopotamia, bordering on the Euphrates.

Palæothere—A fossil pachyderm allied to the tapir.

Pamir—The northern extremity of the Himalayan plateau.

Pan—The god of Nature.

Pandemonium—The council-chamber of the demons.

Pantheon—The whole body of divinities worshipped by a people.

Paramos—Low mountainous districts in South America.

Parsism—The religion of the Parsees, followers of Zoroaster.

Pelagic—Pertaining to the deep sea.

Pelusium—or Avaris—On the frontier wall of Egypt toward Palestine.

Pentacrinus—A fossil crinoid with five-sided pedicle.

Permian—The period closing the Carboniferous age.

Perfervid—Very fervid,—ardent.

Perfoliate—Surrounding the stem at the base.

Pethual—The father of the prophet Joel.

Petiole—The foot-stalk of a leaf.

Phallic—Pertaining to the orgies of Bacchus.

Pharpar—One of the two rivers of Damascus.

Phocas—Name of a small mollusk.

Phœbus—The sun.

Pholad—A genus of mollusks boring rocks and clay.
Photosphere—The luminous envelope of the sun.
Phyllaries—Bracts forming an involucre.
Phyllotaxy—The science of leaf-arrangement on the stems of plants.
Pihahiroth—The third encampment of Israel in Egypt.
Pintadine—The mother-pearl.
Pithom—A store-city in eastern Lower Egypt.
Placental—Animals having a *placenta*.
Placoderm—A bony-plated fish of the Devonian age.
Placoid—A fish with enameled plates for scales.
Pleiads—A group of seven stars in the constellation Taurus.
Pleiosaur—A fossil-swimming saurian.
PLEROMA—The Plenitude of the Godhead: "FULNESS"—John i., 16 ; Col. ii., 9 ; Eph. i., 23.—The Creative Mind in Nature ;—The Second Person of the Trinity.
Plerome—The potence, or fulness, of a seed, or bud, or egg.
Plethoric—Overfull—overloaded.
Plumule—The growing point of young plants and buds.
Plutonian—Relating to unstratified, crystalline rocks.
Pollenius—Personification of the anthers of flowers.
Polypides—Houses, or hives, of coral polyps.
Polyzoa—Lowest order of mollusks ; many animals united.
Prenominate—To forename.
Presto—Suddenly.
Primordial—Pertaining to the lowest geological period.
Prognostic—A prediction,—a foretelling.
Proleptic—Seen before, by anticipation.
Proplasmic—The earliest moulds of living organisms.
Proteaceæ—Flowering shrubs, natives of Australia and South Africa.
Protozoan—A rhizopod—a sponge, etc.
" *Psyche* "—The personification of the mental principle in man.
Psychic—Relating to the living principle in man.
Ptah—Chief god of Memphis—the divine architect.
Pteropod—A wing-footed mollusk.
Puissant—Mighty, powerful,
Purlieus—The outer portions, the environs.
Purpuræ—Mollusks with a violet-colored fluid.
Pyrosoma—A mollusk emitting brilliant phosphorescent light.
Quadrifurcate—Four-branching.

Quaternary—A modern geological epoch.
Quintuple—In fives.
Ra—The sun, represented by Egyptians as a hawk-headed man.
Ragnarok—The darkness of the gods—a day of doom.
Rama—One of the cities of Benjamin.
Rehoboam—The son and successor of Solomon.
Rehoboth—Genesis xxvi., 22.
Rhizopods—Protozoa with fibre-like processes through pores in the shell.
Rig-Veda—The books of sacred hymns among the Hindus.
Rimmon—A deity worshipped by the Syrians of Damascus.
Rorqual—A species of whale.
Rosh—A poisonous plant.
Roteria—Crustaceans moving by means of cilia about the head.
Ruminants—Animals that chew the cud.
Sacrosanct—Sacred, inviolable.
Sargon—The Assyrian monarch that deported Samaria, 722 B.C.
Sauroids—Resembling lizards.
Savannas—Grassy plains destitute of trees.
Seba—Probably in the Upper Nile.
Secular—Pertaining to an age, or a long period.
Semitic—Pertaining to the descendants of Shem.
Septenate—In octaves of seven, the rhythm of natural forces.
Seraphim—Angels of knowledge.
Sesostris—King Rameses of the Exodus.
Sessile—Issuing directly from the stalk,
Shaveh—Gen. xiv.
Shang Ti—A Divine name among Chinese.
Shemite—A descendant of Shem,
Shich plant—Used in incantation.
Shamgar—Son of Anath, judge of Israel before Barak.
Shumir—Lower Chaldea.
Siddim—Same as Sodom.
Sigillards—Large fossil trees marked in regular notches.
Signatures—Marks by which the mystic virtues of things are divined.
Silurian—The earliest Paleozoic age.
Similitudes—Correspondences between the natural and supernatural worlds.
Sin—The southeastern part of the Peninsula of Sinai.

Sinuous—Winding.
Sippara—A Chaldean city on the Euphrates.
Skittle balls—Discs for throwing at ninepins.
Somme—A valley in France rich in fossil remains.
Sprunt—Spread like a male turkey.
Stipule—An appendage at the base of leaves.
Succoth—Jacob built booths (succoth) here and tarried.
Syenite—A crystalline rock composed of quartz, hornblende, and feld-
  spar.
Sybarite—A person devoted to luxury and pleasure.
Synoptical—Affording a general view of the whole.
Tabid—Emaciated, wasted away.
Talisman—A magical figure to which wonderful effects are ascribed
Tartessan—A mountain district in ancient Spain.
Tekoan—A town in the tribe of Judah near Hebron.
Tentacle—An organ of feeling and motion among polyps.
Tephillim—Frontlets ; phylacteries.
Teredo—A boring mollusk ; used figuratively for a coal-miner.
Tessarene—Coined from tessara—*four ;* to denote a group of four.
Tests—Shells.
Theanthropic—Partaking both of divinity and humanity.
Tholoformic—Roof-shaped.
Thoth—A moon-god ; head of an Ibis—(Egyptian).
Tillodon—(Marsh)—Has head of a bear and incisors of a rodent.
Torus—The receptacle on which the carpels of flowers stand.
Tragacanth—A resinous plant.
Trigon—A trine of planets, making a figure of three sides.
Trilobite—A fossil crustacean.
Troll—A supernatural being inhabiting caves.
Tubularia—Having horny tubes.
Tunicata—Mollusks wearing a tunic, or envelope.
Turan—Ancient home of the Turanians in Central Asia.
Typhon—The Egyptian god of evil (Set).
Ungulate—A hoofed quadruped.
Urania—The heavens ;—The Mother of the Sun or Electron.
Uri—The father of Bezaleel, architect of the Tabernacle.
Uru—A great city near the mouth of the Euphrates.
Uz—The grandson of Shem ; the country also of Job.
Uzziah—A son of Amaziah, king of Judah.

Varuna—The all-enveloping heaven—a Vedic deity.
Vascular—Consisting of vessels—as lichens, sea-weeds.
Valvate—Having a valve or valves.
" *Vegetæ* "—Personification of the vegetable principle in Nature.
Vedic—Belonging to the Vedas.
Volzias—Abundant in the Triassic age.
Wassail—A festive liquor.
Wombat—A marsupial of the opossum family.
Xylem—Woody fibre.
Zaphnath paaneah—" Preserver of the age "—name given to Joseph
Zarathustra—A form of spelling Zoroaster.
Zalmanna—One of two kings of Midian captured by Gideon.
Zeba—One of two kings of Midian who fell by the hand of Gideon.
Zephath—A Canaanitish town afterwards called Hormah.
Zeus—The supreme god of the sky, among Greeks and Romans.
Zidon—or Sidon—An ancient and wealthy city of Phœnicia.
Zimri—A Simeonite chieftain slain by Phineas.
Zoöphytes—Polyps branching like plants and resembling flowers.